The Mystery of the Blue Train

Agatha Christie was born in Torquay and encouraged to write by Eden Phillpotts, the Devon playwright. In her first book, *The Mysterious Affair at Styles*, she created the now famous Belgian detective, Hercule Poirot, who is as popular as Conan Doyle's Sherlock Holmes. This was published in 1920, and her acknowledged masterpiece, *The Murder of Roger Ackroyd*, was published in 1926. She wrote over seventy-five detective novels, romantic novels under the pseudonym of Mary Westmacott, and many short stories and plays – including *The Mousetrap*, which is still running after more than twenty years. Many of her stories have been filmed, including *Ten Little Niggers*, *Witness for the Prosecution* and *Murder on the Orient Express*. Hercule Poirot finally died in *Curtain*, which although written twenty years earlier, was published just before Agatha Christie's death in 1976. She was married to Sir Max Mallowan, the well-known archaeologist, and was a Commander of the Order of the British Empire.

Also by Agatha Christie
in Pan Books

Dumb Witness
Murder in the Mews
Poirot Investigates
Sparkling Cyanide
The Thirteen Problems
The Seven Dials Mystery
Why Didn't They Ask Evans?
The ABC Murders
Sad Cypress
The Body in the Library
The Sittaford Mystery
The Big Four
Hercule Poirot's Christmas
Murder in Mesopotamia
The Labours of Hercules

Agatha Christie

The Mystery of the Blue Train

Pan Books
in association with **Collins**

First published 1928 by William Collins Sons & Co. Ltd
This edition published 1954 by Pan Books Ltd,
Cavaye Place, London SW10 9PG
3rd printing 1982
in association with William Collins Sons & Co. Ltd

ISBN 0 330 26439 7
Printed and bound in Great Britain by
Collins, Glasgow

To the two distinguished members of the OFD
Carlotta and Peter

CONTENTS

I	The man with the white hair	*page* 5
II	M. le Marquis	9
III	Heart of fire	12
IV	In Curzon Street	15
V	A useful gentleman	20
VI	Mirelle	28
VII	Letters	32
VIII	Lady Tamplin writes a letter	38
IX	An offer refused	44
X	On the blue train	48
XI	Murder	57
XII	At the Villa Marguerits	66
XIII	Van Aldin gets a telegram	71
XIV	Ada Mason's story	75
XV	The Comte de la Roche	79
XVI	Poirot discusses the case	84
XVII	An aristocratic gentleman	89
XVIII	Derek lunches	96
XIX	An unexpected visitor	98
XX	Katherine makes a friend	104
XXI	At the tennis	108
XXII	M. Papapolous breakfasts	115
XXIII	A new theory	120
XXIV	Poirot gives advice	123
XXV	Defiance	127
XXVI	A warning	132
XXVII	Interview with Mirelle	138
XXVIII	Poirot plays the squirrel	146
XXIX	A letter from home	154
XXX	Miss Viner gives judgment	161
XXXI	Mr Aaron lunches	167
XXXII	Katherine and Poirot compare notes	170
XXXIII	A new theory	174
XXXIV	The blue train again	176
XXXV	Explanations	180
XXXVI	By the sea	187

Chapter 1

THE MAN WITH THE WHITE HAIR

It was close on midnight when a man crossed the Place de la Concorde. In spite of the handsome fur coat which garbed his meagre form, there was something essentially weak and paltry about him.

A little man with a face like a rat. A man, one would say, who could never play a conspicuous part, or rise to prominence in any sphere. And yet, in leaping to such a conclusion, an onlooker would have been wrong. For this man, negligible and inconspicuous as he seemed, played a prominent part in the destiny of the world. In an Empire where rats ruled, he was the king of the rats.

Even now, an Embassy awaited his return. But he had business to do first—business of which the Embassy was not officially cognizant. His face gleamed white and sharp in the moonlight. There was the least hint of a curve in the thin nose. His father had been a Polish Jew, a journeyman tailor. It was business such as his father would have loved that took him abroad to-night.

He came to the Seine, crossed it, and entered one of the less reputable quarters of Paris. Here he stopped before a tall, dilapidated house and made his way up to an apartment on the fourth floor. He had barely time to knock before the door was opened by a woman who had evidently been awaiting his arrival. She gave him no greeting, but helped him off with his overcoat and then led the way into the tawdrily furnished sitting-room. The electric light was shaded with dirty pink festoons, and it softened, but could not disguise, the girl's face with its mask of crude paint. Could not disguise, either, the broad Mongolian cast of her countenance. There was no doubt of Olga Demiroff's profession, nor of her nationality.

"All is well, little one?"

"All is well, Boris Ivanovitch."

He nodded, murmuring: "I do not think I have been followed."

But there was anxiety in his tone. He went to the window, drawing the curtains aside slightly, and peering carefully out. He started away violently.

"There are two men—on the opposite pavement. It looks to me——" He broke off and began gnawing at his nails—a habit he had when anxious.

The Russian girl was shaking her head with a slow, reassuring action.

"They were here before you came."

"All the same, it looks to me as though they were watching this house."

"Possibly," she admitted indifferently.

"But then——"

"What of it? Even if they *know*—it will not be *you* they will follow from here."

A thin, cruel smile came to his lips.

"No," he admitted, "that is true."

He mused for a minute or two, and then observed,

"This damned American—he can look after himself as well as anybody."

"I suppose so."

He went again to the window.

"Tough customers," he muttered, with a chuckle. "Known to the police, I fear. Well, well, I wish Brother Apache good hunting."

Olga Demiroff shook her head.

"If the American is the kind of man they say he is, it will take more than a couple of cowardly apaches to get the better of him." She paused. "I wonder——"

"Well?"

"Nothing. Only twice this evening a man has passed along this street—a man with white hair."

"What of it?"

"This. As he passed those two men, he dropped his glove. One of them picked it up and returned it to him. A threadbare device."

"You mean—that the white-haired man is—their employer?"

"Something of the kind."

The Russian looked alarmed and uneasy.

"You are sure—the parcel is safe? It has not been tampered with? There has been too much talk . . . much too much talk."

He gnawed his nails again.

"Judge for yourself."

She bent to the fireplace, deftly removing the coals. Underneath, from amongst the crumpled balls of newspaper, she selected from the very middle an oblong package wrapped round with grimy newspaper, and handed it to the man.

"Ingenious," he said, with a nod of approval.

"The apartment has been searched twice. The mattress on my bed was ripped open."

"It is as I said," he muttered. "There has been too much talk. This haggling over the price—it was a mistake."

He had unwrapped the newspaper. Inside was a small brown paper parcel. This in turn he unwrapped, verified the contents, and quickly wrapped it up once more. As he did so, an electric bell rang sharply.

"The American is punctual," said Olga, with a glance at the clock.

She left the room. In a minute she returned ushering in a stranger, a big, broad-shouldered man whose transatlantic origin was evident. His keen glance went from one to the other.

"M. Krassnine?" he inquired politely.

"I am he," said Boris. "I must apologise for—for the unconventionality of this meeting-place. But secrecy is urgent. I—I cannot afford to be connected with this business in any way."

"Is that so?" said the American politely.

"I have your word, have I not, that no details of this transaction will be made public? That is one of the conditions of—sale."

The American nodded.

"That has already been agreed upon," he said indifferently. "Now, perhaps, you will produce the goods."

"You have the money—in notes?"

"Yes," replied the other.

He did not, however, make any attempt to produce it. After a moment's hesitation, Krassnine gestured towards the small parcel on the table.

The American took it up and unrolled the wrapping paper. The contents he took over to a small electric lamp and submitted them to a very thorough examination. Satisfied, he drew from his pocket a thick leather wallet and extracted from it a wad of notes. These he handed to the Russian, who counted them carefully.

"All right?"

"I thank you, Monsieur. Everything is correct."

"Ah!" said the other. He slipped the brown paper parcel negligently into his pocket. He bowed to Olga. "Good evening, Mademoiselle. Good evening, M. Krassnine."

He went out, shutting the door behind him. The eyes of the two in the room met. The man passed his tongue over his dry lips.

"I wonder—will he ever get back to his hotel?" he muttered.

By common accord, they both turned to the window. They were just in time to see the American emerge into the street below. He turned to the left and marched along at a good pace without once turning his head. Two shadows stole from a doorway and followed noiselessly. Pursuers and pursued vanished into the night. Olga Demiroff spoke.

"He will get back safely," she said. "You need not fear—or hope—whichever it is."

"Why do you think he will be safe?" asked Krassnine curiously.

"A man who has made as much money as he has could not possibly be a fool," said Olga. "And talking of money——"

She looked significantly at Krassnine.

"Eh?"

"My share, Boris Ivanovitch."

With some reluctance, Krassnine handed over two of the notes. She nodded her thanks, with a complete lack of emotion, and tucked them away in her stocking.

"That is good," she remarked, with satisfaction.

He looked at her curiously.

"You have no regrets, Olga Vassilovna?"

"Regrets? For what?"

"For what has been in your keeping. There are women —most women, I believe, who go mad over such things."

She nodded reflectively.

"Yes, you speak truth there. Most women have that madness. I—have not. I wonder now——" She broke off.

"Well?" asked the other curiously.

"The American will be safe with them—yes, I am sure of that. But afterwards——"

"Eh? What are you thinking of?"

"He will give them, of course, to some woman," said Olga thoughtfully. "I wonder what will happen then. . . ."

She shook herself impatiently and went over to the window. Suddenly she uttered an exclamation and called to her companion.

"See, he is going down the street now—the man I mean."

They both gazed down together. A slim, elegant figure was progressing along at a leisurely pace. He wore an opera hat and a cloak. As he passed a street lamp, the light illumined a thatch of thick white hair.

Chapter 2

M. LE MARQUIS

The man with the white hair continued on his course, unhurried, and seemingly indifferent to his surroundings. He took a side turning to the right and another one to the left. Now and then he hummed a little air to himself.

Suddenly he stopped dead and listened intently. He had heard a certain sound. It might have been the bursting of a tyre or it might have been—a shot. A curious smile played round his lips for a minute. Then he resumed his leisurely walk.

On turning a corner he came upon a scene of some activity. A representative of the law was making notes in a pocketbook, and one or two late passers-by had collected on the spot. To one of these the man with the white hair made a polite request for information.

"Something has been happening, yes?"

"*Mais oui*, Monsieur. Two apaches set upon an elderly American gentleman."

"They did him no injury?"

"No, indeed." The man laughed. "The American, he had a revolver in his pocket, and before they could attack him, he fired shots so closely round them that they took alarm and fled. The police, as usual, arrived too late."

"Ah!" said the inquirer.

He displayed no emotion of any kind.

Placidly and unconcernedly he resumed his nocturnal strolling. Presently he crossed the Seine and came into the richer areas of the city. It was some twenty minutes later that he came to a stop before a certain house in a quiet but aristocratic thoroughfare.

The shop, for shop it was, was a restrained and unpretentious one. D. Papopolous, dealer in antiques, was so known to fame that he needed no advertisement, and indeed most of his business was not done over a counter. M. Papopolous had a very handsome apartment of his own overlooking the Champs Elysées, and it might reasonably be supposed that he would have been found there and not at his place of business at such an hour, but the man with the white hair seemed confident of success as he pressed the obscurely placed bell, having first given a quick glance up and down the deserted street.

His confidence was not misplaced. The door opened and a man stood in the aperture. He wore gold rings in his ears and was of a swarthy cast of countenance.

"Good evening," said the stranger. "Your master is within?"

"The master is here, but he does not see chance visitors at this time of night," growled the other.

"I think he will see me. Tell him that his friend M. le Marquis is here."

The man opened the door a little wider and allowed the visitor to enter.

The man who gave his name as M. le Marquis had shielded

his face with his hand as he spoke. When the man-servant returned with the information that M. Papopolous would be pleased to receive the visitor a further change had taken place in the stranger's appearance. The man-servant must have been very unobservant or very well trained, for he betrayed no surprise at the small black satin mask which hid the other's features. Leading the way to a door at the end of the hall, he opened it and announced in a respectful murmur: "*M. le Marquis*."

The figure which rose to receive this strange guest was an imposing one. There was something venerable and patriarchal about M. Papopolous. He had a high domed forehead and a beautiful white beard. His manner had in it something ecclesiastical and benign.

"My dear friend," said M. Papopolous.

He spoke in French and his tones were rich and unctuous.

"I must apologise," said the visitor, "for the lateness of the hour."

"Not at all. Not at all," said M. Papopolous—"an interesting time of night. You have had, perhaps, an interesting evening?"

"Not personally," said M. le Marquis.

"Not personally," repeated M. Papopolous, "no, no, of course not. And there is news, eh?"

He cast a sharp glance sideways at the other, a glance that was not ecclesiastical or benign in the least.

"There is no news. The attempt failed. I hardly expected anything else."

"Quite so," said M. Papopolous; "anything crude——"

He waved his hand to express his intense distaste for crudity in any form. There was indeed nothing crude about M. Papopolous nor about the goods he handled. He was well known in most European courts, and kings called him Demetrius in a friendly manner. He had the reputation for the most exquisite discretion. That, together with the nobility of his aspect, had carried him through several very questionable transactions.

"The direct attack——" said M. Papopolous. He shook his head. "It answers sometimes—but very seldom."

The other shrugged his shoulders.

"It saves time," he remarked, "and to fail costs nothing—or next to nothing. The other plan—will not fail."

"Ah," said M. Papopolous, looking at him keenly.

The other nodded slowly.

"I have great confidence in your—er—reputation," said the antique dealer.

M. le Marquis smiled gently.

"I think I may say," he murmured, "that your confidence will not be misplaced."

"You have unique opportunities," said the other, with a note of envy in his voice.

"I make them," said M. le Marquis.

He rose and took up the cloak which he had thrown carelessly on the back of a chair.

"I will keep you informed, M. Papopolous, through the usual channels, but there must be no hitch in your arrangements."

M. Papopolous was pained.

"There is *never* a hitch in my arrangements," he complained.

The other smiled, and without any further word of adieu he left the room, closing the door behind him.

M. Papopolous remained in thought for a moment stroking his venerable white beard, and then moved across to a second door which opened inwards. As he turned the handle, a young woman, who only too clearly had been leaning against it with her ear to the keyhole, stumbled headlong into the room. M. Papopolous displayed neither surprise nor concern. It was evidently all quite natural to him.

"Well, Zia?" he asked.

"I did not hear him go," explained Zia.

She was a handsome young woman, built on Junoesque lines, with dark flashing eyes and such a general air of resemblance to M. Papopolous that it was easy to see they were father and daughter.

"It is annoying," she continued vexedly, "that one cannot see through a keyhole and hear through it at the same time."

"It has often annoyed me," said M. Papopolous, with great simplicity.

"So that is M. le Marquis," said Zia slowly. "Does he always wear a mask, Father?"

"Always."

There was a pause.

"It is the rubies, I suppose?" asked Zia.

Her father nodded.

"What do you think, my little one?" he inquired, with a hint of amusement in his beady black eyes.

"Of M. le Marquis?"

"Yes."

"I think," said Zia slowly, "that it is a very rare thing to find a well-bred Englishman who speaks French as well as that."

"Ah!" said M. Papopolous, "so that is what you think."

As usual, he did not commit himself, but he regarded Zia with benign approval.

"I thought, too," said Zia, "that his head was an odd shape."

"Massive," said her father—"a trifle massive. But then that effect is always created by a wig."

They both looked at each other and smiled.

Chapter 3

HEART OF FIRE

Rufus Van Aldin passed through the revolving doors of the Savoy, and walked to the reception desk. The desk clerk smiled a respectful greeting.

"Pleased to see you back again, Mr. Van Aldin," he said.

The American millionaire nodded his head in a casual greeting.

"Everything all right?" he asked.

"Yes, sir. Major Knighton is upstairs in the suite now."

Van Aldin nodded again.

"Any mail?" he vouchsafed.

"They have all been sent up, Mr. Van Aldin. Oh! wait a minute."

He dived into a pigeon hole, and produced a letter.

"Just come this minute," he explained.

Rufus Van Aldin took the letter from him, and as he saw the handwriting, a woman's flowing hand, his face was suddenly transformed. The harsh contours of it softened, and the hard line of his mouth relaxed. He looked a different man. He walked across to the lift with the letter in his hand and the smile still on his lips.

In the drawing-room of his suite, a young man was sitting at a desk nimbly sorting correspondence with the ease born of long practice. He sprang up as Van Aldin entered.

"Hallo, Knighton!"

"Glad to see you back, sir. Had a good time?"

"So so!" said the millionaire unemotionally. "Paris is rather a one-horse city nowadays. Still—I got what I went over for."

He smiled to himself rather grimly.

"You usually do, I believe," said the secretary, laughing.

"That's so," agreed the other.

He spoke in a matter-of-fact manner, as one stating a well-known fact. Throwing off his heavy overcoat, he advanced to the desk.

"Anything urgent?"

"I don't think so, sir. Mostly the usual stuff. I have not quite finished sorting it out."

Van Aldin nodded briefly. He was a man who seldom expressed either blame or praise. His methods with those he employed were simple; he gave them a fair trial and dismissed promptly those who were inefficient. His selections of people were unconventional. Knighton, for instance, he had met casually at a Swiss resort two months previously. He had approved of the fellow, looked up his war record, and found in it the explanation of the limp with which he walked. Knighton had made no secret of the fact that he was looking for a job, and indeed diffidently asked the millionaire if he knew of any available post. Van Aldin remembered, with a grim smile of amusement, the young man's complete astonishment when he had been offered the post of secretary to the great man himself.

"But—but I have no experience of business," he had stammered.

"That doesn't matter a cuss," Van Aldin had replied. "I have got three secretaries already to attend to that kind of thing. But I am likely to be in England for the next six months, and I want an Englishman who—well, knows the ropes—and can attend to the social side of things for me."

So far, Van Aldin had found his judgment confirmed. Knighton had proved quick, intelligent, and resourceful, and he had a distinct charm of manner.

The secretary indicated three or four letters placed by themselves on the top of the desk.

"It might perhaps be as well, sir, if you glanced at these," he suggested. "The top one is about the Colton agreement——"

But Rufus Van Aldin held up a protesting hand.

"I am not going to look at a durned thing to-night," he declared. "They can all wait till the morning. Except this one," he added, looking down at the letter he held in his hand. And again that strange transforming smile stole over his face.

Richard Knighton smiled sympathetically.

"Mrs. Kettering?" he murmured. "She rang up yesterday and to-day. She seems very anxious to see you at once, sir."

"Does she, now!"

The smile faded from the millionaire's face. He ripped open the envelope which he held in his hand and took out the enclosed sheet. As he read it his face darkened, his mouth set grimly in the line which Wall Street knew so well, and his brows knit themselves ominously. Knighton turned tactfully away, and went on opening letters and sorting them. A muttered oath escaped the millionaire, and his clenched fist hit the table sharply.

"I'll not stand for this," he muttered to himself. "Poor little girl, it's a good thing she has her old father behind her."

He walked up and down the room for some minutes, his brows drawn together in a scowl. Knighton still bent assiduously over the desk. Suddenly Van Aldin came to an abrupt halt. He took up his overcoat from the chair where he had thrown it.

"Are you going out again, sir?"

"Yes, I'm going round to see my daughter."

"If Colton's people ring up——?"

"Tell them to go to the devil," said Van Aldin.

"Very well," said the secretary unemotionally.

Van Aldin had his overcoat on by now. Cramming his hat upon his head, he went towards the door. He paused with his hand upon the handle.

"You are a good fellow, Knighton," he said. "You don't worry me when I am rattled."

Knighton smiled a little, but made no reply.

"Ruth is my only child," said Van Aldin, "and there is no one on this earth who knows quite what she means to me."

A faint smile irradiated his face. He slipped his hand into his pocket.

"Care to see something, Knighton?"

He came back towards the secretary.

From his pocket he drew out a parcel carelessly wrapped in brown paper. He tossed off the wrapping and disclosed a big, shabby, red velvet case. In the centre of it were some twisted initials surmounted by a crown. He snapped the case open, and the secretary drew in his breath sharply. Against the slightly dingy white of the interior, the stones glowed like blood.

"My God! sir," said Knighton. "Are they—are they real?"

Van Aldin laughed a quiet little cackle of amusement.

"I don't wonder at your asking that. Amongst these rubies are the three largest in the world. Catherine of Russia wore them, Knighton. That centre one there is known as Heart of Fire. It's perfect—not a flaw in it."

"But," the secretary murmured, "they must be worth a fortune."

"Four or five hundred thousand dollars," said Van Aldin nonchalantly, "and that is apart from the historical interest."

"And you carry them about—like that, loose in your pocket?"

Van Aldin laughed amusedly.

"I guess so. You see, they are my little present for Ruthie."

The secretary smiled discreetly.

"I can understand now Mrs. Kettering's anxiety over the telephone," he murmured.

But Van Aldin shook his head. The hard look returned to his face.

"You are wrong there," he said. "She doesn't know about these; they are my little surprise for her."

He shut the case, and began slowly to wrap it up again.

"It's a hard thing, Knighton," he said, "how little one can do for those one loves. I can buy a good portion of the earth for Ruth, if it would be any use to her, but it isn't. I can hang these things round her neck and give her a moment or two's pleasure, maybe, but——"

He shook his head.

"When a woman is not happy in her home——"

He left the sentence unfinished. The secretary nodded discreetly. He knew, none better, the reputation of the Hon. Derek Kettering. Van Aldin sighed. Slipping the parcel back in his coat pocket, he nodded to Knighton and left the room.

Chapter 4

IN CURZON STREET

The Hon. Mrs. Derek Kettering lived in Curzon Street. The butler who opened the door recognised Rufus Van Aldin at once and permitted himself a discreet smile of greeting. He led the way upstairs to the big double drawing-room on the first floor.

A woman who was sitting by the window started up with a cry.

"Why, Dad, if that isn't too good for anything! I've been telephoning Major Knighton all day to try and get hold of you, but he couldn't say for sure when you were expected back."

Ruth Kettering was twenty-eight years of age. Without being beautiful, or in the real sense of the word even pretty, she was striking looking because of her colouring. Van Aldin had been called Carrots and Ginger in his time, and Ruth's hair was almost pure auburn. With it went dark eyes and very black lashes—the effect somewhat enhanced by art. She was tall and slender, and moved well. At a careless glance it was the face of a Raphael Madonna. Only if one looked closely did one perceive the same line of jaw and chin as in Van Aldin's face, bespeaking the same hardness and determination. It suited the man, but suited the woman less well. From her childhood upward Ruth Van Aldin had been accustomed to having her own way, and anyone who had ever stood up against her soon realised that Rufus Van Aldin's daughter never gave in.

"Knighton told me you'd 'phoned him," said Van Aldin. "I only got back from Paris half an hour ago. What's all this about Derek?"

Ruth Kettering flushed angrily.

"It's unspeakable. It's beyond all limits," she cried. "He—he doesn't seem to listen to anything I say."

There was bewilderment as well as anger in her voice.

"He'll listen to me," said the millionaire grimly.

Ruth went on.

"I've hardly seen him for the last month. He goes about everywhere with that woman."

"With what woman?"

"Mirelle. She dances at the Parthenon, you know."

Van Aldin nodded.

"I was down at Leconbury last week. I—I spoke to Lord Leconbury. He was awfully sweet to me, sympathised entirely. He said he'd give Derek a good talking to."

"Ah!" said Van Aldin.

"What do you mean by 'Ah!' Dad?"

"Just what you think I mean, Ruthie. Poor old Leconbury is a washout. Of course he sympathised with you, of course he tried to soothe you down. Having got his son and heir married to the daughter of one of the richest men in the States, he naturally doesn't want to mess the thing up. But he's got one foot in the grave already, everyone knows that, and anything he may say will cut darned little ice with Derek."

"Can't *you* do anything, Dad?" urged Ruth, after a minute or two.

"I might," said the millionaire. He waited a second reflectively, and then went on. "There are several things I might do, but there's only one that will be any real good. How much pluck have you got, Ruthie?"

She stared at him. He nodded back at her.

"I mean just what I say. Have you got the grit to admit to all the world that you've made a mistake. There's only one way out of this mess, Ruthie. Cut your losses and start afresh."

"You mean——?"

"Divorce."

"Divorce!"

Van Aldin smiled drily.

"You say that word, Ruth, as though you'd never heard it before. And yet your friends are doing it all round you every day."

"Oh! I know that. But——"

She stopped, biting her lip. Her father nodded comprehendingly.

"I know, Ruth. You're like me, you can't bear to let go. But I've learnt, and you've got to learn, that there are times when it's the only way. I might find ways of whistling Derek back to you, but it would all come to the same in the end. *He's no good*, Ruth; he's rotten through and through. And mind you, I blame myself for ever letting you marry him. But you were kind of set on having him, and he seemed in earnest about turning over a new leaf—and well, I'd crossed you once, honey . . ."

He did not look at her as he said the last words. Had he done so, he might have seen the swift colour that came up in her face.

"You did," she said in a hard voice.

"I was too durned soft-hearted to do it a second time. I can't tell you how I wish I had, though. You've led a poor kind of life for the last few years, Ruth."

"It has not been very—agreeable," agreed Mrs. Kettering.

"That's why I say to you that this thing has got to *stop*!" He brought his hand down with a bang on the table. "You may have a hankering after the fellow still. *Cut it out.* Face facts. Derek Kettering married you for your money. That's all there is to it. Get rid of him, Ruth."

Ruth Kettering looked down at the ground for some moments, then she said, without raising her head:

"Supposing he doesn't consent?"

Van Aldin looked at her in astonishment.

"He won't have a say in the matter."

She flushed and bit her lip.

"No—no—of course not. I only meant——"

She stopped. Her father eyed her keenly.

"What did you mean?"

"I meant——" She paused, choosing her words carefully. "He mayn't take it lying down."

The millionaire's chin shot out grimly.

"You mean he'll fight the case? Let him! But, as a matter of fact, you're wrong. He won't fight. Any solicitor he consults will tell him he hasn't a leg to stand upon."

"You don't think"—she hesitated—"I mean—out of sheer spite against me—he might, well, try to make it awkward?"

Her father looked at her in some astonishment.

"Fight the case, you mean?"

He shook his head.

"Very unlikely. You see, he would have to have something to go upon."

Mrs. Kettering did not answer. Van Aldin looked at her sharply.

"Come, Ruth, out with it. There's something troubling you—what is it?"

"Nothing, nothing at all."

But her voice was unconvincing.

"You are dreading the publicity, eh? Is that it? You leave it to me. I'll put the whole thing through so smoothly that there will be no fuss at all."

"Very well, Dad, if you really think it's the best thing to be done."

"Got a fancy for the fellow still, Ruth? Is that it?"

"No."

The word came with no uncertain emphasis. Van Aldin seemed satisfied. He patted his daughter on the shoulder.

"It will be all right, little girl. Don't you worry any. Now let's forget about all this. I have brought you a present from Paris."

"For me? Something very nice?"

"I hope you'll think so," said Van Aldin, smiling.

He took the parcel from his coat pocket and handed it to her. She unwrapped it eagerly, and snapped open the case. A long-drawn "Oh!" came from her lips. Ruth Kettering loved jewels—always had done so.

"Dad, how—how wonderful!"

"Rather in a class by themselves, aren't they?" said the millionaire with satisfaction. "You like them, eh."

"Like them? Dad, they're unique. How did you get hold of them?"

Van Aldin smiled.

"Ah! that's my secret. They had to be bought privately, of course. They are rather well known. See that big stone in the middle? You have heard of it, maybe; that's the historic 'Heart of Fire.'"

"Heart of Fire!" repeated Mrs. Kettering.

She had taken the stones from the case and was holding them against her breast. The millionaire watched her. He was thinking of the series of women who had worn the jewels. The heartaches, the despairs, the jealousies. "Heart of Fire," like all famous stones, had left behind it a trail of tragedy and violence. Held in Ruth Kettering's assured hand, it seemed to lose its potency of evil. With her cool, equable poise, this woman of the western world seemed a negation to tragedy or heart-burnings. Ruth returned the stones to their case; then, jumping up, she flung her arms round her father's neck.

"Thank you, thank you, thank you, Dad. They are wonderful! You do give me the most marvellous presents always."

"That's all right," said Van Aldin, patting her shoulder. "You are all I have, you know, Ruthie."

"You will stay to dinner, won't you, Father?"

"I don't think so. You were going out, weren't you?"

"Yes, but I can easily put that off. Nothing very exciting."

"No," said Van Aldin. "Keep your engagement. I have got a good deal to attend to. See you to-morrow, my dear. Perhaps if I 'phone you, we can meet at Galbraiths'?"

Messrs. Galbraith, Galbraith, Cuthbertson & Galbraith were Van Aldin's London solicitors.

"Very well, Dad." She hesitated. "I suppose it—this—won't keep me from going to the Riviera?"

"When are you off?"

"On the fourteenth."

"Oh, that will be all right. These things take a long time to mature. By the way, Ruth, I shouldn't take those rubies abroad if I were you. Leave them at the bank."

Mrs. Kettering nodded.

"We don't want to have you robbed and murdered for the sake of 'Heart of Fire,'" said the millionaire jocosely.

"And yet you carried it about in your pocket loose," retorted his daughter, smiling.

"Yes——"

Something, some hesitation, caught her attention.

"What is it, Dad?"

"Nothing." He smiled. "Thinking of a little adventure of mine in Paris."

"An adventure?"

"Yes, the night I bought these things."

He made a gesture towards the jewel case.

"Oh, do tell me."

"Nothing to tell, Ruthie. Some apache fellows got a bit fresh and I shot at them and they got off. That's all."

She looked at him with some pride.

"You're a tough proposition, Dad."

"You bet I am, Ruthie."

He kissed her affectionately and departed. On arriving back at the Savoy, he gave a curt order to Knighton.

"Get hold of a man called Goby; you'll find his address in my private book. He's to be here to-morrow morning at half-past nine."

"Yes, sir."

"I also want to see Mr. Kettering. Run him to earth for me if you can. Try his Club—at any rate, get hold of him somehow, and arrange for me to see him here to-morrow morning. Better make it latish, about twelve. His sort aren't early risers."

The secretary nodded in comprehension of these instructions. Van Aldin gave himself into the hands of his valet. His bath was prepared, and as he lay luxuriating in the hot water, his mind went back over the conversation with his daughter. On the whole he was well satisfied. His keen mind had long since accepted the fact that divorce was the only possible way out. Ruth had agreed to the proposed solution with more readiness than he had hoped for. Yet, in spite of her acquiescence, he was left with a vague sense of uneasiness. Something about her manner, he felt, had not been quite natural. He frowned to himself.

"Maybe I'm fanciful," he muttered, "and yet—I bet there's something she has not told me."

Chapter 5

A USEFUL GENTLEMAN

Rufus Van Aldin had just finished the sparse breakfast of coffee and dry toast, which was all he ever allowed himself, when Knighton entered the room.

"Mr. Goby is below, sir, waiting to see you."

The millionaire glanced at the clock. It was just half-past nine.

"All right," he said curtly. "He can come up."

A minute or two later, Mr. Goby entered the room. He was a small, elderly man, shabbily dressed, with eyes that looked carefully all round the room, and never at the person he was addressing.

"Good morning, Goby," said the millionaire. "Take a chair."

"Thank you, Mr. Van Aldin."

Mr. Goby sat down with his hands on his knees, and gazed earnestly at the radiator.

"I have got a job for you."

"Yes, Mr. Van Aldin?"

"My daughter is married to the Hon. Derek Kettering, as you may perhaps know."

Mr. Goby transferred his gaze from the radiator to the left-hand drawer of the desk, and permitted a deprecating smile to pass over his face. Mr. Goby knew a great many things, but he always hated to admit the fact.

"By my advice, she is about to file a petition for divorce.

That, of course, is a solicitor's business. But, for private reasons, I want the fullest and most complete information."

Mr. Goby looked at the cornice and murmured:

"About Mr. Kettering?"

"About Mr. Kettering."

"Very good, sir."

Mr. Goby rose to his feet.

"When will you have it ready for me?"

"Are you in a hurry, sir?"

"I'm always in a hurry," said the millionaire.

Mr. Goby smiled understandingly at the fender.

"Shall we say two o'clock this afternoon, sir?" he asked.

"Excellent," approved the other. "Good morning, Goby."

"Good morning, Mr. Van Aldin."

"That's a very useful man," said the millionaire as Goby went out and his secretary came in. "In his own line he's a specialist."

"What is his line?"

"Information. Give him twenty-four hours and he would lay the private life of the Archbishop of Canterbury bare for you."

"A useful sort of chap," said Knighton, with a smile.

"He has been useful to me once or twice," said Van Aldin. "Now then, Knighton, I'm ready for work."

The next few hours saw a vast quantity of business rapidly transacted. It was half-past twelve when the telephone bell rang, and Mr. Van Aldin was informed that Mr. Kettering had called. Knighton looked at Van Aldin, and interpreted his brief nod.

"Ask Mr. Kettering to come up, please."

The secretary gathered up his papers and departed. He and the visitor passed each other in the doorway, and Derek Kettering stood aside to let the other go out. Then he came in, shutting the door behind him.

"Good morning, sir. You are very anxious to see me, I hear."

The lazy voice with its slightly ironic inflection roused memories in Van Aldin. There was charm in it—there had always been charm in it. He looked piercingly at his son-in-law. Derek Kettering was thirty-four, lean of build, with a dark, narrow face, which had even now something indescribably boyish in it.

"Come in," said Van Aldin curtly. "Sit down."

Kettering flung himself lightly into an arm-chair. He looked at his father-in-law with a kind of tolerant amusement.

"Not seen you for a long time, sir," he remarked pleasantly. "About two years, I should say. Seen Ruth yet?"

"I saw her last night," said Van Aldin.

"Looking very fit, isn't she?" said the other lightly.

"I didn't know you had had much opportunity of judging," said Van Aldin drily.

Derek Kettering raised his eyebrows.

"Oh, we sometimes meet at the same night club, you know," he said airily.

"I am not going to beat about the bush," Van Aldin said curtly. "I have advised Ruth to file a petition for divorce."

Derek Kettering seemed unmoved.

"How drastic!" he murmured. "Do you mind if I smoke, sir?"

He lit a cigarette, and puffed out a cloud of smoke as he added nonchalantly:

"And what did Ruth say?"

"Ruth proposes to take my advice," said her father.

"Does she really?"

"Is that all you have got to say?" demanded Van Aldin sharply.

Kettering flicked his ash into the grate.

"I think, you know," he said, with a detached air, "that she's making a great mistake."

"From your point of view she doubtless is," said Van Aldin grimly.

"Oh, come now," said the other; "don't let's be personal. I really wasn't thinking of myself at the moment. I was thinking of Ruth. You know my poor old Governor really can't last much longer; all the doctors say so. Ruth had better give it a couple more years, then I shall be Lord Leconbury, and she can be châtelaine of Leconbury, which is what she married me for."

"I won't have any of your darned impudence," roared Van Aldin.

Derek Kettering smiled at him unmoved.

"I agree with you. It's an obsolete idea," he said. "There's nothing in a title nowadays. Still, Leconbury is a very fine old place, and, after all, we are one of the oldest families in England. It will be very annoying for Ruth if she divorces me to find me marrying again, and some other woman queening it at Leconbury instead of her."

"I am serious, young man," said Van Aldin.

"Oh, so am I," said Kettering. "I am in very low water financially; it will put me in a nasty hole if Ruth divorces me, and, after all, if she has stood it for ten years, why not stand it a little longer? I give you my word of honour that the old man can't possibly last out another eighteen months, and, as I said before, it's a pity Ruth shouldn't get what she married me for."

"You suggest that my daughter married you for your title and position?"

Derek Kettering laughed a laugh that was not all amusement.

"You don't think it was a question of a love match?" he asked.

"I know," said Van Aldin slowly, "that you spoke very differently in Paris ten years ago."

"Did I? Perhaps I did. Ruth was very beautiful, you know—rather like an angel or a saint, or something that had stepped down from a niche in a church. I had fine ideas, I remember, of turning over a new leaf, of settling down and living up to the highest traditions of English home-life with a beautiful wife who loved me."

He laughed again, rather more discordantly.

"But you don't believe that, I suppose?" he said.

"I have no doubt at all that you married Ruth for her money," said Van Aldin unemotionally.

"And that she married me for love?" asked the other ironically.

"Certainly," said Van Aldin.

Derek Kettering stared at him for a minute or two, then he nodded reflectively.

"I see you believe that," he said. "So did I at the time.

I can assure you, my dear father-in-law, I was very soon undeceived."

"I don't know what you are getting at," said Van Aldin, "and I don't care. You have treated Ruth darned badly."

"Oh, I have," agreed Kettering lightly, "but she's tough, you know. She's your daughter. Underneath the pink-and-white softness of her she's as hard as granite. You have always been known as a hard man, so I have been told, but Ruth is harder than you are. You, at any rate, love one person better than yourself. Ruth never has and never will."

"That is enough," said Van Aldin. "I asked you here so that I could tell you fair and square what I meant to do. My girl has got to have some happiness, and remember this, I am behind her."

Derek Kettering got up and stood by the mantelpiece. He tossed away his cigarette. When he spoke, his voice was very quiet.

"What exactly do you mean by that, I wonder?" he said.

"I mean," said Van Aldin, "that you had better not try to defend the case."

"Oh," said Kettering, "is that a threat?"

"You can take it any way you please," said Van Aldin.

Kettering drew a chair up to the table. He sat down fronting the millionaire.

"And supposing," he said softly, "that, just for argument's sake, I did defend the case?"

Van Aldin shrugged his shoulders.

"You have not got a leg to stand upon, you young fool. Ask your solicitors, they will soon tell you. Your conduct has been notorious, the talk of London."

"Ruth has been kicking up a row about Mirelle, I suppose. Very foolish of her. I don't interfere with her friends."

"What do you mean?" said Van Aldin sharply.

Derek Kettering laughed.

"I see you don't know everything, sir," he said. "You are, perhaps naturally, prejudiced."

He took up his hat and stick and moved towards the door.

"Giving advice is not much in my line." He delivered his final thrust. "But, in this case, I should advise most strongly perfect frankness between father and daughter."

He passed quickly out of the room and shut the door behind him just as the millionaire sprang up.

"Now, what the hell did he mean by that?" said Van Aldin as he sank back into his chair again.

All his uneasiness returned in full force. There was something here that he had not yet got to the bottom of. The telephone was by his elbow; he seized it, and asked for the number of his daughter's house.

"Hallo! Hallo! Is that Mayfair 81907? Mrs. Kettering in? Oh, she's out, is she? Yes, out to lunch. What time will she be in? You don't know? Oh, very good; no, there's no message."

He slammed the receiver down again angrily. At two o'clock he was pacing the floor of his room waiting expectantly for Goby. The latter was ushered in at ten minutes past two.

"Well?" barked the millionaire sharply.

But little Mr. Goby was not to be hurried. He sat down at the table, produced a very shabby pocket-book, and proceeded to read from it in a monotonous voice. The millionaire listened attentively, with an increasing satisfaction. Goby came to a full stop, and looked attentively at the wastepaper-basket.

"Um!" said Van Aldin. "That seems pretty definite. The case will go through like winking. The hotel evidence is all right, I suppose?"

"Cast iron," said Mr. Goby, and looked malevolently at a gilt arm-chair.

"And financially he's in very low water. He's trying to raise a loan now, you say? Has already raised practically all he can upon his expectations from his father. Once the news of the divorce gets about, he won't be able to raise another cent, and not only that, his obligations can be bought up and pressure can be put upon him from that quarter. We have got him, Goby; we have got him in a cleft stick."

He hit the table a bang with his fist. His face was grim and triumphant.

"The information," said Mr. Goby in a thin voice, "seems satisfactory."

"I have got to go round to Curzon Street now," said the

millionaire. "I am much obliged to you, Goby. You are the goods all right."

A pale smile of gratification showed itself on the little man's face.

"Thank you, Mr. Van Aldin," he said; "I try to do my best."

Van Aldin did not go direct to Curzon Street. He went first to the City, where he had two interviews which added to his satisfaction. From there he took the tube to Down Street. As he was walking along Curzon Street, a figure came out of No. 160, and turned up the street towards him, so that they passed each other on the pavement. For a moment, the millionaire had fancied it might be Derek Kettering himself; the height and build were not unlike. But as they came face to face, he saw that the man was a stranger to him. At least—no, not a stranger; his face awoke some call of recognition in the millionaire's mind, and it was associated definitely with something unpleasant. He cudgelled his brains in vain, but the thing eluded him. He went on, shaking his head irritably. He hated to be baffled.

Ruth Kettering was clearly expecting him. She ran to him and kissed him when he entered.

"Well, Dad, how are things going?"

"Very well," said Van Aldin; "but I have got a word or two to say to you, Ruth."

Almost insensibly he felt the change in her; something shrewd and watchful replaced the impulsiveness of her greeting. She sat down in a big arm-chair.

"Well, Dad?" she asked. "What is it?"

"I saw your husband this morning," said Van Aldin.

"You saw Derek?"

"I did. He said a lot of things, most of which were darned cheek. Just as he was leaving, he said something that I didn't understand. He advised me to be sure that there was perfect frankness between father and daughter. What did he mean by that, Ruthie?"

Mrs. Kettering moved a little in her chair.

"I—I don't know, Dad. How should I?"

"Of course you know," said Van Aldin. "He said something else, about his having his friends and not interfering with yours. What did he mean by that?"

"I don't know," said Ruth Kettering again.

Van Aldin sat down. His mouth set itself in a grim line.

"See here, Ruth. I am not going into this with my eyes closed. I am not at all sure that that husband of yours doesn't mean to make trouble. Now, he can't do it, I am sure of that. I have got the means to silence him, to shut his mouth for good and all, but I have got to know if there's any need to use those means. What did he mean by your having your own friends?"

Mrs. Kettering shrugged her shoulders.

"I have got lots of friends," she said uncertainly. "I don't know what he meant, I am sure."

"You do," said Van Aldin.

He was speaking now as he might have spoken to a business adversary.

"I will put it plainer. Who is the man?"

"What man?"

"*The man.* That's what Derek was driving at. Some special man who is a friend of yours. You needn't worry, honey, I know there is nothing in it, but we have got to look at everything as it might appear to the Court. They can twist these things about a good deal, you know. I want to know who the man is, and just how friendly you have been with him."

Ruth didn't answer. Her hands were kneading themselves together in intense nervous absorption.

"Come, honey," said Van Aldin in a softer voice. "Don't be afraid of your old Dad. I was not too harsh, was I, even that time in Paris?—By gosh!"

He stopped, thunderstruck.

"That's who it was," he murmured to himself. "I thought I knew his face."

"What are you talking about, Dad? I don't understand."

The millionaire strode across to her and took her firmly by the wrist.

"See here, Ruth, have you been seeing that fellow again?"

"What fellow?"

"The one we had all that fuss about years ago. You know who I mean well enough."

"You mean"—she hesitated—"you mean the Comte de la Roche?"

"Comte de la Roche!" snorted Van Aldin. "I told you at the time that the man was no better than a swindler. You had entangled yourself with him then very deeply, but I got you out of his clutches."

"Yes, you did," said Ruth bitterly. "And I married Derek Kettering."

"You wanted to," said the millionaire sharply.

She shrugged her shoulders.

"And now," said Van Aldin slowly, "you have been seeing him again—after all I told you. He has been in the house to-day. I met him outside, and couldn't place him for the moment."

Ruth Kettering had recovered her composure.

"I want to tell you one thing, Dad; you are wrong about Armand—the Comte de la Roche, I mean. Oh, I know there were several regrettable incidents in his youth—he has told me about them; but—well, he has cared for me always. It broke his heart when you parted us in Paris, and now——"

She was interrupted by the snort of indignation her father gave.

"So you fell for that stuff, did you? You, a daughter of mine! My God!"

He threw up his hands.

"That women can be such darned fools!"

Chapter 6

MIRELLE

Derek Kettering emerged from Van Aldin's suite so precipitantly that he collided with a lady passing across the corridor. He apologised, and she accepted his apologies with a smiling reassurance and passed on, leaving with him a pleasant impression of a soothing personality and rather fine grey eyes.

For all his nonchalance, his interview with his father-in-law had shaken him more than he cared to show. He had a solitary lunch, and after it, frowning to himself a little, he went round to the sumptuous flat that housed the lady known as Mirelle. A trim Frenchwoman received him with smiles.

"But enter then, Monsieur. Madame reposes herself."

He was ushered into the long room with its Eastern setting which he knew so well. Mirelle was lying on the divan, supported by an incredible number of cushions, all in varying shades of amber, to harmonise with the yellow ochre of her complexion. The dancer was a beautifully made woman, and if her face, beneath its mask of yellow, was in truth somewhat haggard, it had a bizarre charm of its own, and her orange lips smiled invitingly at Derek Kettering.

He kissed her, and flung himself into a chair.

"What have you been doing with yourself? Just got up, I suppose?"

The orange mouth widened into a long smile.

"No," said the dancer. "I have been at work."

She flung out a long, pale hand towards the piano, which was littered with untidy music scores.

"Ambrose has been here. He has been playing me the new Opera."

Kettering nodded without paying much attention. He was profoundly uninterested in Claud Ambrose and the latter's operatic setting of Ibsen's *Peer Gynt*. So was Mirelle, for that matter, regarding it merely as a unique opportunity for her own presentation as Anitra.

"It is a marvellous dance," she murmured. "I shall put all the passion of the desert into it. I shall dance hung over with jewels—ah! and, by the way, *mon ami*, there is a pearl that I saw yesterday in Bond Street—a black pearl."

She paused, looking at him invitingly.

"My dear girl," said Kettering, "it's no use talking of black pearls to me. At the present minute, as far as I am concerned, the fat is in the fire."

She was quick to respond to his tone. She sat up, her big black eyes widening.

"What is that you say, Dereek? What has happened?"

"My esteemed father-in-law," said Kettering, "is preparing to go off the deep end."

"Eh?"

"In other words, he wants Ruth to divorce me."

"How stupid!" said Mirelle. "Why should she want to divorce you?"

Derek Kettering grinned.

"Mainly because of you, *chérie*!" he said.

Mirelle shrugged her shoulders.

"That is foolish," she observed in a matter-of-fact voice.

"Very foolish," agreed Derek.

"What are you going to do about it?" demanded Mirelle.

"My dear girl, what can I do? On the one side, the man with unlimited money; on the other side, the man with unlimited debts. There is no question as to who will come out on top."

"They are extraordinary, these Americans," commented Mirclle. "It is not as though your wife were fond of you."

"Well," said Derek, "what are we going to do about it?"

She looked at him inquiringly. He came over and took both her hands in his.

"Are you going to stick to me?"

"What do you mean? After——?"

"Yes," said Kettering. "After, when the creditors come down like wolves on the fold. I am damned fond of you, Mirelle; are you going to let me down?"

She pulled her hands away from him.

"You know I adore you, Dereek."

He caught the note of evasion in her voice.

"So that's that, is it? The rats will leave the sinking ship."

"Ah, Dereek!"

"Out with it," he said violently. "You will fling me over; is that it?"

She shrugged her shoulders.

"I am very fond of you, *mon ami*—indeed I am fond of you. You are very charming—*un beau garçon*, but *ce n'est pas pratique*."

"You are a rich man's luxury, eh? Is that it?"

"If you like to put it that way.

She leaned back on the cushions, her head flung back.

"All the same, I am fond of you, Dereek."

He went over to the window and stood there some time

looking out, with his back to her. Presently the dancer raised herself on her elbow and stared at him curiously.

"What are you thinking of, *mon ami*?"

He grinned at her over his shoulder, a curious grin, that made her vaguely uneasy.

"As it happened, I was thinking of a woman, my dear."

"A woman, eh?"

Mirelle pounced on something that she could understand.

"You are thinking of some other woman, is that it?"

"Oh, you needn't worry; it is purely a fancy portrait. 'Portrait of a lady with grey eyes.'"

Mirelle said sharply, "When did you meet her?"

Derek Kettering laughed, and his laughter had a mocking, ironical sound.

"I ran into the lady in the corridor of the Savoy Hotel."

"Well! What did she say?"

"As far as I can remember, I said 'I beg your pardon,' and she said, 'It doesn't matter,' or words to that effect."

"And then?" persisted the dancer.

Kettering shrugged his shoulders.

"And then—nothing. That was the end of the incident."

"I don't understand a word of what you are talking about," declared the dancer.

"Portrait of a lady with grey eyes," murmured Derek reflectively. "Just as well I am never likely to meet her again."

"Why?"

"She might bring me bad luck. Women do."

Mirelle slipped quietly from her couch, and came across to him, laying one long, snake-like arm round his neck.

"You are foolish, Dereek," she murmured. "You are very foolish. You are *beau garçon*, and I adore you, but I am not made to be poor—no, decidedly I am not made to be poor. Now listen to me; everything is very simple. You must make it up with your wife."

"I am afraid that's not going to be actually in the sphere of practical politics," said Derek drily.

"How do you say? I do not understand."

"Van Aldin, my dear, is not taking any. He is the kind of man who makes up his mind and sticks to it."

"I have heard of him," nodded the dancer. "He is very rich, is he not? Almost the richest man in America. A few days ago, in Paris, he bought the most wonderful ruby in the world—'Heart of Fire' it is called."

Kettering did not answer. The dancer went on musingly:

"It is a wonderful stone—a stone that should belong to a woman like me. I love jewels, Dereek; they say something to me. Ah! to wear a ruby like 'Heart of Fire.'"

She gave a little sigh, and then became practical once more.

"You don't understand these things, Dereek; you are only a man. Van Aldin will give these rubies to his daughter, I suppose. Is she his only child?"

"Yes."

"Then when he dies, she will inherit all his money. She will be a rich woman."

"She is a rich woman already," said Kettering drily. "He settled a couple of millions on her at her marriage."

"A couple of million! But that is immense. And if she died suddenly, eh? That would all come to you?"

"As things stand at present," said Kettering slowly, "it would. As far as I know she has not made a will."

"*Mon Dieu!*" said the dancer. "If she were to die, what a solution that would be."

There was a moment's pause, and then Derek Kettering laughed outright.

"I like your simple, practical mind, Mirelle, but I am afraid what you desire won't come to pass. My wife is an extremely healthy person."

"*Eh bien!*" said Mirelle; "there are accidents."

He looked at her sharply but did not answer.

She went on.

"But you are right, *mon ami*, we must not dwell on possibilities. See now, my little Dereek, there must be no more talk of this divorce. Your wife must give up the idea."

"And if she won't?"

The dancer's eyes narrowed to slits.

"I think she will, my friend. She is one of those who would not like the publicity. There are one or two pretty stories that she would not like her friends to read in the newspapers."

"What do you mean?" asked Kettering sharply.

Mirelle laughed, her head thrown back.

"*Parbleu!* I mean the gentleman who calls himself the Comte de la Roche. I know all about him. I am Parisienne, you remember. He was her lover before she married you, was he not?"

Kettering took her sharply by the shoulders.

"That is a damned lie," he said, "and please remember that, after all, you are speaking of my wife."

Mirelle was a little sobered.

"You are extraordinary, you English," she complained. "All the same, I dare say that you may be right. The Americans are so cold, are they not? But you will permit me to say, *mon ami*, that she was *in love with him* before she married you, and her father stepped in and sent the Comte about his business. And the little Mademoiselle, she wept many tears! But she obeyed. Still, you must know as well as I do, Dereek, that it is a very different story now. She sees him nearly every day, and on the fourteenth she goes to Paris to meet him."

"How do you know all this?" demanded Kettering.

"Me? I have friends in Paris, my dear Dereek, who know the Comte intimately. It is all arranged. She is going to the Riviera, so she says, but in reality the Comte meets her in Paris and—who knows! Yes, yes, you can take my word for it, it is all arranged."

Derek Kettering stood motionless.

"You see," purred the dancer, "if you are clever, you have her in the hollow of your hand. You can make things very awkward for her."

"Oh, for God's sake be quiet," cried Kettering. "Shut your cursed mouth!"

Mirelle flung herself down again on the divan with a laugh. Kettering caught up his hat and coat and left the flat, banging the door violently. And still the dancer sat on the divan and laughed softly to herself. She was not displeased with her work.

Chapter 7

LETTERS

"Mrs. Samuel Harfield presents her compliments to Miss Katherine Grey and wishes to point out that under the circumstances Miss Grey may not be aware——"

Mrs. Harfield, having written so far fluently, came to a dead stop, held up by what has proved an insuperable difficulty to many other people—namely, the difficulty of expressing oneself fluently in the third person.

After a minute or two of hesitation, Mrs. Harfield tore up the sheet of notepaper and started afresh.

"Dear Miss Grey,—Whilst fully appreciating the adequate way you discharged your duties to my Cousin Emma (whose recent death has indeed been a severe blow to us all), I cannot but feel——"

Again Mrs. Harfield came to a stop. Once more the letter was consigned to the wastepaper-basket. It was not until four false starts had been made that Mrs. Harfield at last produced an epistle that satisfied her. It was duly sealed and stamped and addressed to Miss Katherine Grey, Little Crampton, St. Mary Mead, Kent, and it lay beside the lady's plate on the following morning at breakfast-time in company with a more important-looking communication in a long blue envelope.

Katherine Grey opened Mrs. Harfield's letter first. The finished production ran as follows:

"Dear Miss Grey,—My husband and I wish to express our thanks to you for your services to my poor cousin, Emma. Her death has been a great blow to us, though we were, of course, aware that her mind has been failing for some time past. I understand that her latter testamentary dispositions have been of a most peculiar character, and they would not hold good, of course, in any court of law. I have no doubt that, with your usual good sense, you have already realised this fact. If these matters can be arranged privately it is always so much better, my husband says. We shall be pleased to recommend you most highly for a similar post, and hope that you will also accept a small present. Believe me, dear Miss Grey, yours cordially,

MARY ANNE HATFIELD."

Katherine Grey read the letter through, smiled a little, and read it a second time. Her face as she laid the letter down after the second reading was distinctly amused. Then she took up the second letter. After one brief perusal she laid it down and stared very straight in front of her. This time she did not smile. Indeed, it would have been hard for anyone watching her to guess what emotions lay behind that quiet, reflective gaze.

Katherine Grey was thirty-three. She came of good family, but her father had lost all his money, and Katherine had had to work for her living from an early age. She had been just twenty-three when she had come to old Mrs. Harfield as companion.

It was generally recognised that old Mrs. Harfield was "difficult." Companions came and went with startling rapidity. They arrived full of hope and they usually left in tears. But from the moment Katherine Grey set foot in Little Crampton, ten years ago, perfect peace had reigned. No one knows how these things come about. Snake-charmers, they say, are born, not made. Katherine Grey was born with the power of managing old ladies, dogs, and small boys, and she did it without any apparent sense of strain.

At twenty-three she had been a quiet girl with beautiful eyes. At thirty-three she was a quiet woman, with those same grey eyes, shining steadily out on the world with a kind of happy serenity that nothing could shake. Moreover, she had been born with, and still possessed, a sense of humour.

As she sat at the breakfast-table, staring in front of her, there was a ring at the bell, accompanied by a very energetic rat-a-tat-tat at the knocker. In another minute the little maid-servant opened the door and announced rather breathlessly:

"Dr. Harrison."

The big, middle-aged doctor came bustling in with the energy and breeziness that had been fore-shadowed by his onslaught on the knocker.

"Good morning, Miss Grey."

"Good morning, Dr. Harrison."

"I dropped in early," began the doctor, "in case you should have heard from one of those Harfield cousins. Mrs. Samuel, she calls herself—a perfectly poisonous person."

Without a word, Katherine picked up Mrs. Harfield's letter from the table and gave it to him. With a good deal of amusement she watched his perusal of it, the drawing together of the bushy eyebrows, the snorts and grunts of violent disapproval. He dashed it down again on the table.

"Perfectly monstrous," he fumed. "Don't you let it worry you, my dear. They're talking through their hat. Mrs. Harfield's intellect was as good as yours or mine, and you won't get anyone to say the contrary. They wouldn't have a leg to stand upon, and they know it. All that talk of taking it into court is pure bluff. Hence this attempt to get round you in a hole-and-corner way. And look here, my dear, don't let them get round you with soft soap either. Don't get fancying it's your duty to hand over the cash, or any tomfoolery of conscientious scruples."

"I'm afraid it hasn't occurred to me to have scruples," said Katherine. "All these people are distant relatives of Mrs. Harfield's husband, and they never came near her or took any notice of her in her lifetime."

"You're a sensible woman," said the doctor. "I know, none better, that you've had a hard life of it for the last ten years. You're fully entitled to enjoy the old lady's savings, such as they were."

Katherine smiled thoughtfully.

"Such as they were," she repeated. "You've no idea of the amount, doctor?"

"Well—enough to bring in five hundred a year or so, I suppose."

Katherine nodded.

"That's what I thought," she said. "Now read this."

She handed him the letter she had taken from the long blue envelope. The doctor read and uttered an exclamation of utter astonishment.

"Impossible," he muttered. "Impossible."

"She was one of the original shareholders in Mortaulds.

Forty years ago she must have had an income of eight or ten thousand a year. She has never, I am sure, spent more than four hundred a year. She was always terribly careful about money. I always believed that she was obliged to be careful about every penny."

"And all the time the income has accumulated at compound interest. My dear, you're going to be a very rich woman."

Katherine Grey nodded.

"Yes," she said, "I am."

She spoke in a detached, impersonal tone, as though she were looking at the situation from outside.

"Well," said the doctor, preparing to depart, "you have all my congratulations." He flicked Mrs. Samuel Harfield's letter with his thumb. "Don't worry about that woman and her odious letter."

"It really isn't an odious letter," said Miss Grey tolerantly. "Under the circumstances, I think it's really quite a natural thing to do."

"I have the gravest suspicions of you sometimes," said the doctor.

"Why?"

"The things that you find perfectly natural."

Katherine Grey laughed.

Doctor Harrison retailed the great news to his wife at lunch-time. She was very excited about it.

"Fancy old Mrs. Harfield—with all that money. I'm glad she left it to Katherine Grey. That girl's a saint."

The doctor made a wry face.

"Saints I always imagined must have been difficult people. Katherine Grey is too human for a saint."

"She's a saint with a sense of humour," said the doctor's wife, twinkling. "And, though I don't suppose you've ever noticed the fact, she's extremely good looking."

"Katherine Grey?" The doctor was honestly surprised. "She's got very nice eyes, I know."

"Oh, you men!" cried his wife. "Blind as bats. Katherine's got all the makings of a beauty in her. All she wants is clothes!"

"Clothes? What's wrong with her clothes? She always looks very nice."

Mrs. Harrison gave an exasperated sigh, and the doctor rose preparatory to starting on his rounds.

"You might look in on her, Polly," he suggested.

"I'm going to," said Mrs. Harrison promptly.

She made her call about three o'clock.

"My dear, I'm so glad," she said warmly, as she squeezed Katherine's hand. "And everyone in the village will be glad too."

"It's very nice of you to come and tell me," said Katherine. "I hoped you would come in because I wanted to ask about Johnnie."

"Oh! Johnnie. Well——"

Johnnie was Mrs. Harrison's youngest son. In another minute she was off, retailing a long history in which Johnnie's adenoids and tonsils bulked largely. Katherine listened sympathetically. Habits die hard. Listening had been her portion for ten years now. "My dear, I wonder if I ever told you about the naval ball at Portsmouth? When Lord Charles admired my gown?" And composedly, kindly, Katherine would reply: "I rather think you have, Mrs. Harfield, but I've forgotten about it. Won't you tell it me again?" And then the old lady would start off full swing, with numerous corrections, and stops, and remembered details. And half of Katherine's mind would be listening, saying the right things mechanically when the old lady paused . . .

Now, with the same curious feeling of duality to which she was accustomed, she listened to Mrs. Harrison.

At the end of half an hour, the latter recalled herself suddenly.

"I've been talking about myself all this time," she exclaimed. "And I came here to talk about you and your plans."

"I don't know that I've got any yet."

"My dear—you're not going to stay on *here*."

Katherine smiled at the horror in the other's tone.

"No; I think I want to travel. I've never seen much of the world, you know."

"I should think not. It must have been an awful life for you cooped up here all these years."

"I don't know," said Katherine. "It gave me a lot of freedom."

She caught the other's gasp, and reddened a little.

"It must sound foolish—saying that. Of course, I hadn't much freedom in the downright physical sense——"

"I should think not," breathed Mrs. Harrison, remembering that Katherine had seldom had that useful thing, a "day off."

"But in a way, being tied physically gives you lots of scope mentally. You're always free to think. I've had a lovely feeling always of mental freedom."

Mrs. Harrison shook her head.

"I can't understand that."

"Oh! you would if you'd been in my place. But, all the same, I feel I want a change. I want—well, I want things to happen. Oh! not to me—I don't mean that. But to be in the midst of things—exciting things—even if I'm only the looker-on. You know, things don't happen in St. Mary Mead."

"They don't indeed," said Mrs. Harrison, with fervour.

"I shall go to London first," said Katherine. "I have to see the solicitors, anyway. After that, I shall go abroad, I think."

"Very nice."

"But, of course, first of all——"

"Yes?"

"I must get some clothes."

"Exactly what I said to Arthur this morning," cried the doctor's wife. "You know, Katherine, you could look possibly positively beautiful if you tried."

Miss Grey laughed unaffectedly.

"Oh! I don't think you could ever make a beauty out of me," she said sincerely. "But I shall enjoy having some really good clothes. I'm afraid I'm talking about myself an awful lot."

Mrs. Harrison looked at her shrewdly.

"It must be quite a novel experience for you," she said drily.

Katherine went to say good-bye to old Miss Viner before

leaving the village. Miss Viner was two years older than Mrs. Harfield, and her mind was mainly taken up with her own success in out-living her dead friend.

"You wouldn't have thought I'd have outlasted Jane Harfield, would you?" she demanded triumphantly of Katherine. "We were at school together, she and I. And here we are, she taken, and I left. Who would have thought it?"

"You've always eaten brown bread for supper, haven't you?" murmured Katherine mechanically.

"Fancy your remembering that, my dear. Yes; if Jane Harfield had had a slice of brown bread every evening and taken a little stimulant with her meals she might be here to-day."

The old lady paused, nodding her head triumphantly; then added in sudden remembrance:

"And so you've come into a lot of money, I hear? Well, well. Take care of it. And you're going up to London to have a good time? Don't think you'll get married, though, my dear, because you won't. You're not the kind to attract the men. And, besides, you're getting on. How old are you now?"

"Thirty-three," Katherine told her.

"Well," remarked Miss Viner doubtfully, "that's not so very bad. You've lost your first freshness, of course."

"I'm afraid so," said Katherine, much entertained.

"But you're a very nice girl," said Miss Viner kindly. "And I'm sure there's many a man might do worse than take you for a wife instead of one of these flibbertigibbets running about nowadays showing more of their legs than the Creator ever intended them to. Good-bye, my dear, and I hope you'll enjoy yourself, but things are seldom what they seem in this life."

Heartened by these prophecies, Katherine took her departure. Half the village came to see her off at the station, including the little maid of all work, Alice, who brought a stiff wired nosegay and cried openly.

"There ain't a many like her," sobbed Alice when the train had finally departed. "I'm sure when Charlie went back on me with that girl from the Dairy, nobody could have been kinder than Miss Grey was, and though particular about the brasses and the dust, she was always one to notice when you'd give a thing an extra rub. Cut myself in little pieces for her, I would, any day. A real lady, that's what I call her."

Such was Katherine's departure from St. Mary Mead.

Chapter 8

LADY TAMPLIN WRITES A LETTER

"Well," said Lady Tamplin, "well."

She laid down the continental *Daily Mail* and stared out across the blue waters of the Mediterranean. A branch of golden mimosa, hanging just above her head, made an effective frame for a very charming picture. A golden-haired, blue-eyed lady in a very becoming *négligée.* That the golden hair owed something to art, as did the pink-and-white complexion, was undeniable, but the blue of the eyes was Nature's gift, and at forty-four Lady Tamplin could still rank as a beauty.

Charming as she looked, Lady Tamplin was, for once, not thinking of herself. That is to say, she was not thinking of her appearance. She was intent on graver matters.

Lady Tamplin was a well-known figure on the Riviera, and her parties at the Villa Marguerite were justly celebrated. She was a woman of considerable experience, and had had four husbands. The first had been merely an indiscretion, and so was seldom referred to by the lady. He had had the good sense to die with commendable promptitude, and his widow thereupon espoused a rich manufacturer of buttons. He too had departed for another sphere after three years of married life—it was said after a congenial evening with some boon companions. After him came Viscount Tamplin, who had placed Rosalie securely on those heights where she wished to tread. She retained her title when she married for a fourth time. This fourth venture had been undertaken for pure pleasure. Mr. Charles Evans, an extremely good-looking young man of twenty-seven, with delightful manners, a keen love of sport, and an appreciation of this world's goods, had no money of his own whatsoever.

Lady Tamplin was very pleased and satisfied with life generally, but she had occasional faint preoccupations about money. The button manufacturer had left his widow a considerable fortune, but, as Lady Tamplin was wont to say, "what with one thing and another——" (one thing being the depreciation of stocks owing to the War, and the other the extravagances of the late Lord Tamplin). She was still comfortably off. But to be merely comfortably off was hardly satisfactory to one of Rosalie Tamplin's temperament.

So, on this particular January morning, she opened her blue eyes extremely wide as she read a certain item of news and uttered that non-committal monosyllable "Well." The only other occupant of the balcony was her daughter, the Hon. Lenox Tamplin. A daughter such as Lenox was a sad thorn in Lady Tamplin's side, a girl with no kind of tact, who actually looked older than her age, and whose peculiar sardonic form of humour was, to say the least of it, uncomfortable.

"Darling," said Lady Tamplin, "just fancy."

"What is it?"

Lady Tamplin picked up the *Daily Mail*, handed it to her daughter, and indicated with an agitated forefinger the paragraph of interest.

Lenox read it without any of the signs of agitation shown by her mother. She handed back the paper.

"What about it?" she asked. "It is the sort of thing that is always happening. Cheese-paring old women are always dying in villages and leaving fortunes of millions to their humble companions."

"Yes, dear, I know," said her mother, "and I dare say the fortune is not anything like as large as they say it is; newspapers are so inaccurate. But even if you cut it down by half——"

"Well," said Lenox, "it has not been left to us."

"Not exactly, dear," said Lady Tamplin, "but this girl, this Katherine Grey, is actually a cousin of mine. One of the Worcestershire Greys, the Edgeworth lot. My very own cousin! Fancy!"

"Ah-ha," said Lenox.

"And I was wondering——" said her mother.

"What there is in it for us," finished Lenox, with that sideways smile that her mother always found difficult to understand.

"Oh, darling," said Lady Tamplin, on a faint note of reproach.

It was very faint, because Rosalie Tamplin was used to her daughter's outspokenness and to what she called Lenox's uncomfortable way of putting things.

"I was wondering," said Lady Tamplin, again drawing her artistically pencilled brows together, "whether—oh, good morning, Chubby darling: are you going to play tennis? How nice!"

Chubby, thus addressed, smiled kindly at her, remarked perfunctorily, "How topping you look in that peach-coloured thing," and drifted past them and down the steps.

"The dear thing," said Lady Tamplin, looking affectionately after her husband. "Let me see, what was I saying? Ah!" She switched her mind back to business once more. "I was wondering——"

"Oh, for God's sake get on with it. That is the third time you have said that."

"Well, dear," said Lady Tamplin, "I was thinking that it would be very nice if I wrote to dear Katherine and suggested that she should pay us a little visit out here. Naturally, she is quite out of touch with Society. It would be nicer for her to be launched by one of her own people. An advantage for her and an advantage for us."

"How much do you think you would get her to cough up?" asked Lenox.

Her mother looked at her reproachfully and murmured:

"We should have to come to some financial arrangement, of course. What with one thing and another—the War—your poor father——"

"And Chubby now," said Lenox. "He is an expensive luxury if you like."

"She was a nice girl as I remember her," murmured Lady Tamplin, pursuing her own line of thought—"quiet, never wanted to shove herself forward, not a beauty, and never a man-hunter."

" She will leave Chubby alone, then?" said Lenox.

Lady Tamplin looked at her in protest. " Chubby would never——" she began.

" No," said Lenox, " I don't believe he would; he knows a jolly sight too well which way his bread is buttered."

" Darling," said Lady Tamplin, " you have such a coarse way of putting things."

" Sorry," said Lenox.

Lady Tamplin gathered up the *Daily Mail* and her *négligée*, a vanity bag, and various odd letters.

" I shall write to dear Katherine at once," she said, " and remind her of the dear old days at Edgeworth."

She went into the house, a light of purpose shining in her eyes.

Unlike Mrs. Samuel Harfield, correspondence flowed easily from her pen. She covered four sheets without pause or effort, and on re-reading it found no occasion to alter a word.

Katherine received it on the morning of her arrival in London. Whether she read between the lines of it or not is another matter. She put it in her handbag and started out to keep the appointment she had made with Mrs. Harfield's lawyers.

The firm was an old-established one in Lincoln's Inn Fields, and after a few minutes' delay Katherine was shown into the presence of the senior partner, a kindly, elderly man with shrewd blue eyes and a fatherly manner.

They discussed Mrs. Harfield's will and various legal matters for some twenty minutes, then Katherine handed the lawyer Mrs. Samuel's letter.

" I had better show you this, I suppose," she said, " though it is really rather ridiculous."

He read it with a slight smile.

" Rather a crude attempt, Miss Grey. I need hardly tell you, I suppose, that these people have no claim of any kind upon the estate, and if they endeavour to contest the will no court will uphold them."

" I thought as much."

"Human nature is not always very wise. In Mrs. Samuel Harfield's place, I should have been more inclined to make an appeal to your generosity."

"That is one of the things I want to speak to you about. I should like a certain sum to go to these people."

"There is no obligation."

"I know that."

"And they will not take it in the spirit it is meant. They will probably regard it as an attempt to pay them off, though they will not refuse it on that account."

"I can see that, and it can't be helped."

"I should advise you, Miss Grey, to put that idea out of your mind."

Katherine shook her head. "You are quite right, I know, but I should like it done all the same."

"They will grab at the money and abuse you all the more afterwards."

"Well," said Katherine, "let them if they like. We all have our own ways of enjoying ourselves. They were, after all, Mrs. Harfield's only relatives, and though they despised her as a poor relation and paid no attention to her when she was alive, it seems to me unfair that they should be cut off with nothing."

She carried her point, though the lawyer was still unwilling, and she presently went out into the streets of London with a comfortable assurance that she could spend money freely and make what plans she liked for the future. Her first action was to visit the establishment of a famous dressmaker.

A slim, elderly Frenchwoman, rather like a dreaming duchess, received her, and Katherine spoke with a certain *naïveté*.

"I want, if I may, to put myself in your hands. I have been very poor all my life and know nothing about clothes, but now I have come into some money and want to look really well dressed."

The Frenchwoman was charmed. She had an artist's temperament, which had been soured earlier in the morning by a visit from an Argentine meat queen, who had insisted on having those models least suited to her flamboyant type of beauty. She scrutinised Katherine with keen, clever eyes. "Yes—yes, it will be a pleasure. Mademoiselle has a very good figure; for her the simple lines will be best. She is also *très anglaise*. Some people it would offend them if I said that, but Mademoiselle no. *Une belle Anglaise*, there is no style more delightful."

The demeanour of a dreaming duchess was suddenly put off. She screamed out directions to various mannequins. "Clothilde, Virginie, quickly, my little ones, the little *tailleur gris clair* and the *robe de soirée 'soupir d'automne.'* Marcelle, my child, the little mimosa suit of crêpe de chine."

It was a charming morning. Marcelle, Clothilde, Virginie, bored and scornful, passed slowly round, squirming and wriggling in the time-honoured fashion of mannequins. The Duchess stood by Katherine and made entries in a small note-book.

"An excellent choice, Mademoiselle. Mademoiselle has great *goût*. Yes, indeed. Mademoiselle cannot do better than those little suits if she is going to the Riviera, as I suppose, this winter."

"Let me see that evening dress once more," said Katherine—"the pinky mauve one."

Virginie appeared, circling slowly.

"That is the prettiest of all," said Katherine, as she surveyed the exquisite draperies of mauve and grey and blue. "What do you call it?"

"*Soupir d'automne*; yes, yes, that is truly the dress of Mademoiselle."

What was there in these words that came back to Katherine with a faint feeling of sadness after she had left the dressmaking establishment.

"'*Soupir d'automne; that is truly the dress of Mademoiselle.*'" Autumn, yes, it was autumn for her. She who had never known spring or summer, and would never know them now. Something she had lost never could be given to her again. These years of servitude in St. Mary Mead—and all the while life passing by.

"I am an idiot," said Katherine. "I am an idiot. What do I want? Why, I was more contented a month ago than I am now."

She drew out from her handbag the letter she had received that morning from Lady Tamplin. Katherine was no fool. She understood the *nuances* of that letter as well as anybody and the reason of Lady Tamplin's sudden show of affection towards a long-forgotten cousin was not lost upon her. It was for profit and not for pleasure that Lady Tamplin was so anxious for the company of her dear cousin. Well, why not? There would be profit on both sides.

"I will go," said Katherine.

She was walking down Piccadilly at the moment, and turned into Cook's to clinch the matter then and there. She had to wait for a few minutes. The man with whom the clerk was engaged was also going to the Riviera. Everyone, she felt, was going. Well, for the first time in her life, she, too, would be doing what "everybody" did.

The man in front of her turned abruptly, and she stepped into his place. She made her demand to the clerk, but at the same time half of her mind was busy with something else. That man's face—in some vague way it was familiar to her. Where had she seen him before? Suddenly she remembered. It was in the Savoy outside her room that morning. She had collided with him in the passage. Rather an odd coincidence that she should run into him twice in a day. She glanced over her shoulder, rendered uneasy by something, she knew not what. The man was standing in the doorway looking back at her. A cold shiver passed over Katherine; she had a haunting sense of tragedy, of doom impending. . . .

Then she shook the impression from her with her usual good sense and turned her whole attention to what the clerk was saying.

Chapter 9

AN OFFER REFUSED

It was rarely that Derek Kettering allowed his temper to get the better of him. An easy-going insouciance was his chief characteristic, and it had stood him in good stead in more than one tight corner. Even now, by the time he had left Mirelle's flat, he had cooled down. He had need of coolness. The corner he was in now was a tighter one than he had ever been in before, and unforeseen factors had arisen with which, for the moment, he did not know how to deal.

He strolled along deep in thought. His brow was furrowed, and there was none of the easy, jaunty manner which sat so well upon him. Various possibilities floated through his mind. It might have been said of Derek Kettering that he was less of a fool than he looked. He saw several roads that he might take—one in particular. If he shrank from it, it was for the moment only. Desperate ills need desperate remedies. He had gauged his father-in-law correctly. A war between Derek Kettering and Rufus Van Aldin could end only one way. Derek damned money and the power of money vehemently to himself. He walked up St. James's Street, across Piccadilly, and strolled along it in the direction of Piccadilly Circus. As he passed the offices of Messrs. Thomas Cook & Sons his footsteps slackened. He walked on, however, still turning the matter over in his mind. Finally, he gave a brief nod of his head, turned sharply—so sharply as to collide with a couple of pedestrians who were following in his footsteps, and went back the way he had come. This time he did not pass Cook's, but went in. The office was comparatively empty, and he got attended to at once.

"I want to go to Nice next week. Will you give me particulars?"

"What date, sir?"

"The fourteenth. What is the best train?"

"Well, of course, *the* best train is what they call 'The Blue Train.' You avoid the tiresome Customs business at Calais."

Derek nodded. He knew all this, none better.

"The fourteenth," murmured the clerk; "that is rather soon. The Blue Train is nearly always all booked up."

"See if there is a berth left," said Derek. "If there is not——" He left the sentence unfinished, with a curious smile on his face.

The clerk disappeared for a few minutes, and presently returned. "That is all right, sir, still three berths left. I will book you one of them. What name?"

"Pavett," said Derek. He gave the address of his rooms in Jermyn Street.

The clerk nodded, finished writing it down, wished Derek good morning politely, and turned his attention to the next client.

"I want to go to Nice—on the fourteenth. Isn't there a train called the Blue Train?"

Derek looked round sharply.

Coincidence—a strange coincidence. He remembered his own half-whimsical words to Mirelle. "*Portrait of a lady with grey eyes. I don't suppose I shall ever see her again.*" But he *had* seen her again, and, what was more, she proposed to travel to the Riviera on the same day as he did.

Just for a moment a shiver passed over him; in some ways he was superstitious. He had said, half-laughingly, that this woman might bring him bad luck. Suppose—suppose that should prove to be true. From the doorway he looked back at her as she stood talking to the clerk. For once his memory had not played him false. A lady—a lady in every sense of the word. Not very young, not singularly beautiful. But with something—grey eyes that might perhaps see too much. He knew as he went out of the door that in some way he was afraid of this woman. He had a sense of fatality.

He went back to his rooms in Jermyn Street and summoned his man.

"Take this cheque, Pavett, and go round to Cook in Piccadilly. They will have some tickets there booked in your name, pay for them, and bring them back."

"Very good, sir."

Pavett withdrew.

Derek strolled over to a side-table and picked up a handful of letters. They were of a type only too familiar. Bills, small bills and large bills, one and all pressing for payment. The tone of the demands was still polite. Derek knew how soon that polite tone would change if—if certain news became public property.

He flung himself moodily into a large, leather-covered chair. A damned hole—that was what he was in. Yes, a damned hole! And ways of getting out of that damned hole were not too promising.

Pavett appeared with a discreet cough.

"A gentleman to see you—sir—Major Knighton."

"Knighton, eh?"

Derek sat up, frowned, became suddenly alert. He said in a softer tone, almost to himself: "Knighton—I wonder what is in the wind now?"

"Shall I—er—show him in, sir?"

His master nodded. When Knighton entered the room he found a charming and genial host awaiting him.

"Very good of you to look me up," said Derek.

Knighton was nervous.

The other's keen eyes noticed that at once. The errand on which the secretary had come was clearly distasteful to him. He replied almost mechanically to Derek's easy flow of conversation. He declined a drink, and, if anything, his manner became stiffer than before. Derek appeared at last to notice it.

"Well," he said cheerfully, "what does my esteemed father-in-law want with me? You have come on his business, I take it?"

Knighton did not smile in reply.

"I have, yes," he said carefully. "I—I wish Mr. Van Aldin had chosen someone else."

Derek raised his eyebrows in mock dismay.

"Is it as bad as all that? I am not very thin skinned, I can assure you, Knighton."

"No," said Knighton; "but this——"

He paused.

Derek eyed him keenly.

"Go on, out with it," he said kindly. "I can imagine my dear father-in-law's errands might not always be pleasant ones."

Knighton cleared his throat. He spoke formally in tones that he strove to render free of embarrassment.

"I am directed by Mr. Van Aldin to make you a definite offer."

"An offer?" For a moment Derek showed his surprise. Knighton's opening words were clearly not what he had expected. He offered a cigarette to Knighton, lit one himself, and sank back in his chair, murmuring in a slightly sardonic voice:

"An offer? That sounds rather interesting."

"Shall I go on?"

"Please. You must forgive my surprise, but it seems to me that my dear father-in-law has rather climbed down since our chat this morning. And climbing down is not what one associates with strong men, Napoleons of finance, etc. It shows —I think it shows that he finds his position weaker than he thought it."

Knighton listened politely to the easy, mocking voice, but no sign of any kind showed itself on his rather stolid countenance. He waited until Derek had finished, and then he said quietly:

"I will state the proposition in the fewest possible words."

"Go on."

Knighton did not look at the other. His voice was curt and matter-of-fact.

"The matter is simply this. Mrs. Kettering, as you know, is about to file a petition for divorce. If the case goes undefended you will receive one hundred thousand on the day that the decree is made absolute."

Derek, in the act of lighting his cigarette, suddenly stopped dead. "A hundred thousand!" he said sharply. "Dollars?"

"Pounds."

There was dead silence for at least two minutes. Kettering had his brows together thinking. A hundred thousand pounds. It meant Mirelle and a continuance of his pleasant, careless life. It meant that Van Aldin knew something. Van Aldin did not pay for nothing. He got up and stood by the chimney-piece.

"And in the event of my refusing his handsome offer?" he asked, with a cold, ironical politeness.

Knighton made a deprecating gesture.

"I can assure you, Mr. Kettering," he said earnestly, "that it is with the utmost unwillingness that I came here with this message."

"That's all right," said Kettering. "Don't distress yourself; it's not your fault. Now then—I asked you a question, will you answer it?"

Knighton also rose. He spoke more reluctantly than before.

"In the event of your refusing this proposition," he said,

"Mr. Van Aldin wished me to tell you in plain words that he proposes to break you. Just that."

Kettering raised his eyebrows, but he retained his light, amused manner.

"Well, well!" he said, "I suppose he can do it. I certainly should not be able to put up much of a fight against America's man of many millions. A hundred thousand! If you are going to bribe a man there is nothing like doing it thoroughly. Supposing I were to tell you that for two hundred thousand I'd do what he wanted, what then?"

"I would take your message back to Mr. Van Aldin," said Knighton unemotionally. "Is that your answer?"

"No," said Derek; "funnily enough it is not. You can go back to my father-in-law and tell him to take himself and his bribes to hell. Is that clear?"

"Perfectly," said Knighton. He got up, hesitated, and then flushed. "I—you will allow me to say, Mr. Kettering, that I am glad you have answered as you have."

Derek did not reply. When the other had left the room he remained for a minute or two lost in thought. A curious smile came to his lips.

"And that is that," he said softly.

Chapter 10

ON THE BLUE TRAIN

"Dad!"

Mrs. Kettering started violently. Her nerves were not completely under control this morning. Very perfectly dressed in a long mink coat and a little hat of Chinese lacquer red, she had been walking along the crowded platform of Victoria deep in thought, and her father's sudden appearance and hearty greeting had an unlooked-for effect upon her.

"Why, Ruth, how you jumped!"

"I didn't expect to see you, I suppose, Dad. You said good-bye to me last night and said you had a conference this morning."

"So I have," said Van Aldin, "but you are more to me than any number of darned conferences. I came to take a last look at you, since I am not going to see you for some time."

"That is very sweet of you, Dad. I wish you were coming too."

"What would you say if I did?"

The remark was merely a joking one. He was surprised to see the quick colour of flame in Ruth's cheeks. For a moment he almost thought he saw dismay flash out of her eyes. She laughed uncertainly and nervously.

"Just for a moment I really thought you meant it," she said.

"Would you have been pleased?"

"Of course." She spoke with exaggerated emphasis.

"Well," said Van Aldin, "that's good."

"It isn't really for very long, Dad," continued Ruth; "you know, you are coming out next month."

"Ah!" said Van Aldin unemotionally, "sometimes I guess I will go to one of these big guys in Harley Street and have him tell me that I need sunshine and change of air right away."

"Don't be so lazy," cried Ruth; "next month is ever so much nicer than this month out there. You have got all sorts of things you can't possibly leave just now."

"Well, that's so, I suppose," said Van Aldin, with a sigh. "You had better be getting on board this train of yours, Ruth. Where is your seat?"

Ruth Kettering looked vaguely up at the train. At the door of one of the Pullman cars a thin, tall woman dressed in black was standing—Ruth Kettering's maid. She drew aside as her mistress came up to her.

"I have put your dressing-case under your seat, Madam, in case you should need it. Shall I take the rugs, or will you require one?"

"No, no, I shan't want one. Better go and find your own seat now, Mason."

"Yes, Madam."

The maid departed.

Van Aldin entered the Pullman car with Ruth. She found her seat, and Van Aldin deposited various papers and magazines on the table in front of her. The seat opposite to her was already taken, and the American gave a cursory glance at its occupant. He had a fleeting impression of attractive grey eyes and a neat travelling costume. He indulged in a little more desultory conversation with Ruth, the kind of talk peculiar to those seeing other people off by train.

Presently, as whistles blew, he glanced at his watch.

"I had best be clearing out of here. Good-bye, my dear. Don't worry. I will attend to things."

"Oh, Father!"

He turned back sharply. There had been something in Ruth's voice, something so entirely foreign to her usual manner, that he was startled. It was almost a cry of despair. She had made an impulsive movement towards him, but in another minute she was mistress of herself once more.

"Till next month," she said cheerfully.

Two minutes later the train started.

Ruth sat very still, biting her under lip and trying hard to keep the unaccustomed tears from her eyes. She felt a sudden sense of horrible desolation. There was a wild longing upon her to jump out of the train and to go back before it was too late. She, so calm, so self-assured, for the first time in her life felt like a leaf swept by the wind. If her father knew—what would he say?

Madness! Yes, just that, madness! For the first time in her life she was swept away by emotion, swept away to the point of doing a thing which even she knew to be incredibly foolish and reckless. She was enough Van Aldin's daughter to realise her own folly, and level-headed enough to condemn her own action. But she was his daughter in another sense also. She had that same iron determination that would have what it wanted, and once it had made up its mind would not be balked. From her cradle she had been self-willed; the very circumstances of her life had developed that self-will in her. It drove her now remorselessly. Well, the die was cast. She must go through with it now.

She looked up, and her eyes met those of the woman sitting opposite. She had a sudden fancy that in some way this other woman had read her mind. She saw in those grey eyes understanding and—yes—compassion.

It was only a fleeting impression. The faces of both

women hardened to well-bred impassiveness. Mrs. Kettering took up a magazine, and Katherine Grey looked out of the window and watched a seemingly endless vista of depressing streets and suburban homes.

Ruth found an increasing difficulty in fixing her mind on the printed page in front of her. In spite of herself, a thousand apprehensions preyed on her mind. What a fool she had been! What a fool she was! Like all cool and self-sufficient people, when she did lose her self-control she lost it thoroughly. It was too late. . . . Was it too late? Oh, for someone to speak to, for someone to advise her. She had never before had such a wish; she would have scorned the idea of relying on any judgment other than her own, but now —what was the matter with her? Panic. Yes, that would describe it best—panic. She, Ruth Kettering, was completely and utterly panic stricken.

She stole a covert glance at the figure opposite. If only she knew someone like that, some nice, cool, calm, sympathetic creature. That was the sort of person one could talk to. But you can't, of course, confide in a stranger. And Ruth smiled to herself a little at the idea. She picked up the magazine again. Really she must control herself. After all she had thought all this out. She had decided of her own free will. What happiness had she ever had in her life up to now? She said to herself restlessly: "Why shouldn't I be happy? No one will ever know."

It seemed no time before Dover was reached. Ruth was a good sailor. She disliked the cold, and was glad to reach the shelter of the private cabin she had telegraphed for. Although she would not have admitted the fact, Ruth was in some ways superstitious. She was of the order of people to whom coincidence appeals. After disembarking at Calais and settling herself down with her maid in her double compartment in the Blue Train, she went along to the luncheon car. It was with a little shock of surprise that she found herself set down to a small table with, opposite her, the same woman who had been her *vis-à-vis* in the Pullman. A faint smile came to the lips of both women.

"This is quite a coincidence," said Mrs. Kettering.

"I know," said Katherine; "it is odd the way things happen."

A flying attendant shot up to them with the wonderful velocity always displayed by the Compagnie Internationale des Wagons-Lits and deposited two cups of soup. By the time the omelette succeeded the soup they were chatting together in friendly fashion.

"It will be heavenly to get into the sunshine," sighed Ruth.

"I am sure it will be a wonderful feeling."

"You know the Riviera well?"

"No; this is my first visit."

"Fancy that."

"You go every year, I expect?"

"Practically. January and February in London are horrible."

"I have always lived in the country. They are not very inspiring months there either. Mostly mud."

"What made you suddenly decide to travel?"

"Money," said Katherine. "For ten years I have been a paid companion with just enough money of my own to buy myself strong country shoes; now I have been left what seems to me a fortune, though I dare say it would not seem so much to you."

"Now I wonder why you said that—that it would not seem so to me."

Katherine laughed. "I don't really know. I suppose one forms impressions without thinking of it. I put you down in my own mind as one of the very rich of the earth. It was just an impression. I dare say I am wrong."

"No," said Ruth, "you are not wrong." She had suddenly become very grave. "I wish you would tell me what other impressions you formed about me."

"I——"

Ruth swept on disregarding the other's embarrassment. "Oh, please, don't be conventional. I want to know. As we left Victoria I looked across at you, and I had the sort of feeling that you—well, understood what was going on in my mind."

"I can assure you I am not a mind reader," said Katherine smiling.

"No, but will you tell me, please, just what you thought." Ruth's eagerness was so intense and so sincere that she carried her point.

"I will tell you if you like, but you must not think me impertinent. I thought that for some reason you were in great distress of mind, and I was sorry for you."

"You are right. You are quite right. I am in terrible trouble. I—I should like to tell you something about it, if I may."

"Oh, dear," Katherine thought to herself, "how extraordinarily alike the world seems to be everywhere! People were always telling me things in St. Mary Mead, and it is just the same thing here, and I don't really want to hear anybody's troubles!"

She replied politely:

"Do tell me."

They were just finishing their lunch. Ruth gulped down her coffee, rose from her seat, and quite oblivious of the fact that Katherine had not begun to sip her coffee, said: "Come to my compartment with me."

They were two single compartments with a communicating door between them. In the second of them a thin maid, whom Katherine had noticed at Victoria, was sitting very upright on the seat, clutching a big scarlet morocco case with the initials R. V. K. on it. Mrs. Kettering pulled the communicating door to and sank down on the seat. Katherine sat down beside her.

"I am in trouble and I don't know what to do. There is a man whom I am fond of—very fond of indeed. We cared for each other when we were young, and we were thrust apart most brutally and unjustly. Now we have come together again."

"Yes?"

"I—I am going to meet him now. Oh! I dare say you think it is all wrong, but you don't know the circumstances. My husband is impossible. He has treated me disgracefully."

"Yes," said Katherine again.

"What I feel so badly about is this. I have deceived my father—it was he who came to see me off at Victoria to-day. He wishes me to divorce my husband, and, of course, he has no idea—that I am going to meet this other man. He would think it extraordinarily foolish."

"Well, don't you think it is?"

"I—I suppose it is."

Ruth Kettering looked down at her hands; they were shaking violently.

"But I can't draw back now."

"Why not?"

"I—it is all arranged, and it would break his heart."

"Don't you believe it," said Katherine robustly; "hearts are pretty tough."

"He will think I have no courage, no strength of purpose."

"It seems to me an awfully silly thing that you are going to do," said Katherine. "I think you realise that yourself."

Ruth Kettering buried her face in her hands. "I don't know—I don't know. Ever since I left Victoria I have had a horrible feeling of something—something that is coming to me very soon—that I can't escape."

She clutched convulsively at Katherine's hand.

"You must think I am mad talking to you like this, but I tell you I know something horrible is going to happen."

"Don't think it," said Katherine; "try to pull yourself together. You could send your father a wire from Paris, if you like, and he would come to you at once."

The other brightened.

"Yes, I could do that. Dear old Dad. It is queer—but I never knew until to-day how terribly fond of him I am." She sat up and dried her eyes with a handkerchief. "I have been very foolish. Thank you so much for letting me talk to you. I don't know why I got into such a queer, hysterical state."

She got up. "I am quite all right now. I suppose, really, I just needed someone to talk to. I can't think now why I have been making such an absolute fool of myself."

Katherine got up too.

"I am glad you feel better," she said, trying to make her voice sound as conventional as possible. She was only too well aware that the aftermath of confidences is embarrassment. She added tactfully:

"I must be going back to my own compartment."

She emerged into the corridor at the same time as the maid

was also coming out from the next door. The latter looked towards Katherine, over her shoulder, and an expression of intense surprise showed itself on her face. Katherine turned also, but by that time whoever it was who had aroused the maid's interest had retreated into his or her compartment, and the corridor was empty. Katherine walked down it to regain her own place, which was in the next coach. As she passed the end compartment the door opened and a woman's face looked out for a moment and then pulled the door to sharply. It was a face not easily forgotten, as Katherine was to know when she saw it again. A beautiful face, oval and dark, very heavily made up in a bizarre fashion. Katherine had a feeling that she had seen it before somewhere.

She regained her own compartment without other adventure and sat for some time thinking of the confidence which had just been made to her. She wondered idly who the woman in the mink coat might be, wondered also how the end of her story would turn out.

"If I had stopped anyone from making an idiot of themselves, I suppose I have done good work," she thought to herself. "But who knows? That is the kind of woman who is hard-headed and egotistical all her life, and it might be good for her to do the other sort of thing for a change. Oh, well—I don't suppose I shall ever see her again. She certainly won't want to see *me again.* That is the worst of letting people tell you things. They never do."

She hoped that she would not be given the same place at dinner. She reflected, not without humour, that it might be awkward for both of them. Leaning back with her head against a cushion she felt tired and vaguely depressed. They had reached Paris, and the slow journey round the *ceinture*, with its interminable stops and waits, was very wearisome. Whey they arrived at the Gare de Lyon she was glad to get out and walk up and down the platform. The keen cold air was refreshing after the steam-heated train. She observed with a smile that her friend of the mink coat was solving the possible awkwardness of the dinner problem in her own way. A dinner basket was being handed up and received through the window by the maid.

When the train started once more, and dinner was announced by a violent ringing of bells, Katherine went along to it much relieved in mind. Her *vis-à-vis* to-night was of an entirely different kind—a small man, distinctly foreign in appearance, with a rigidly waxed moustache and an egg-shaped head which he carried rather on one side. Katherine had taken in a book to dinner with her. She found the little man's eyes fixed upon it with a kind of twinkling amusement.

"I see, Madame, that you have a *roman policier*. You are fond of such things?"

"They amuse me," Katherine admitted.

The little man nodded with the air of complete understanding.

"They have a good sale always, so I am told. Now why is that, eh, Mademoiselle? I ask of you as a student of human nature—why should that be?"

Katherine felt more and more amused.

"Perhaps they give one the illusion of living an exciting life," she suggested.

He nodded gravely.

"Yes; there is something in that."

"Of course, one knows that such things don't really happen," Katherine was continuing, but he interrupted her sharply.

"Sometimes, Mademoiselle! Sometimes! I who speak to you—they have happened to *me*."

She threw him a quick, interested glance.

"Some day, who knows, *you* might be in the thick of things," he went on. "It is all chance."

"I don't think it is likely," said Katherine. "Nothing of that kind ever happens to me."

He leaned forward.

"Would you like it to?"

The question startled her, and she drew in her breath sharply.

"It is my fancy, perhaps," said the little man, as he dexterously polished one of the forks, "but I think that you have a yearning in you for interesting happenings. *Eh bien*, Mademoiselle, all through my life I have observed one thing—'All one wants one gets!' Who knows?" His face screwed itself up comically. "You may get more than you bargain for."

"Is that a prophecy?" asked Katherine, smiling as she rose from the table.

The little man shook his head.

"I never prophesy," he declared pompously. "It is true that I have the habit of being always right—but I do not boast of it. Good-night, Mademoiselle, and may you sleep well."

Katherine went back along the train amused and entertained by her little neighbour. She passed the open door of her friend's compartment and saw the conductor making up the bed. The lady in the mink coat was standing looking out of the window. The second compartment, as Katherine saw through the communicating door, was empty, with rugs and bags heaped up on the seat. The maid was not there.

Katherine found her own bed prepared, and since she was tired, she went to bed and switched off her light about half-past nine.

She woke with a sudden start; how much time had passed she did not know. Glancing at her watch, she found that it had stopped. A feeling of intense uneasiness pervaded her and grew stronger moment by moment. At last she got up, threw her dressing-gown round her shoulders, and stepped out into the corridor. The whole train seemed wrapped in slumber. Katherine let the window down and sat by it for some minutes, drinking in the cool night air and trying vainly to calm her uneasy fears. She presently decided that she would go along to the end and ask the conductor for the right time so that she could set her watch. She found, however, that his little chair was vacant. She hesitated for a moment and then walked through into the next coach. She looked down the long, dim line of the corridor and saw, to her surprise, that a man was standing with his hand on the door of the compartment occupied by the lady in the mink coat. That is to say, she thought it was the compartment. Probably, however, she was mistaken. He stood there for a moment or two with his back to her, seeming uncertain and hesitating in his attitude. Then he slowly turned, and with an odd feeling of fatality, Katherine recognised him as the same man whom she had noticed twice before—once in the corridor of the Savoy Hotel and once in Cook's offices. Then he opened the door of the compartment and passed in, drawing it to behind him.

An idea flashed across Katherine's mind. Could this be the man of whom the other woman had spoken—the man she was journeying to meet.

Then Katherine told herself that she was romancing. In all probability she had mistaken the compartment.

She went back to her own carriage. Five minutes later the train slackened speed. There was the long plaintive hiss of the Westinghouse brake, and a few minutes later the train came to a stop at Lyons.

Chapter 11

MURDER

Katherine wakened the next morning to brilliant sunshine. She went along to breakfast early, but met none of her acquaintances of the day before. When she returned to her compartment it had just been restored to its daytime appearance by the conductor, a dark man with a drooping moustache and melancholy face.

"Madame is fortunate," he said; "the sun shines. It is always a great disappointment to passengers when they arrive on a grey morning."

"I should have been disappointed, certainly," said Katherine.

The man prepared to depart.

"We are rather late, Madame," he said. "I will let you know just before we get to Nice."

Katherine nodded. She sat by the window, entranced by the sunlit panorama. The palm trees, the deep blue of the sea, the bright yellow mimosa came with all the charm of novelty to the woman who for fourteen years had known only the drab winters of England.

When they arrived at Cannes, Katherine got out and walked up and down the platform. She was curious about the lady in the mink coat, and looked up at the windows of her compartment. The blinds were still drawn down—the only ones to be so on the whole train. Katherine wondered a little, and when she re-entered the train she passed along the corridor and noticed that these two compartments were still shuttered and closed. The lady of the mink coat was clearly no early riser.

Presently the conductor came to her and told her that in a few minutes the train would arrive at Nice. Katherine handed him a tip; the man thanked her, but still lingered. There was something odd about him. Katherine, who had at first wondered whether the tip had not been big enough, was now convinced that something far more serious was amiss. His face was of a sickly pallor, he was shaking all over, and looked as if he had been frightened out of his life. He was eyeing her in a curious manner. Presently he said abruptly: "Madame will excuse me, but is she expecting friends to meet her at Nice?"

"Probably," said Katherine. "Why?"

But the man merely shook his head and murmured something that Katherine could not catch and moved away, not reappearing until the train came to rest at the station, when he started handing her belongings down from the window.

Katherine stood for a moment or two on the platform rather at a loss, but a fair young man with an ingenuous face came up to her and said rather hesitatingly:

"Miss Grey, is it not?"

Katherine said that it was, and the young man beamed upon her seraphically and murmured: "I am Chubby, you know—Lady Tamplin's husband. I expect she mentioned me, but perhaps she forgot. Have you got your *billet de bagages*? I lost mine when I came out this year, and you would not believe the fuss they made about it. Regular French red tape!"

Katherine produced it, and was just about to move off beside him when a very gentle and insidious voice murmured in her ear:

"A little moment, Madame, if you please."

Katherine turned to behold an individual who made up for insignificance of stature by a large quantity of gold lace and uniform. The individual explained. "There were certain formalities. Madame would perhaps be so kind as to accompany him. The regulations of the police——" He threw up his arms. "Absurd, doubtless, but there it was."

Mr. Chubby Evans listened with a very imperfect comprehension, his French being of a limited order.

"So like the French," murmured Mr. Evans. He was one of those staunch patriotic Britons who, having made a portion of a foreign country their own, strongly resent the original inhabitants of it. "Always up to some silly dodge or other. They've never tackled people on the station before, though. This is something quite new. I suppose you'll have to go."

Katherine departed with her guide. Somewhat to her surprise, he led her towards a siding where a coach of the departed train had been shunted. He invited her to mount into this, and, preceding her down the corridor, held aside the door of one of the compartments. In it was a pompous-looking official personage, and with him a nondescript being who appeared to be a clerk. The pompous-looking personage rose politely, bowed to Katherine, and said:

"You will excuse me, Madame, but there are certain formalities to be complied with. Madame speaks French, I trust?"

"Sufficiently, I think, Monsieur," replied Katherine in that language.

"That is good. Pray be seated, Madame. I am M. Caux, the Commissary of Police." He blew out his chest importantly, and Katherine tried to look sufficiently impressed.

"You wish to see my passport?" she inquired. "Here it is."

The Commissary eyed her keenly and gave a little grunt.

"Thank you, Madame," he said, taking the passport from her. He cleared his throat. "But what I really desire is a little information."

"Information?"

The Commissary nodded his head slowly.

"About a lady who has been a fellow-passenger of yours. You lunched with her yesterday."

"I am afraid I can't tell you anything about her. We fell into conversation over our meal, but she is a complete stranger to me. I have never seen her before."

"And yet," said the Commissary sharply, "you returned to her compartment with her after lunch and sat talking for some time?"

"Yes," said Katherine; "that is true."

The Commissary seemed to expect her to say something more. He looked at her encouragingly.

"Yes, Madame?"

"Well, Monsieur?" said Katherine.

"You can, perhaps, give me some kind of idea of that conversation?"

"I could," said Katherine, "but at the moment I see no reason to do so."

In a somewhat British fashion she felt annoyed. This foreign official seemed to her impertinent.

"No reason?" cried the Commissary. "Oh yes, Madame, I can assure you that there *is* a reason."

"Then perhaps you will give it to me."

The Commissary rubbed his chin thoughtfully for a minute or two without speaking.

"Madame," he said at last, "the reason is very simple. The lady in question was found dead in her compartment this morning."

"Dead!" gasped Katherine. "What was it—heart failure?"

"No," said the Commissary in a reflective, dreamy voice. "No—she was murdered."

"Murdered!" cried Katherine.

"So you see, Madame, why we are anxious for any information we can possibly get."

"But surely her maid——"

"The maid has disappeared."

"Oh!" Katherine paused to assemble her thoughts.

"Since the conductor had seen you talking with her in her compartment, he quite naturally reported the fact to the police, and that is why, Madame, we have detained you, in the hope of gaining some information."

"I am very sorry," said Katherine; "I don't even know her name."

"Her name is Kettering. That we know from her passport and from the labels on her luggage. If we——"

There was a knock on the compartment door. M. Caux frowned. He opened it about six inches.

"What is the matter?" he said peremptorily. "I cannot be disturbed."

The egg-shaped head of Katherine's dinner acquaintance showed itself in the aperture. On his face was a beaming smile.

"My name," he said, "is Hercule Poirot."

"Not," the Commissary stammered, "not *the* Hercule Poirot?"

"The same," said M. Poirot. "I remember meeting you once, M. Caux, at the *Sûreté* in Paris, though doubtless you have forgotten me?"

"Not at all, Monsieur, not at all," declared the Commissary heartily. "But enter, I pray you. You know of this——?"

"Yes, I know," said Hercule Poirot. "I came to see if I might be of any assistance?"

"We should be flattered," replied the Commissary promptly. "Let me present you, M. Poirot, to"—he consulted the passport he still held in his hand—"to Madame—er—Mademoiselle Grey."

Poirot smiled across at Katherine.

"It is strange, is it not," he murmured, "that my words should have come true so quickly?"

"Mademoiselle, alas! can tell us very little," said the Commissary.

"I have been explaining," said Katherine, "that this poor lady was a complete stranger to me."

Poirot nodded.

"But she talked to you, did she not?" he said gently. "You formed an impression—is it not so?"

"Yes," said Katherine thoughtfully. "I suppose I did."

"And that impression was——?"

"Yes, Mademoiselle"—the Commissary jerked himself forward—"let us by all means have your impressions."

Katherine sat turning the whole thing over in her mind. She felt in a way as if she were betraying a confidence, but with that ugly word "Murder" ringing in her ears she dared not keep anything back. Too much might hang upon it. So, as nearly as she could, she repeated word for word the conversation she had had with the dead woman.

"That is interesting," said the Commissary, glancing at the

other. "Eh, M. Poirot, that is interesting? Whether it has anything to do with the crime——" He left the sentence unfinished.

"I suppose it could not be suicide," said Katherine, rather doubtfully.

"No," said the Commissary, "it could not be suicide. She was strangled with a length of black cord."

"Oh!" Katherine shivered. M. Caux spread out his hands apologetically. "It is not nice—no. I think that our train robbers are more brutal than they are in your country."

"It is horrible."

"Yes, yes"—he was soothing and apologetic—"but you have great courage, Mademoiselle. At once, as soon as I saw you, I said to myself, 'Mademoiselle has great courage.' That is why I am going to ask you to do something more—something distressing, but I assure you very necessary."

Katherine looked at him apprehensively.

He spread out his hands apologetically.

"I am going to ask you, Mademoiselle, to be so good as to accompany me to the next compartment."

"Must I?" asked Katherine in a low voice.

"Someone must identify her," said the Commissary, "and since the maid has disappeared"—he coughed significantly—"you appear to be the person who has seen most of her since she joined the train."

"Very well," said Katherine quietly; "if it is necessary——"

She rose. Poirot gave her a little nod of approval.

"Mademoiselle is sensible," he said. "May I accompany you, M. Caux?"

"Enchanted, my dear M. Poirot."

They went out into the corridor, and M. Caux unlocked the door of the dead woman's compartment. The blinds on the far side had been drawn half-way up to admit light. The dead woman lay on the berth to their left, in so natural a posture that one could have thought her asleep. The bedclothes were drawn up over her, and her head was turned to the wall, so that only the red auburn curls showed. Very gently M. Caux laid a hand on her shoulder and turned the body back so that the face came into view. Katherine flinched a little and dug her nails into her palms. A heavy blow had disfigured the features almost beyond recognition. Poirot gave a sharp exclamation.

"When was that done, I wonder?" he demanded. "Before death or after?"

"The doctor says after," said M. Caux.

"Strange," said Poirot, drawing his brows together. He turned to Katherine. "Be brave, Mademoiselle; look at her well. Are you sure that this is the woman you talked to in the train yesterday?"

Katherine had good nerves. She steeled herself to look long and earnestly at the recumbent figure. Then she leaned forward and took up the dead woman's hand.

"I am quite sure," she replied at length. "The face is too disfigured to recognise, but the build and carriage and hair are exact, and besides I noticed *this*"—she pointed to a tiny mole on the dead woman's wrist—"while I was talking to her."

"*Bon*," approved Poirot. "You are an excellent witness, Mademoiselle. There is, then, no question as to the identity, but it is strange, all the same." He frowned down on the dead woman in perplexity.

M. Caux shrugged his shoulders.

"The murderer was carried away by rage, doubtless," he suggested.

"If she had been struck down, it would have been comprehensible," mused Poirot, "but the man who strangled her slipped up behind and caught her unawares. A little choke—a little gurgle—that is all that would be heard, and then afterwards—that smashing blow on her face. Now why? Did he hope that if the face were unrecognisable she might not be identified? Or did he hate her so much that he could not resist striking that blow even after she was dead?"

Katherine shuddered, and he turned at once to her kindly.

"You must not let me distress you, Mademoiselle," he said. "To you this is all very new and terrible. To me, alas! it is an old story. One moment, I pray of you both."

They stood against the door watching him as he went quickly round the compartment. He noted the dead woman's clothes neatly folded on the end of the berth, the big fur coat that hung from a hook, and the little red lacquer hat tossed on the rack. Then he passed through into the adjoining compartment, that in which Katherine had seen the maid sitting. Here the berth had not been made up. Three or four rugs were piled loosely on the seat; there was a hat-box and a couple of suit-cases. He turned suddenly to Katherine.

"You were in here yesterday," he said. "Do you see anything changed, anything missing?"

Katherine looked carefully round both compartments.

"Yes," she said, "there is something missing—a scarlet morocco case. It had the initials 'R. V. K.' on it. It might have been a small dressing-case or a big jewel-case. When I saw it, the maid was holding it."

"Ah!" said Poirot.

"But, surely," said Katherine, "I—of course, I don't know anything about such things, but surely it is plain enough, if the maid and the jewel-case are missing?"

"You mean that it was the maid who was the thief? No, Mademoiselle, there is a very good reason against that."

"What?"

"The maid was left behind in Paris."

He turned to Poirot. "I should like you to hear the conductor's story yourself," he murmured confidentially. "It is very suggestive."

"Mademoiselle would doubtless like to hear it also," said Poirot. "You do not object, Monsieur le Commissaire?"

"No," said the Commissary, who clearly did object very much. "No, certainly, M. Poirot, if you say so. You have finished here?"

"I think so. One little minute."

He had been turning over the rugs, and now he took one to the window and looked at it, picking something off it with his fingers.

"What is it?" demanded M. Caux sharply.

"Four auburn hairs." He bent over the dead woman. "Yes, they are from the head of Madame."

"And what of it? Do you attach importance to them?"

Poirot let the rug drop back on the seat.

"What is important? What is not? One cannot say at this stage. But we must note each little fact carefully."

They went back again into the first compartment, and in a

minute or two the conductor of the carriage arrived to be questioned.

"Your name is Pierre Michel?" said the Commissary.

"Yes, Monsieur le Commissaire."

"I should like you to repeat to this gentleman"—he indicated Poirot—"the story that you told me as to what happened in Paris."

"Very good, Monsieur le Commissaire. It was after we had left the Gare de Lyon I came along to make the beds, thinking that Madame would be at dinner, but she had a dinner-basket in her compartment. She said to me that she had been obliged to leave her maid behind in Paris, so that I only need make up one berth. She took her dinner basket into the adjoining compartment, and sat there while I made up the bed; then she told me that she did not wish to be wakened early in the morning, that she liked to sleep on. I told her I quite understood, and she wished me 'good-night.'"

"You yourself did not go into the adjoining compartment?"

"No, Monsieur."

"Then you did not happen to notice if a scarlet morocco case was amongst the luggage there?"

"No, Monsieur, I did not."

"Would it have been possible for a man to have been concealed in the adjoining compartment?"

The conductor reflected.

"The door was half open," he said. "If a man had stood behind that door I should not have been able to see him, but he would, of course, have been perfectly visible to Madame when she went in there."

"Quite so," said Poirot. "Is there anything more you have to tell us?"

"I think that is all, Monsieur. I can remember nothing else."

"And now this morning?" prompted Poirot.

"As Madame had ordered, I did not disturb her. It was not until just before Cannes that I ventured to knock at the door Getting no reply, I opened it. The lady appeared to be in her bed asleep. I took her by the shoulder to rouse her, and then——"

"And then you saw what had happened," volunteered Poirot. "*Très bien.* I think I know all I want to know."

"I hope, Monsieur le Commissaire, it is not that I have been guilty of any negligence," said the man piteously. "Such an affair to happen on the Blue Train! It is horrible."

"Console yourself," said the Commissary. "Everything will be done to keep the affair as quiet as possible, if only in the interests of justice. I cannot think you have been guilty of any negligence."

"And Monsieur le Commissaire will report as much to the Company?"

"But certainly, but certainly," said M. Caux, impatiently. "That will do now."

The conductor withdrew.

"According to the medical evidence," said the Commissary, "the lady was probably dead before the train reached Lyons. Who then was the murderer? From Mademoiselle's story, it seems clear that somewhere on her journey she was to meet this man of whom she spoke. Her action in getting rid of the maid seems significant. Did the man join the train at Paris, and did she conceal him in the adjoining compartment? If so, they may have quarrelled, and he may have killed her in a fit of rage. That is one possibility. The other, and the more likely to my mind, is that her assailant was a train robber travelling on the train; that he stole along the corridor unseen by the conductor, killed her, and went off with the red morocco case, which doubtless contained jewels of some value. In all probability he left the train at Lyons, and we have already telegraphed to the station there for full particulars of anyone seen leaving the train."

"Or he might have come on to Nice," suggested Poirot.

"He might," agreed the Commissary, "but that would be a very bold course."

Poirot let a minute or two go by before speaking, and then he said:

"In the latter case you think the man was an ordinary train robber?"

The Commissary shrugged his shoulders.

"It depends. We must get hold of the maid. It is possible

that she has the red morocco case with her. If so, then the man of whom she spoke to Mademoiselle may be concerned in the case, and the affair is a crime of passion. I myself think the solution of a train robber is the more probable. These bandits have become very bold of late."

Poirot looked suddenly across at Katherine.

"And you, Mademoiselle," he said, "you heard and saw nothing during the night?"

"Nothing," said Katherine.

Poirot turned to the Commissary.

"We need detain Mademoiselle no longer, I think," he suggested.

The latter nodded.

"She will leave us her address?" he said.

Katherine gave him the name of Lady Tamplin's villa. Poirot made her a little bow.

"You permit that I see you again, Mademoiselle?" he said. "Or have you so many friends that your time will be all taken up?"

"On the contrary," said Katherine, "I shall have plenty of leisure, and I shall be very pleased to see you again."

"Excellent," said Poirot, and gave her a little friendly nod. "This shall be a '*roman policier*' *à nous*. We will investigate this affair together."

Chapter 12

AT THE VILLA MARGUERITE

"Then you were really in the thick of it all!" said Lady Tamplin enviously. "My dear, how thrilling!" She opened her china blue eyes very wide and gave a little sigh.

"A real murder," said Mr. Evans gloatingly.

"Of course Chubby had no idea of anything of the kind," went on Lady Tamplin, "he simply could not imagine why the police wanted you. My dear, what an opportunity! I think, you know—yes, I certainly think something might be made out of this."

A calculating look rather marred the ingenuousness of the blue eyes.

Katherine felt slightly uncomfortable. They were just finishing lunch, and she looked in turn at the three people sitting round the table. Lady Tamplin, full of practical schemes; Mr. Evans, beaming with naïve appreciation, and Lenox with a queer crooked smile on her dark face.

"Marvellous luck," murmured Chubby; "I wish I could have gone along with you—and seen—all the exhibits." His tone was wistful and childlike.

Katherine said nothing. The police had laid no injunctions of secrecy upon her, and it was clearly impossible to suppress the bare facts or try to keep them from her hostess. But she did rather wish it had been possible to do so.

"Yes," said Lady Tamplin, coming suddenly out of her reverie, "I do think something might be done. A little account, you know, cleverly written up. An eye-witness, a feminine touch: '*How I chatted with the dead woman, little thinking*——' that sort of thing, you know."

"Rot!" said Lenox.

"You have no idea," said Lady Tamplin in a soft, wistful voice, "what newspapers will pay for a little titbit! Written, of course, by someone of really unimpeachable social position. You would not like to do it yourself, I dare say, Katherine dear, but just give me the bare bones of it, and *I* will manage the whole thing for you. Mr. de Haviland is a special friend of mine. We have a little understanding together. A most delightful man—not at all reporterish. How does the idea strike you, Katherine?"

"I would much prefer to do nothing of the kind," said Katherine bluntly.

Lady Tamplin was rather disconcerted at this uncompromising refusal. She sighed and turned to the elucidation of further details.

"A very striking-looking woman, you said? I wonder now who she could have been. You didn't hear her name?"

"It was mentioned," Katherine admitted, "but I can't remember it. You see, I was rather upset."

"I should think so," said Mr. Evans; "it must have been a beastly shock."

It is to be doubted whether, even if Katherine had remembered the name, she would have admitted the fact. Lady Tamplin's remorseless cross-examination was making her restive. Lenox, who was observant in her own way, noticed this, and offered to take Katherine upstairs to see her room. She left her there, remarking kindly before she went: "You mustn't mind Mother; she would make a few pennies' profit out of her dying grandmother if she could."

Lenox went down again to find her mother and her step-father discussing the newcomer.

"Presentable," said Lady Tamplin, "quite presentable. Her clothes are all right. That grey thing is the same model that Gladys Cooper wore in *Palm Trees in Egypt*."

"Have you noticed her eyes—what?" interposed Mr. Evans.

"Never mind her eyes, Chubby," said Lady Tamplin tartly; "we are discussing things that really matter."

"Oh, quite," said Mr. Evans, and retired into his shell.

"She doesn't seem to me very—malleable," said Lady Tamplin, rather hesitating to choose the right word.

"She has all the instincts of a lady, as they say in books," said Lenox, with a grin.

"Narrow-minded," murmured Lady Tamplin. "Inevitable under the circumstances, I suppose."

"I expect you will do your best to broaden her," said Lenox, with a grin, "but you will have your work cut out. Just now, you noticed, she stuck down her fore feet and laid back her ears and refused to budge."

"Anyway," said Lady Tamplin hopefully, "she doesn't look to me at all mean. Some people, when they come into money, seem to attach undue importance to it."

"Oh, you'll easily touch her for what you want," said Lenox; "and, after all, that is all that matters, isn't it? That is what she is here for."

"She is my own cousin," said Lady Tamplin, with dignity.

"Cousin, eh?" said Mr. Evans, waking up again. "I suppose I call her Katherine, don't I?"

"It is of no importance at all what you call her, Chubby," said Lady Tamplin.

"Good," said Mr. Evans; "then I will. Do you suppose she plays tennis?" he added hopefully.

"Of course not," said Lady Tamplin. "She has been a companion, I tell you. Companions don't play tennis—or golf. They might possibly play golf-croquet, but I have always understood that they wind wool and wash dogs most of the day."

"O God!" said Mr. Evans; "do they really?"

Lenox drifted upstairs again to Katherine's room. "Can I help you?" she asked rather perfunctorily.

On Katherine's disclaimer, Lenox sat on the edge of the bed and stared thoughtfully at her guest.

"Why did you come?" she said at last. "To us, I mean. We're not your sort."

"Oh, I am anxious to get into Society."

"Don't be an ass," said Lenox promptly, detecting the flicker of a smile. "You know what I mean well enough. You are not a bit what I thought you would be. I say, you *have* got some decent clothes." She sighed. "Clothes are no good to me. I was born awkward. It's a pity, because I love them."

"I love them too," said Katherine, "but it has not been much use my loving them up to now. Do you think this is nice?"

She and Lenox discussed several models with artistic fervour.

"I like you," said Lenox suddenly. "I came up to warn you not to be taken in by Mother, but I think now that there is no need to do that. You are frightfully sincere and upright and all those queer things, but you are not a fool. Oh hell! what is it now?"

Lady Tamplin's voice was calling plaintively from the hall:

"Lenox, Derek has just rung up. He wants to come to dinner to-night. Will it be all right? I mean, we haven't got anything awkward, like quails, have we?"

Lenox reassured her and came back into Katherine's room. Her face looked brighter and less sullen.

"I'm glad old Derek is coming," she said; "you'll like him."

"Who is Derek?"

"He is Lord Leconbury's son, married a rich American woman. Women are simply potty about him."

"Why?"

"Oh, the usual reason—very good-looking and a regular bad lot. Everyone goes off their head about him."

"Do you?"

"Sometimes I do," said Lenox, "and sometimes I think I would like to marry a nice curate and live in the country and grow things in frames." She paused a minute, and then added, "An Irish curate would be best, and then I should hunt."

After a minute or two she reverted to her former theme. "There is something queer about Derek. All that family are a bit potty—mad gamblers, you know. In the old days they used to gamble away their wives and their estates, and did most reckless things just for the love of it. Derek would have made a perfect highwayman—debonair and gay, just the right manner." She moved to the door. "Well, come down when you feel like it."

Left alone, Katherine gave herself up to thought. Just at present she felt thoroughly ill at ease and jarred by her surroundings. The shock of the discovery in the train and the reception of the news by her new friends jarred upon her susceptibilities. She thought long and earnestly about the murdered woman. She had been sorry for Ruth, but she could not honestly say that she had liked her. She had divined only too well the ruthless egoism that was the keynote of her personality, and it repelled her.

She had been amused and a trifle hurt by the other's cool dismissal of her when she had served her turn. That she had come to some decision, Katherine was quite certain, but she wondered now what that decision had been. Whatever it was, death had stepped in and made all decisions meaningless. Strange that it should have been so, and that a brutal crime should have been the ending of that fateful journey. But suddenly Katherine remembered a small fact that she ought, perhaps, to have told the police—a fact that had for the moment escaped her memory. Was it of any real importance? She had certainly thought that she had seen a man going into that particular compartment, but she realised that she might easily have been mistaken. It might have been the compartment next door, and certainly the man in question could be no train robber. She recalled him very clearly as she had seen him on those two previous occasions—once at the Savoy and once at Cook's office. No, doubtless she had been mistaken. He had not gone into the dead woman's compartment, and it was perhaps as well that she had said nothing to the police. She might have done incalculable harm by doing so.

She went down to join the others on the terrace outside. Through the branches of mimosa, she looked out over the blue of the Mediterranean, and, whilst listening with half an ear to Lady Tamplin's chatter, she was glad that she had come. This was better than St. Mary Mead.

That evening she put on the mauvy pink dress that went by the name of *soupir d'automne*, and after smiling at her reflection in the mirror, went downstairs with, for the first time in her life, a faint feeling of shyness.

Most of Lady Tamplin's guests had arrived, and since noise was the essential of Lady Tamplin's parties, the din was already terrific. Chubby rushed up to Katherine, pressed a cocktail upon her, and took her under his wing.

"Oh, here you are, Derek," cried Lady Tamplin, as the door opened to admit the last comer. "Now at last we can have something to eat. I am starving."

Katherine looked across the room. She was startled. So this—was Derek, and she realised that she was not surprised. She had always known that she would some day meet the man whom she had seen three times by such a curious chain of coincidences. She thought, too, that he recognised her. He paused abruptly in what he was saying to Lady Tamplin, and went on again as though with an effort. They all went in to dinner, and Katherine found that he was placed beside her. He turned to her at once with a vivid smile.

"I knew I was going to meet you soon," he remarked, "but I never dreamt that it would be here. It had to be, you know. Once at the Savoy and once at Cook's—never twice without three times. Don't say you can't remember me or never noticed me. I insist upon your pretending that you noticed me, anyway."

"Oh, I did," said Katherine; "but this is not the third time. It is the fourth. I saw you on the Blue Train."

"On the Blue Train!" Something undefinable came over his manner; she could not have said just what it was. It was as though he had received a check, a set-back. Then he said carelessly:

"What was the rumpus this morning? Somebody had died, hadn't they?"

"Yes," said Katherine slowly; "somebody had died."

"You shouldn't die on a train," remarked Derek flippantly. "I believe it causes all sorts of legal and international complications, and it gives the train an excuse for being even later than usual."

"Mr. Kettering?" A stout American lady, who was sitting opposite, leaned forward and spoke to him with the deliberate intonation of her race. "Mr. Kettering, I do believe you have forgotten me, and I thought you such a perfectly lovely man."

Derek leaned forward, answering her, and Katherine sat almost dazed.

Kettering! That was the name, of course! She remembered it now—but what a strange, ironical situation! Here was this man whom she had seen go into his wife's compartment last night, who had left her alive and well, and now he was sitting at dinner, quite unconscious of the fate that had befallen her. Of that there was no doubt. He did not know.

A servant was leaning over Derek, handing him a note and murmuring in his ear. With a word of excuse to Lady Tamplin, he broke it open, and an expression of utter astonishment came over his face as he read; then he looked at his hostess.

"This is most extraordinary. I say, Rosalie, I am afraid I will have to leave you. The Prefect of Police wants to see me at once. I can't think what about."

"Your sins have found you out," remarked Lenox.

"They must have," said Derek; "probably some idiotic nonsense, but I suppose I shall have to push off to the Prefecture. How dare the old boy rout me out from dinner? It ought to be something deadly serious to justify that," and he laughed as he pushed back his chair and rose to leave the room.

Chapter 13

VAN ALDIN GETS A TELEGRAM

On the afternoon of the 15th February a thick yellow fog had settled down on London. Rufus Van Aldin was in his suite at the Savoy and was making the most of the atmospheric conditions by working double time. Knighton was overjoyed. He had found it difficult of late to get his employer to concentrate on the matters in hand. When he had ventured to urge certain courses, Van Aldin had put him off with a curt word. But now Van Aldin seemed to be throwing himself into work with redoubled energy, and the secretary made the most of his opportunities. Always tactful, he plied the spur so unobtrusively that Van Aldin never suspected it.

Yet in the middle of this absorption in business matters, one little fact lay at the back of Van Aldin's mind. A chance remark of Knighton's, uttered by the secretary in all unconsciousness, had given rise to it. It now festered unseen, gradually reaching further and further forward into Van Aldin's consciousness, until at last, in spite of himself, he had to yield to its insistence.

He listened to what Knighton was saying with his usual air of keen attention, but in reality not one word of it penetrated his mind. He nodded automatically, however, and the secretary turned to some other paper. As he was sorting them out, his employer spoke:

"Do you mind telling me that over again, Knighton?"

For a moment Knighton was at a loss.

"You mean about this, sir?" He held up a closely written Company report.

"No, no," said Van Aldin; "what you told me about seeing Ruth's maid in Paris last night. I can't make it out. You must have been mistaken."

"I can't have been mistaken, sir; I actually spoke to her."

"Well, tell me the whole thing again."

Knighton complied.

"I had fixed up the deal with Bartheimers," he explained, "and had gone back to the Ritz to pick up my traps preparatory to having dinner and catching the nine o'clock train from the Gare du Nord. At the reception desk I saw a woman whom I was quite sure was Mrs. Kettering's maid. I went up to her and asked if Mrs. Kettering was staying there."

"Yes, yes," said Van Aldin. "Of course. Naturally. And she told you that Ruth had gone on to the Riviera and had sent her to the Ritz to await further orders there?"

"Exactly that, sir."

"It is very odd," said Van Aldin. "Very odd, indeed, unless the woman had been impertinent or something of that kind."

"In that case," objected Knighton, "surely Mrs. Kettering would have paid her down a sum of money, and told her to go back to England. She would hardly have sent her to the Ritz."

"No," muttered the millionaire; "that's true."

He was about to say something further, but checked himself. He was fond of Knighton and liked and trusted him, but he could hardly discuss his daughter's private affairs with his secretary. He had already felt hurt by Ruth's lack of frankness, and this chance information which had come to him did nothing to allay his misgivings.

Why had Ruth got rid of her maid in Paris? What possible object or motive could she have had in so doing?

He reflected for a moment or two on the curious combination of chance. How should it have occurred to Ruth, except as the wildest coincidence, that the first person that the maid should run across in Paris should be her father's secretary? Ah, but that was the way things happened. That was the way things got found out.

He winced at the last phrase; it had arisen with complete naturalness to his mind. Was there then "something to be found out"? He hated to put this question to himself; he had no doubt of the answer. The answer was—he was sure of it—Armand de la Roche.

It was bitter to Van Aldin that a daughter of his should be

gulled by such a man, yet he was forced to admit that she was in good company—that other well-bred and intelligent women had succumbed just as easily to the Count's fascination. Men saw through him, women did not.

He sought now for a phrase that would allay any suspicion that his secretary might have felt.

"Ruth is always changing her mind about things at a moment's notice," he remarked, and then he added in a would-be careless tone: "The maid didn't give any—er—reason for this change of plan?"

Knighton was careful to make his voice as natural as possible as he replied:

"She said, sir, that Mrs. Kettering had met a friend unexpectedly."

"Is that so?"

The secretary's practised ears caught the note of strain underlying the seemingly casual tone.

"Oh, I see. Man or woman?"

"I think she said a man, sir."

Van Aldin nodded. His worst fears were being realised. He rose from his chair, and began pacing up and down the room, a habit of his when agitated. Unable to contain his feelings any longer, he burst forth:

"There is one thing no man can do, and that is to get a woman to listen to reason. Somehow or other, they don't seem to have any kind of *sense*. Talk of woman's instinct—why, it is well known all the world over that a woman is the surest mark for any rascally swindler. Not one in ten of them knows a scoundrel when she meets one; they can be preyed on by any good-looking fellow with a soft side to his tongue. If I had my way——"

He was interrupted. A page-boy entered with a telegram. Van Aldin tore it open, and his face went a sudden chalky white. He caught hold of the back of a chair to steady himself, and waved the page-boy from the room.

"What's the matter, sir?"

Knighton had risen in concern.

"Ruth!" said Van Aldin hoarsely.

"Mrs. Kettering?"

"Killed!"

"An accident to the train?"

Van Aldin shook his head.

"No. From this it seems she has been robbed as well. They don't use the word, Knighton, but my poor girl has been murdered."

"Oh, my God, sir!"

Van Aldin tapped the telegram with his forefinger.

"This is from the police at Nice. I must go out there by the first train."

Knighton was efficient as ever. He glanced at the clock.

"Five o'clock from Victoria, sir."

"That's right. You will come with me, Knighton. Tell my man, Archer, and pack your own things. See to everything here. I want to go round to Curzon Street."

The telephone rang sharply, and the secretary lifted the receiver.

"Yes; who is it?"

Then to Van Aldin:

"Mr. Goby, sir."

"Goby? I can't see him now. No—wait, we have plenty of time. Tell them to send him up."

Van Aldin was a strong man. Already he had recovered that iron calm of his. Few people would have noticed anything amiss in his greeting to Mr. Goby.

"I am pressed for time, Goby. Got anything important to tell me?"

Mr. Goby coughed.

"The movements of Mr. Kettering, sir. You wished them reported to you."

"Yes—well?"

"Mr. Kettering, sir, left London for the Riviera yesterday morning."

"What?"

Something in his voice must have startled Mr. Goby. That worthy gentleman departed from his usual practice of never looking at the person to whom he was talking, and stole a fleeting glance at the millionaire.

"What train did he go on?" demanded Van Aldin.

"The Blue Train, sir."

Mr. Goby coughed again and spoke to the clock on the mantelpiece.

"Mademoiselle Mirelle, the dancer from the Parthenon, went by the same train."

Chapter 14

ADA MASON'S STORY

"I cannot repeat to you often enough, Monsieur, our horror, our consternation, and the deep sympathy we feel for you."

Thus M. Carrège, the Juge d'Instruction, addressed Van Aldin. M. Caux, the Commissary, made sympathetic noises in his throat. Van Aldin brushed away horror, consternation, and sympathy with an abrupt gesture. The scene was the Examining Magistrate's room at Nice. Besides M. Carrège, the Commissary, and Van Aldin, there was a further person in the room. It was that person who now spoke.

"M. Van Aldin," he said, "desires action—swift action."

"Ah!" cried the Commissary, "I have not yet presented you. M. Van Aldin, this is M. Hercule Poirot; you have doubtless heard of him. Although he has retired from his profession for some years now, his name is still a household word as one of the greatest living detectives."

"Pleased to meet you, M. Poirot," said Van Aldin, falling back mechanically on a formula that he had discarded some years ago. "You have retired from your profession?"

"That is so, Monsieur. Now I enjoy the world."

The little man made a grandiloquent gesture.

"M. Poirot happened to be travelling on the Blue Train," explained the Commissary, "and he has been so kind as to assist us out of his vast experience."

The millionaire looked at Poirot keenly. Then he said unexpectedly:

"I am a very rich man, M. Poirot. It is usually said that a rich man labours under the belief that he can buy everything and everyone. That is not true. I am a big man in my way, and one big man can ask a favour from another big man."

Poirot nodded a quick appreciation.

"That is very well said, M. Van Aldin. I place myself entirely at your service."

"Thank you," said Van Aldin. "I can only say call upon me at any time, and you will not find me ungrateful. And now, gentlemen, to business."

"I propose," said M. Carrège, "to interrogate the maid, Ada Mason. You have her here, I understand?"

"Yes," said Van Aldin. "We picked her up in Paris in passing through. She was very upset to hear of her mistress's death, but she tells her story coherently enough."

"We will have her in, then," said M. Carrège.

He rang the bell on his desk, and in a few minutes Ada Mason entered the room.

She was very neatly dressed in black, and the tip of her nose was red. She had exchanged her grey travelling gloves for a pair of black suède ones. She cast a look round the Examining Magistrate's office in some trepidation, and seemed relieved at the presence of her mistress's father. The Examining Magistrate prided himself on his geniality of manner, and did his best to put her at her ease. He was helped in this by Poirot, who acted as interpreter, and whose friendly manner was reassuring to the Englishwoman.

"Your name is Ada Mason; is that right?"

"Ada Beatrice I was christened, sir," said Mason primly.

"Just so. And we can understand, Mason, that this has all been very distressing."

"Oh, indeed it has, sir. I have been with many ladies and always given satisfaction, I hope, and I never dreamt of anything of this kind happening in any situation where I was."

"No, no," said M. Carrège.

"Naturally, I have read of such things, of course, in the Sunday papers. And then I always have understood that those foreign trains——" She suddenly checked her flow, remembering that the gentlemen who were speaking to her were of the same nationality as the trains.

"Now let us talk this affair over," said M. Carrège. "There

was, I understand, no question of your staying in Paris when you started from London?"

"Oh no, sir. We were to go straight through to Nice."

"Have you ever been abroad with your mistress before?"

"No, sir. I had only been with her two months, you see."

"Did she seem quite as usual when starting on this journey?"

"She was worried like and a bit upset, and she was rather irritable and difficult to please."

M. Carrège nodded.

"Now then, Mason, what was the first you heard of your stopping in Paris?"

"It was at the place they call the Gare de Lyon, sir. My mistress was thinking of getting out and walking up and down the platform. She was just going out into the corridor when she gave a sudden exclamation, and came back into her compartment with a gentleman. She shut the door between her carriage and mine, so that I didn't see or hear anything, till she suddenly opened it again and told me that she had changed her plans. She gave me some money and told me to get out and go to the Ritz. They knew her well there, she said, and would give me a room. I was to wait there until I heard from her; she would wire me what she wanted me to do. I had just time to get my things together and jump out of the train before it started off. It was a rush."

"While Mrs. Kettering was telling you this, where was the gentleman?"

"He was standing in the other compartment, sir, looking out of the window."

"Can you describe him to us?"

"Well, you see, sir, I hardly saw him. He had his back to me most of the time. He was a tall gentleman and dark; that's all I can say. He was dressed very like another gentleman in a dark blue overcoat and a grey hat."

"Was he one of the passengers on the train?"

"I don't think so, sir; I took it that he had come to the station to see Mrs. Kettering in passing through. Of course he might have been one of the passengers; I never thought of that."

Mason seemed a little flurried by the suggestion.

"Ah!" M. Carrège passed lightly to another subject. "Your mistress later requested the conductor not to rouse her early in the morning. Was that a likely thing for her to do, do you think?"

"Oh yes, sir. The mistress never ate any breakfast and she didn't sleep well at nights, so that she liked sleeping on in the morning."

Again M. Carrège passed to another subject.

"Amongst the luggage there was a scarlet morocco case, was there not?" he asked. "Your mistress's jewel-case?"

"Yes, sir."

"Did you take that case to the Ritz?"

"*Me* take the mistress's jewel-case to the Ritz! Oh no, indeed, sir." Mason's tones were horrified.

"You left it behind you in the carriage?"

"Yes, sir."

"Had your mistress many jewels with her, do you know?"

"A fair amount, sir; made me a bit uneasy sometimes, I can tell you, with those nasty tales you hear of being robbed in foreign countries. They were insured, I know, but all the same it seemed a frightful risk. Why, the rubies alone, the mistress told me, were worth several hundred thousand pounds."

"The rubies! What rubies?" barked Van Aldin suddenly.

Mason turned to him. "I think it was you who gave them to her, sir, not very long ago."

"My God!" cried Van Aldin. "You don't say she had those rubies with her? I told her to leave them at the bank."

Mason gave once more the discreet cough which was apparently part of her stock-in-trade as a lady's maid. This time it expressed a good deal. It expressed far more clearly than words could have done, that Mason's mistress had been a lady who took her own way.

"Ruth must have been mad," muttered Van Aldin. "What on earth could have possessed her?"

M. Carrège in turn gave vent to a cough, again a cough of significance. It riveted Van Aldin's attention on him.

"For the moment," said M. Carrège, addressing Mason, "I think that is all. If you will go into the next room, Mademoiselle, they will read over to you the questions and answers, and you will sign accordingly."

Mason went out escorted by the clerk, and Van Aldin said immediately to the Magistrate:

"Well?"

M. Carrège opened a drawer in his desk, took out a letter, and handed it across to Van Aldin.

"This was found in Madame's handbag."

"CHERE AMIE" (the letter ran),—"I will obey you; I will be prudent, discreet—all those things that a lover most hates. Paris would perhaps have been unwise, but the Isles d'Or are far away from the world, and you may be assured that nothing will leak out. It is like you and your divine sympathy to be so interested in the work on famous jewels that I am writing. It will, indeed, be an extraordinary privilege to actually see and handle these historic rubies. I am devoting a special passage to 'Heart of Fire.' My wonderful one! Soon I will make up to you for all those sad years of separation and emptiness.—Your ever-adoring,

"ARMAND."

Chapter 15

THE COMTE DE LA ROCHE

Van Aldin read the letter through in silence. His face turned a dull angry crimson. The men watching him saw the veins start out on his forehead, and his big hands clench themselves unconsciously. He handed back the letter without a word. M. Carrège was looking with close attention at his desk, M. Caux's eyes were fixed upon the ceiling, and M. Hercule Poirot was tenderly brushing a speck of dust from his coat sleeve. With the greatest tact they none of them looked at Van Aldin.

It was M. Carrège, mindful of his status and his duties, who tackled the unpleasant subject.

"Perhaps, Monsieur," he murmured, "you are aware by whom—er—this letter was written?"

"Yes, I know," said Van Aldin heavily.

"Ah?" said the magistrate inquiringly.

"A scoundrel who calls himself the Comte de la Roche."

There was a pause; then M. Poirot leaned forward, straightened a ruler on the judge's desk, and addressed the millionaire directly.

"M. Van Aldin, we are all sensible, deeply sensible, of the pain it must give you to speak of these matters, but believe me, Monsieur, it is not the time for concealments. If justice is to be done, we must know everything. If you will reflect a little minute you will realise the truth of that clearly for yourself."

Van Aldin was silent for a moment or two, then almost reluctantly he nodded his head in agreement.

"You are quite right, M. Poirot," he said. "Painful as it is, I have no right to keep anything back."

The Commissary gave a sigh of relief, and the Examining Magistrate leaned back in his chair and adjusted a pince-nez on his long thin nose.

"Perhaps you will tell us in your own words, M. Van Aldin," he said, "all that you know of this gentleman."

"It began eleven or twelve years ago—in Paris. My daughter was a young girl then, full of foolish, romantic notions, like all young girls are. Unknown to me, she made the acquaintance of this Comte de la Roche. You have heard of him, perhaps?"

The Commissary and Poirot nodded in assent.

"He calls himself the Comte de la Roche," continued Van Aldin, "but I doubt if he has any right to the title."

"You would not have found his name in the *Almanac de Gotha*," agreed the Commissary.

"I discovered as much," said Van Aldin. "The man was a good-looking, plausible scoundrel, with a fatal fascination for women. Ruth was infatuated with him, but I soon put a stop to the whole affair. The man was no better than a common swindler."

"You are quite right," said the Commissary. "The Comte de la Roche is well known to us. If it were possible, we should have laid him by the heels before now, but *ma foi*! it is not easy; the fellow is cunning, his affairs are always conducted with ladies of high social position. If he obtains money from them under false pretences or as the fruit of blackmail, *eh bien!* naturally they will not prosecute. To look foolish in the eyes of the world, oh no, that would never do, and he has an extraordinary power over women."

"That is so," said the millionaire heavily. "Well, as I told you, I broke the affair up pretty sharply. I told Ruth exactly what he was, and she had, perforce, to believe me. About a year afterwards, she met her present husband and married him. As far as I knew, that was the end of the matter; but only a week ago, I discovered, to my amazement, that my daughter had resumed her acquaintance with the Comte de la Roche. She had been meeting him frequently in London and Paris. I remonstrated with her on her imprudence, for I may tell you gentlemen that, on my insistence, she was preparing to bring a suit for divorce against her husband."

"That is interesting," murmured Poirot softly, his eyes on the ceiling.

Van Aldin looked at him sharply, and then went on.

"I pointed out to her the folly of continuing to see the Comte under the circumstances. I thought she agreed with me."

The Examining Magistrate coughed delicately.

"But according to this letter——" he began, and then stopped.

Van Aldin's jaw set itself squarely.

"I know. It's no good mincing matters. However unpleasant, we have got to face facts. It seems clear that Ruth had arranged to go to Paris and meet de la Roche there. After my warnings to her, however, she must have written to the Count suggesting a change of rendezvous."

"The Isles d'Or," said the Commissary thoughtfully, "are situated just opposite Hyères, a remote and idyllic spot."

Van Aldin nodded.

"My God! How could Ruth be such a fool?" he exclaimed bitterly. "All this talk about writing a book on jewels! Why, he must have been after the rubies from the first."

"There are some very famous rubies," said Poirot, "originally part of the Crown jewels of Russia; they are unique in character, and their value is almost fabulous. There has been a rumour that they have lately passed into the possession of an American. Are we right in concluding, Monsieur, that you were the purchaser?"

"Yes," said Van Aldin. "They came into my possession in Paris about ten days ago."

"Pardon me, Monsieur, but you have been negotiating for their purchase for some time?"

"A little over two months. Why?"

"These things became known," said Poirot. "There is always a pretty formidable crowd on the track of jewels such as these."

A spasm distorted the other's face.

"I remember," he said brokenly, "a joke I made to Ruth when I gave them to her. I told her not to take them to the Riviera with her, as I could not afford to have her robbed and murdered for the sake of the jewels. My God! the things one says—never dreaming or knowing they will come true."

There was a sympathetic silence, and then Poirot spoke in a detached manner.

"Let us arrange our facts with order and precision. According to our present theory, this is how they run. The Comte de la Roche knows of your purchase of these jewels. By an easy stratagem he induces Madame Kettering to bring the stones with her. He, then, is the man Mason saw in the train at Paris."

The other three nodded in agreement.

"Madame is surprised to see him, but he deals with the situation promptly. Mason is got out of the way; a dinner basket is ordered. We know from the conductor that he made up the berth for the first compartment, but he did not go into the second compartment, and that a man could quite well have been concealed from him. So far the Comte could have been hidden to a marvel. No one knows of his presence on the train except Madame; he has been careful that the maid did not see his face. All that she could say is that he was tall and dark. It is all most conveniently vague. They are alone—and the train rushes through the night. There would be no outcry, no struggle, for the man is, so she thinks, her lover."

He turned gently to Van Aldin.

"Death, Monsieur, must have been almost instantaneous. We will pass over that quickly. The Comte takes the jewel-case which lies ready to his hand. Shortly afterwards the train draws into Lyons."

M. Carrège nodded his approval.

"Precisely. The conductor without descends. It would be easy for our man to leave the train unseen; it would be easy to catch a train back to Paris or anywhere he pleases. And the crime would be put down as an ordinary train robbery. But for the letter found in Madame's bag, the Comte would not have been mentioned."

"It was an oversight on his part not to search that bag," declared the Commissary.

"Without doubt he thought she had destroyed that letter. It was—pardon me, Monsieur—it was an indiscretion of the first water to keep it."

"And yet," murmured Poirot, "it was an indiscretion the Comte might have foreseen."

"You mean?"

"I mean we are all agreed on one point, and that is that the Comte de la Roche knows one subject *à fond*: Women. How was it that, knowing women as he does, he did not foresee that Madame would have kept that letter?"

"Yes—yes," said the Examining Magistrate doubtfully, "there is something in what you say. But at such times, you understand, a man is not master of himself. He does not reason calmly. *Mon Dieu!*" he added, with feeling, "if our criminals kept their heads and acted with intelligence, how should we capture them?"

Poirot smiled to himself.

"It seems to me a clear case," said the other, "but a difficult one to prove. The Comte is a slippery customer, and unless the maid can identify him——"

"Which is most unlikely," said Poirot.

"True, true." The Examining Magistrate rubbed his chin. "It is going to be difficult."

"If he did indeed commit the crime——" began Poirot. M. Caux interrupted.

"If—you say *if*?"

"Yes, Monsieur le Commissaire, I say *if*."

The other looked at him sharply. "You are right," he said at last, "we go too fast. It is possible that the Comte may have an alibi. Then we should look foolish."

"*Ah, ça par exemple*," replied Poirot, "that is of no importance whatever. Naturally, if he committed the crime he will have an alibi. A man with the Comte's experience does not neglect to take precautions. No, I said *if* for a very definite reason."

"And what was that?"

Poirot wagged an emphatic forefinger. "The psychology."

"Eh?" said the Commissary.

"The psychology is at fault. The Comte is a scoundrel—yes. The Comte is a swindler—yes. The Comte preys upon women—yes. He proposes to steal Madame's jewels—again yes. Is he the kind of man to commit murder? I say *no*! A man of the type of the Comte is always a coward; he takes no risks. He plays the safe, the mean, what the English call the lowdown game; but murder, a hundred times no!" He shook his head in a dissatisfied manner.

The Examining Magistrate, however, did not seem disposed to agree with him.

"The day always comes when such gentry lose their heads and go too far," he observed sagely. "Doubtless that is the case here. Without wishing to disagree with you, M. Poirot——"

"It was only an opinion," Poirot hastened to explain. "The case is, of course, in your hands, and you will do what seems fit to you."

"I am satisfied in my own mind the Comte de la Roche is the man we need to get hold of," said M. Carrège. "You agree with me, Monsieur le Commissaire?"

"Perfectly."

"And you, M. Van Aldin?"

"Yes," said the millionaire. "Yes; the man is a thorough paced villain, no doubt about it."

"It will be difficult to lay hands on him, I am afraid," said the Magistrate, "but we will do our best. Telegraphed instructions shall go out at once."

"Permit me to assist you," said Poirot. "There need be no difficulty."

"Eh?"

The others stared at him. The little man smiled beamingly back at them.

"It is my business to know things," he explained. "The Comte is a man of intelligence. He is at present at a villa he has leased, the Villa Marina at Antibes."

Chapter 16

POIROT DISCUSSES THE CASE

Everybody looked respectfully at Poirot. Undoubtedly the little man had scored heavily. The Commissary laughed—on a rather hollow note.

"You teach us all our business," he cried. "M. Poirot knows more than the police."

Poirot gazed complacently at the ceiling, adopting a mock-modest air.

"What will you; it is my little hobby," he murmured, "to know things. Naturally I have the time to indulge it. I am not overburdened with affairs."

"Ah!" said the Commissary shaking his head portentously. "As for me——"

He made an exaggerated gesture to represent the cares that lay on his shoulders.

Poirot turned suddenly to Van Aldin.

"You agree, Monsieur, with this view? You feel certain that the Comte de la Roche is the murderer?"

"Why, it would seem so—yes, certainly."

Something guarded in the answer made the Examining Magistrate look at the American curiously. Van Aldin seemed aware of his scrutiny and made an effort as though to shake off some preoccupation.

"What about my son-in-law?" he asked. "You have acquainted him with the news? He is in Nice, I understand."

"Certainly, Monsieur." The Commissary hesitated, and then murmured very discreetly: "You are doubtless aware,

M. Van Aldin, that M. Kettering was also one of the passengers on the Blue Train that night?"

The millionaire nodded.

"Heard it just before I left London," he vouchsafed laconically.

"He tells us," continued the Commissary, "that he had no idea his wife was travelling on the train."

"I bet he hadn't," said Van Aldin grimly. "It would have been rather a nasty shock to him if he'd come across her on it."

The three men looked at him questioningly.

"I'm not going to mince matters," said Van Aldin savagely. "No one knows what my poor girl has had to put up with. Derek Kettering wasn't alone. He had a lady with him."

"Ah?"

"Mirelle—the dancer."

M. Carrège and the Commissary looked at each other and nodded as though confirming some previous conversation. M. Carrège leaned back in his chair, joined his hands, and fixed his eyes on the ceiling.

"Ah!" he murmured again. "One wondered." He coughed. "One has heard rumours."

"The lady," said M. Caux, "is very notorious."

"And also," murmured Poirot softly, "very expensive."

Van Aldin had gone very red in the face. He leant forward and hit the table a bang with his fist.

"See here," he cried, "my son-in-law is a damned scoundrel!"

He glared at them, looking from one face to another.

"Oh, I don't know," he went on. "Good looks and a charming, easy manner. It took me in once upon a time. I suppose he pretended to be broken-hearted when you broke the news to him—that is, if he didn't know it already."

"Oh, it came as a surprise to him. He was overwhelmed."

"Darned young hypocrite," said Van Aldin. "Simulated great grief, I suppose?"

"N—no," said the Commissary cautiously. "I would not quite say that—eh, M. Carrège?"

The Magistrate brought the tips of his fingers together, and half closed his eyes.

"Shock, bewilderment, horror—these things, yes," he declared judicially. "Great sorrow—no—I should not say that."

Hercule Poirot spoke once more.

"Permit me to ask, M. Van Aldin, does M. Kettering benefit by the death of his wife?"

"He benefits to the tune of a couple of millions," said Van Aldin.

"Dollars?"

"Pounds. I settled that sum on Ruth absolutely on her marriage. She made no will and leaves no children, so the money will go to her husband."

"Whom she was on the point of divorcing," murmured Poirot. "Ah, yes—*précisément*."

The Commissary turned and looked sharply at him.

"Do you mean——?" he began.

"I mean nothing," said Poirot. "I arrange the facts, that is all."

Van Aldin stared at him with awakening interest.

The little man rose to his feet.

"I do not think I can be of any further service to you, M. le Juge," he said politely, bowing to M. Carrège. "You will keep me informed of the course of events? It will be a kindness."

"But certainly—most certainly."

Van Aldin rose also.

"You don't want me any more at present?"

"No, Monsieur; we have all the information we need for the moment."

"Then I will walk a little way with M. Poirot. That is, if he does not object?"

"Enchanted, Monsieur," said the little man, with a bow.

Van Aldin lighted a large cigar, having first offered one to Poirot, who declined it and lit one of his own tiny cigarettes. A man of great strength of character, Van Aldin already appeared to be his everyday, normal self once more. After strolling along for a minute or two in silence, the millionaire spoke:

"I take it, M. Poirot, that you no longer exercise your profession?"

"That is so, Monsieur. I enjoy the world."

"Yet you are assisting the police in this affair?"

"Monsieur, if a doctor walks along the street and an accident happens, does he say, 'I have retired from my profession, I will continue my walk,' when there is someone bleeding to death at his feet? If I had been already in Nice, and the police had sent to me and asked me to assist them, I should have refused. But this affair, the good God thrust it upon me."

"You were on the spot," said Van Aldin thoughtfully. "You examined the compartment, did you not?"

Poirot nodded.

"Doubtless you found things that were, shall we say, suggestive to you?"

"Perhaps," said Poirot.

"I hope you see what I am leading up to?" said Van Aldin. "It seems to me that the case against this Comte de la Roche is perfectly clear, but I am not a fool. I have been watching you for this last hour or so, and I realise that for some reason of your own you don't agree with that theory?"

Poirot shrugged his shoulders.

"I may be wrong."

"So we come to the favour I want to ask you. Will you act in this matter for me?"

"For you, personally?"

"That was my meaning."

Poirot was silent for a moment or two. Then he said:

"You realise what you are asking?"

"I guess so," said Van Aldin.

"Very well," said Poirot. "I accept. But in that case, I must have frank answers to my questions."

"Why, certainly. That is understood."

Poirot's manner changed. He became suddenly brusque and business-like.

"This question of a divorce," he said. "It was you who advised your daughter to bring the suit?"

"Yes."

"When?"

"About ten days ago. I had had a letter from her complaining of her husband's behaviour, and I put it to her very strongly that divorce was the only remedy."

"In what way did she complain of his behaviour?"

"He was being seen about with a *very* notorious lady—the one we have been speaking of—Mirelle."

"The dancer. Ah-ha! And Madame Kettering objected? Was she very devoted to her husband?"

"I would not say that," said Van Aldin, hesitating a little.

"It was not her heart that suffered, it was her pride—is that what you would say?"

"Yes, I suppose you might put it like that."

"I gather that the marriage has not been a happy one from the beginning?"

"Derek Kettering is rotten to the core," said Van Aldin. "He is incapable of making any woman happy."

"He is, as you say in England, a bad lot. That is right, is it not?"

Van Aldin nodded.

"*Très bien!* You advise Madame to seek a divorce, she agrees; you consult your solicitors. When does M. Kettering get news of what is in the wind?"

"I sent for him myself, and explained the course of action I proposed to take."

"And what did he say?" murmured Poirot softly.

Van Aldin's face darkened at the remembrance.

"He was infernally impudent."

"Excuse the question, Monsieur, but did he refer to the Comte de la Roche?"

"Not by name," growled the other unwillingly, "but he showed himself cognizant of the affair."

"What, if I may ask, was Mr. Kettering's financial position at the time?"

"How do you suppose I should know that?" asked Van Aldin, after a very brief hesitation.

"It seemed likely to me that you would inform yourself on that point."

"Well—you are quite right, I did. I discovered that Kettering was on the rocks."

"And now he has inherited two million pounds! *La vie*—it is a strange thing, is it not?"

Van Aldin looked at him sharply.

"What do you mean?"

"I moralise," said Poirot, "I reflect, I speak the philosophy. But to return to where we were. Surely M. Kettering did not propose to allow himself to be divorced without making a fight for it?"

Van Aldin did not answer for a minute or two, then he said:

"I don't exactly know what his intentions were."

"Did you hold any further communications with him?"

Again a slight pause, then Van Aldin said:

"No."

Poirot stopped dead, took off his hat, and held out his hand.

"I must wish you good-day, Monsieur. I can do nothing for you."

"What are you getting at?" demanded Van Aldin angrily.

"If you do not tell me the truth, I can do nothing."

"I don't know what you mean."

"I think you do. You may rest assured, M. Van Aldin, that I know how to be discreet."

"Very well, then," said the millionaire. "I'll admit that I was not speaking the truth just now. I *did* have further communication with my son-in-law."

"Yes?"

"To be exact, I sent my secretary, Major Knighton, to see him, with instructions to offer him the sum of one hundred thousand pounds in cash if the divorce went through undefended."

"A pretty sum of money," said Poirot appreciatively: "and the answer of Monsieur your son-in-law?"

"He sent back word that I could go to hell," replied the millionaire succinctly.

"Ah!" said Poirot.

He betrayed no emotion of any kind. At the moment he was engaged in methodically recording facts.

"Monsieur Kettering has told the police that he neither saw nor spoke to his wife on the journey from England. Are you inclined to believe that statement, Monsieur?"

"Yes, I am," said Van Aldin. "He would take particular pains to keep out of her way, I should say."

"Why?"

"Because he had got that woman with him."

"Mirelle?"

"Yes."

"How did you come to know that fact?"

"A man of mine, whom I had put on to watch him, reported to me that they both left by that train."

"I see," said Poirot. "In that case, as you said before, he would not be likely to attempt to hold any communication with Madame Kettering."

The little man fell silent for some time. Van Aldin did not interrupt his meditation.

Chapter 17

AN ARISTOCRATIC GENTLEMAN

"You have been to the Riviera before, Georges?" said Poirot to his valet the following morning.

George was an intensely English, rather wooden-faced individual.

"Yes, sir. I was here two years ago when I was in the service of Lord Edward Frampton."

"And to-day," murmured his master, "you are here with Hercule Poirot. How one mounts in the world!"

The valet made no reply to this observation. After a suitable pause he asked:

"The brown lounge suit, sir? The wind is somewhat chilly to-day."

"There is a grease spot on the waistcoat," objected Poirot. "A *morceau* of *Filet de sole à la Jeanette* alighted there when I was lunching at the Ritz last Tuesday."

"There is no spot there now, sir," said George reproachfully. "I have removed it."

"*Très bien!*" said Poirot. "I am pleased with you, Georges."

"Thank you, sir."

There was a pause, and then Poirot murmured dreamily:

"Supposing, my good Georges, that you had been born in

the same social sphere as your late master, Lord Edward Frampton—that, penniless yourself, you had married an extremely wealthy wife, but that wife proposed to divorce you, with excellent reasons, what would you do about it?"

"I should endeavour, sir," replied George, "to make her change her mind."

"By peaceful or by forcible methods?"

George looked shocked.

"You will excuse me, sir," he said, "but a gentleman of the aristocracy would not behave like a Whitechapel coster. He would not do anything low."

"Would he not, Georges? I wonder now. Well, perhaps you are right."

There was a knock on the door. George went to it and opened it a discreet inch or two. A low murmured colloquy went on, and then the valet returned to Poirot.

"A note, sir."

Poirot took it. It was from M. Caux, the Commissary of Police.

"We are about to interrogate the Comte de la Roche. The Juge d'Instruction begs that you will be present."

"Quickly, my suit, Georges! I must hasten myself."

A quarter of an hour later, spick and span in his brown suit, Poirot entered the Examining Magistrate's room. M. Caux was already there, and both he and M. Carrège greeted Poirot with polite *empressement*.

"The affair is somewhat discouraging," murmured M. Caux.

"It appears that the Comte arrived in Nice the day before the murder."

"If that is true, it will settle your affair nicely for you," responded Poirot.

M. Carrège cleared his throat.

"We must not accept this alibi without very cautious inquiry," he declared. He struck the bell upon the table with his hand.

In another minute a tall dark man, exquisitely dressed, with a somewhat haughty cast of countenance, entered the room. So very aristocratic-looking was the Count, that it would have seemed sheer heresy even to whisper that his father had been an obscure corn-chandler in Nantes—which, as a matter of fact, was the case. Looking at him, one would have been prepared to swear that innumerable ancestors of his must have perished by the guillotine in the French Revolution.

"I am here, gentlemen," said the Count haughtily. "May I ask why you wish to see me?"

"Pray be seated, Monsieur le Comte," said the Examining Magistrate politely. "It is the affair of the death of Madame Kettering that we are investigating."

"The death of Madame Kettering? I do not understand."

"You were—ahem!—acquainted with the lady, I believe, Monsieur le Comte?"

"Certainly I was acquainted with her. What has that to do with the matter?"

Sticking an eyeglass in his eye, he looked coldly round the room, his glance resting longest on Poirot, who was gazing at him with a kind of simple, innocent admiration which was most pleasing to the Count's vanity. M. Carrège leaned back in his chair and cleared his throat.

"You do not perhaps know, Monsieur le Comte"—he paused—"that Madame Kettering was murdered?"

"Murdered? *Mon Dieu*, how terrible!"

The surprise and the sorrow were excellently done—so well done, indeed, as to seem wholly natural.

"Madame Kettering was strangled between Paris and Lyons," continued M. Carrège, "and her jewels were stolen."

"It is iniquitous!" cried the Count warmly; "the police should do something about these train bandits. Nowadays no one is safe."

"In Madame's handbag," continued the Judge, "we found a letter to her from you. She had, it seemed, arranged to meet you?"

The Count shrugged his shoulders and spread out his hands.

"Of what use are concealments," he said frankly. "We are all men of the world. Privately and between ourselves, I admit the affair."

"You met her in Paris and travelled down with her, I believe?" said M. Carrège.

"That was the original arrangement, but by Madame's wish it was changed. I was to meet her at Hyères."

"You did not meet her on the train at Gare de Lyon on the evening of the 14th?"

"On the contrary, I arrived in Nice on the morning of that day, so what you suggest is impossible."

"Quite so, quite so," said M. Carrège. "As a matter of form, you would perhaps give me an account of your movements during the evening and night of the 14th."

The Count reflected for a minute.

"I dined in Monte Carle at the Café de Paris. Afterwards I went to the Le Sporting. I won a few thousand francs," he shrugged his shoulders. "I returned home at perhaps one o'clock."

"Pardon me, Monsieur, but how did you return home?"

"In my own two-seater car."

"No one was with you?"

"No one."

"You could produce witnesses in support of this statement?"

"Doubtless many of my friends saw me there that evening. I dined alone."

"Your servant admitted you on your return to your villa?"

"I let myself in with my own latch-key."

"Ah!" murmured the Magistrate.

Again he struck the bell on the table with his hand. The door opened, and a messenger appeared.

"Bring in the maid, Mason," said M. Carrège.

"Very good, Monsieur le Juge."

Ada Mason was brought in.

"Will you be so good, Mademoiselle, as to look at this gentleman. To the best of your ability was it he who entered your mistress's compartment in Paris?"

The woman looked long and searchingly at the Count, who was, Poirot fancied, rather uneasy under this scrutiny.

"I could not say, sir, I am sure," said Mason at last. "It might be and again it might not. Seeing as how I only saw his back, it's hard to say. I rather think it *was* the gentleman."

"But you are not sure?"

"No—o," said Mason unwillingly; "n—no, I am not sure."

"You have seen this gentleman before in Curzon Street?"

Mason shook her head.

"I should not be likely to see any visitors that come to Curzon Street," she explained, "unless they were staying in the house."

"Very well, that will do," said the Examining Magistrate sharply.

Evidently he was disappointed.

"One moment," said Poirot. "There is a question I would like to put to Mademoiselle, if I may?"

"Certainly, M. Poirot—certainly, by all means."

Poirot addressed himself to the maid.

"What happened to the tickets?"

"The tickets, sir?"

"Yes; the tickets from London to Nice. Did you or your mistress have them?"

"The mistress had her own Pullman ticket, sir; the others were in my charge."

"What happened to them?"

"I gave them to the conductor on the French train, sir; he said it was usual. I hope I did right, sir?"

"Oh, quite right, quite right. A mere matter of detail."

Both M. Caux and the Examining Magistrate looked at him curiously. Mason stood uncertainly for a minute or two, and then the magistrate gave her a brief nod of dismissal, and she went out. Poirot scribbled something on a scrap of paper and handed it across to M. Carrège. The latter read it and his brow cleared.

"Well, gentlemen," demanded the Count haughtily, "am I to be detained further?"

"Assuredly not, assuredly not," M. Carrège hastened to say, with a great deal of amiability. "Everything is now cleared up as regards your own position in this affair. Naturally, in view of Madame's letter, we were bound to question you."

The Count rose, picked up his handsome stick from the corner, and, with rather a curt bow, left the room.

"And that is that," said M. Carrège. "You were quite right, M. Poirot—much better to let him feel he is not suspected. Two of my men will shadow him night and day, and at the same time we will go into the question of the alibi. It seems to me rather—er—a fluid one."

"Possibly," agreed Poirot thoughtfully.

"I asked M. Kettering to come here this morning," continued the Magistrate, "though really I doubt if we have much to ask him, but there are one or two suspicious circumstances ——" He paused, rubbing his nose.

"Such as?" asked Poirot.

"Well"—the Magistrate coughed—"this lady with whom he is said to be travelling—Mademoiselle Mirelle. She is staying at one hotel and he at another. That strikes me—er—as rather odd."

"It looks," said M. Caux, "as though they were being careful."

"Exactly," said M. Carrège triumphantly; "and what should they have to be careful about?"

"An excess of caution is suspicious, eh?" said Poirot.

"*Précisément.*"

"We might, I think," murmured Poirot, "ask M. Kettering one or two questions."

The Magistrate gave instructions. A moment or two later, Derek Kettering, debonair as ever, entered the room.

"Good morning, Monsieur," said the Judge politely.

"Good morning," said Derek Kettering curtly. "You sent for me. Has anything fresh turned up?"

"Pray sit down, Monsieur."

Derek took a seat and flung his hat and stick on the table.

"Well?" he asked impatiently.

"We have, so far, no fresh data," said M. Carrège cautiously.

"That's very interesting," said Derek drily. "Did you send for me here in order to tell me that?"

"We naturally thought, Monsieur, that you would like to be informed of the progress of the case," said the Magistrate severely.

"Even if the progress is non-existent."

"We also wished to ask you a few questions."

"Ask away."

"You are quite sure that you neither saw nor spoke with your wife on the train."

"I've answered that already. I did not."

"You had, no doubt, your reasons."

Derek stared at him suspiciously.

"I—did—not—know—she—was—on—the—train," he explained, spacing his words elaborately, as though to someone dull of intellect.

"That is what you say, yes," murmured M. Carrège.

A quick frown suffused Derek's face.

"I should like to know what you are driving at. Do you know what I think, M. Carrège?"

"What do you think, Monsieur?"

"I think the French police are vastly overrated. Surely you must have some data as to these gangs of train robbers. It's outrageous that such a thing could happen on a *train de luxe* like that, and that the French police should be helpless to deal with the matter."

"We are dealing with it, Monsieur, never fear."

"Madame Kettering, I understand, did not leave a will," interposed Poirot suddenly. His finger-tips were joined together, and he was looking intently at the ceiling.

"I don't think she ever made one," said Kettering. "Why?"

"It is a very pretty little fortune that you inherit there," said Poirot—"a very pretty little fortune."

Although his eyes were still on the ceiling, he managed to see the dark flush that rose to Derek Kettering's face.

"What do you mean, and who are you?"

Poirot gently uncrossed his knees, withdrew his gaze from the ceiling, and looked the young man full in the face.

"My name is Hercule Poirot," he said quietly, "and I am probably the greatest detective in the world. You are quite sure that you did not see or speak to your wife on that train?"

"What are you getting at? Do you—do you mean to insinuate that I—I killed her?"

He laughed suddenly.

"I mustn't lose my temper; it's too palpably absurd. Why, if I killed her I should have had no need to steal her jewels, would I?"

"That is true," murmured Poirot, with a rather crestfallen air. "I did not think of that."

"If ever there were a clear case of murder and robbery this is it," said Derek Kettering. "Poor Ruth, it was those damned rubies did for her. It must have got about she had them with her. There has been murder done for those same stones before now, I believe."

Poirot sat up suddenly in his chair. A very faint green light glowed in his eyes. He looked extraordinarily like a sleek, well-fed cat.

"One more question, M. Kettering," he said. "Will you give me the date when you last saw your wife?"

"Let me see," Kettering reflected. "It must have been—yes, over three weeks ago. I am afraid I can't give you the date exactly."

"No matter," said Poirot drily; "that is all I wanted to know."

"Well," said Derek Kettering impatiently, "anything further?"

He looked towards M. Carrège. The latter sought inspiration from Poirot, and received it in a very faint shake of the head.

"No, M. Kettering," he said politely; "no, I do not think we need trouble you any further. I wish you good morning."

"Good morning," said Kettering. He went out, banging the door behind him.

Poirot leaned forward and spoke sharply, as soon as the young man was out of the room.

"Tell me," he said peremptorily, "when did you speak of these rubies to M. Kettering?"

"I have not spoken of them," said M. Carrège. "It was only yesterday afternoon that we learnt about them from M. Van Aldin."

"Yes; but there was a mention of them in the Comte's letter."

M. Carrège looked pained.

"Naturally I did not speak of that letter to M. Kettering," he said in a shocked voice. "It would have been most indiscreet at the present juncture of affairs."

Poirot leaned forward and tapped the table.

"*Then how did he know about them?*" he demanded softly. "Madame could not have told him, for he has not seen her for three weeks. It seems unlikely that either M. Van Aldin or his secretary would have mentioned them; their interviews with him have been on entirely different lines, and there has not been any hint or reference to them in the newspapers."

He got up and took his hat and stick.

"And yet," he murmured to himself, "our gentleman knows all about them. I wonder now, yes, I wonder!"

Chapter 18

DEREK LUNCHES

Derek Kettering went straight to the Negresco, where he ordered a couple of cocktails and disposed of them rapidly; then he stared moodily out over the dazzling blue sea. He noted the passers-by mechanically—a damned dull crowd, badly dressed, and painfully uninteresting; one hardly ever saw anything worthwhile nowadays. Then he corrected this last impression rapidly, as a woman placed herself at a table a little distance away from him. She was wearing a marvellous confection of orange and black, with a little hat that shaded her face. He ordered a third cocktail; again he stared out to sea, and then suddenly he started. A well-known perfume assailed his nostrils, and he looked up to see the orange-and-black lady standing beside him. He saw her face now, and recognised her. It was Mirelle. She was smiling that insolent, seductive smile he knew so well.

"Dereek!" she murmured. "You are pleased to see me, no?"

She dropped into a seat the other side of the table.

"But welcome me, then, stupid one," she mocked.

"This is an unexpected pleasure," said Derek. "When did you leave London?"

She shrugged her shoulders.

"A day or two ago?"

"And the Parthenon?"

"I have, how do you say it?—given them the chuck!"

"Really?"

"You are not very amiable, Dereek."

"Do you expect me to be?"

Mirelle lit a cigarette and puffed at it for a few minutes before saying:

"You think, perhaps, that it is not prudent so soon?"

Derek stared at her, then he shrugged his shoulders, and remarked formally:

"You are lunching here?"

"*Mais oui.* I am lunching with you."

"I am exceedingly sorry," said Derek. "I have a very important engagement."

"*Mon Dieu!* But you men are like children," exclaimed the dancer. "But yes, it is the spoilt child that you act to me, ever since that day in London when you flung yourself out of my flat, you sulk. Ah! *mais c'est inouï!*"

"My dear girl," said Derek, "I really don't know what you are talking about. We agreed in London that rats desert a sinking ship, that is all that there is to be said."

In spite of his careless words, his face looked haggard and strained. Mirelle leaned forward suddenly.

"You cannot deceive me," she murmured. "I know—I know what you have done for me."

He looked up at her sharply. Some undercurrent in her voice arrested his attention. She nodded her head at him.

"Ah! have no fear; I am discreet. You are magnificent! You have a superb courage, but, all the same, it was I who gave you the idea that day, when I said to you in London that accidents sometimes happened. And you are not in danger? The police do not suspect you?"

"What the devil——?"

"Hush!"

She held up a slim olive hand with one big emerald on the little finger.

"You are right, I should not have spoken so in a public place. We will not speak of the matter again, but our troubles are ended; our life together will be wonderful—wonderful!"

Derek laughed suddenly—a harsh, disagreeable laugh.

"So the rats come back, do they? Two million makes a difference—of course it does. I ought to have known that." He laughed again. "You will help me to spend that two million, won't you, Mirelle? You know how, no woman better." He laughed again.

" Hush!" cried the dancer. " What is the matter with you, Dereek? See—people are turning to stare at you."

" Me? I will tell you what is the matter. I have finished with you, Mirelle. Do you hear? Finished!"

Mirelle did not take it as he expected her to do. She looked at him for a minute or two, and then she smiled softly.

" But what a child! You are angry—you are sore, and all because I am practical. Did I not always tell you that I adored you?"

She leaned forward.

" But I know you, Dereek. Look at me—see, it is Mirelle who speaks to you. You cannot live without her, you know it. I loved you before, I will love you a hundred times more now. I will make life wonderful for you—but wonderful. There is no one like Mirelle."

Her eyes burned into his. She saw him grow pale and draw in his breath, and she smiled to herself contentedly. She knew her own magic and power over men.

" That is settled," she said softly, and gave a little laugh. " And now, Dereek, will you give me lunch?"

" No."

He drew in his breath sharply and rose to his feet.

" I am sorry, but I told you—I have got an engagement."

" You are lunching with someone else? Bah! I don't believe it."

" I am lunching with that lady over there."

He crossed abruptly to where a lady in white had just come up the steps. He addressed her a little breathlessly.

" Miss Grey, will you—will you have lunch with me? You met me at Lady Tamplin's, if you remember."

Katherine looked at him for a minute or two with those thoughtful grey eyes that said so much.

" Thank you," she said, after a moment's pause; " I should like to very much."

Chapter 19

AN UNEXPECTED VISITOR

The Comte de la Roche had just finished *déjeuner*, consisting of an *omelette fines herbes*, an *entrecôte Bearnaise*, and a *Savarin au Rhum*. Wiping his fine black moustache delicately with his table napkin, the Comte rose from the table. He passed through the salon of the villa, noting with appreciation the few *objets d'art* which were carelessly scattered about. The Louis XV snuff-box, the satin shoe worn by Marie Antoinette, and the other historic trifles that were part of the Comte's *mise en scène*. They were, he would explain to his fair visitors, heirlooms in his family. Passing through on to the terrace the Comte looked out on to the Mediterranean with an unseeing eye. He was in no mood for appreciating the beauties of scenery. A fully matured scheme had been rudely brought to naught, and his plans had to be cast afresh. Stretching himself out in a basket chair, a cigarette held between his white fingers, the Comte pondered deeply.

Presently Hipolyte, his man-servant, brought out coffee and a choice of liqueurs. The Comte selected some very fine old brandy.

As the man-servant was preparing to depart, the Comte arrested him with a slight gesture. Hipolyte stood respectfully to attention. His countenance was hardly a prepossessing one, but the correctitude of his demeanour went far to obliterate the fact. He was now the picture of respectful attention.

"It is possible," said the Comte, "that in the course of the next few days various strangers may come to the house. They will endeavour to scrape acquaintance with you and with Marie. They will probably ask you various questions concerning me."

"Yes, Monsieur le Comte."

"Perhaps this has already happened?"

"No, Monsieur le Comte."

"There have been no strangers about the place? You are certain?"

"There has been no one, Monsieur le Comte."

"That is well," said the Comte drily; "nevertheless they will come—I am sure of it. They will ask questions."

Hipolyte looked at his master in intelligent anticipation.

The Comte spoke slowly, without looking at Hipolyte.

"As you know, I arrived here last Tuesday morning. If the police or any other inquirer should question you, do not forget that fact. I arrived on Tuesday, the 14th—not Wednesday, the 15th. You understand?"

"Perfectly, Monsieur le Comte."

"In an affair where a lady is concerned, it is always necessary to be discreet. I feel certain, Hipolyte, that you can be discreet."

"I can be discreet, Monsieur."

"And Marie?"

"Marie also. I will answer for her."

"That is well then," murmured the Comte.

When Hipolyte had withdrawn, the Comte sipped his black coffee with a reflective air. Occasionally he frowned, once he shook his head slightly, twice he nodded it. Into the midst of these cogitations came Hipolyte once more.

"A lady, Monsieur."

"A lady?"

The Comte was surprised. Not that a visit from a lady was an unusual thing at the Villa Marina, but at this particular moment the Comte could not think who the lady was likely to be.

"She is, I think, a lady not known to Monsieur," murmured the valet helpfully.

The Comte was more and more intrigued.

"Show her out here, Hipolyte," he commanded.

A moment later a marvellous vision in orange and black stepped out in the terrace, accompanied by a strong perfume of exotic blossoms.

"Monsieur le Comte de la Roche?"

"At your service, Mademoiselle," said the Comte, bowing.

"My name is Mirelle. You may have heard of me."

"Ah, indeed, Mademoiselle, but who has not been enchanted by the dancing of Mademoiselle Mirelle? Exquisite!"

The dancer acknowledged this compliment with a brief mechanical smile.

"My descent upon you is unceremonious," she began.

"But seat yourself, I beg of you, Mademoiselle," cried the Comte, bringing forward a chair.

Behind the gallantry of his manner he was observing her narrowly. There were very few things that the Comte did not know about women. True, his experience had not lain much in ladies of Mirelle's class, who were themselves predatory. He and the dancer were, in a sense, birds of a feather. His arts, the Comte knew, would be thrown away on Mirelle. She was a Parisienne, and a shrewd one. Nevertheless, there was one thing that the Comte could recognise infallibly when he saw it. He knew at once that he was in the presence of a very angry woman, and an angry woman, as the Comte was well aware, always says more than is prudent, and is occasionally a source of profit to a level-headed gentleman who keeps cool.

"It is most amiable of you, Mademoiselle, to honour my poor abode thus."

"We have mutual friends in Paris," said Mirelle. "I have heard of you from them, but I come to see you to-day for another reason. I have heard of you since I came to Nice—in a different way, you understand."

"Ah?" said the Comte softly.

"I will be brutal," continued the dancer; "nevertheless, believe that I have your welfare at heart. They are saying in Nice, Monsieur le Comte, that you are the murderer of the English lady, Madame Kettering."

"I!—the murderer of Madame Kettering? Bah! But how absurd!"

He spoke more languidly than indignantly, knowing that he would thus provoke her further.

"But yes," she insisted, "it is as I tell you."

"It amuses people to talk," murmured the Comte indifferently. "It would be beneath me to take such wild accusations seriously."

"You do not understand." Mirelle bent forward, her dark eyes flashing. "It is not the idle talk of those in the streets. It is the police."

"The police—ah?"

The Comte sat up, alert once more.

Mirelle nodded her head vigorously several times.

"Yes, yes. You comprehend me—I have friends everywhere. The Prefect himself——" She left the sentence unfinished, with an eloquent shrug of the shoulders.

"Who is not indiscreet where a beautiful woman is concerned?" murmured the Count politely.

"The police believe that you killed Madame Kettering. But they are wrong."

"Certainly they are wrong," agreed the Comte easily.

"You say that, but you do not know the truth. I do."

The Comte looked at her curiously.

"You know who killed Madame Kettering? Is that what you would say, Mademoiselle?"

Mirelle nodded vehemently.

"Yes."

"Who was it?" asked the Comte sharply.

"Her husband." She leant across to the Comte, speaking in a low voice that vibrated with anger and excitement. "It was her husband who killed her."

The Comte leaned back in his chair. His face was a mask.

"Let me ask you, Mademoiselle—how do you know this?"

"How do I know it?" Mirelle sprang to her feet, with a laugh. "He boasted of it beforehand. He was ruined, bankrupt, dishonoured. Only the death of his wife could save him. He told me so. He travelled on the same train—but she was not to know it. Why was that, I ask you? So that he might creep upon her in the night—— Ah!"—she shut her eyes—"I can see it happening . . ."

The Count coughed.

"Perhaps—perhaps," he murmured. "But surely, Mademoiselle, in that case he would not steal the jewels?"

"The jewels!" breathed Mirelle. "The jewels. Ah! Those rubies . . ."

Her eyes grew misty, a far-away light in them. The Comte looked at her curiously, wondering for the hundredth time at the magical influence of precious stones on the female sex. He recalled her to practical matters.

"What do you want me to do, Mademoiselle?"

Mirelle became alert and business-like once more.

"Surely it is simple. You will go to the police. You will say to them that M. Kettering committed this crime."

"And if they do not believe me? If they ask for proof?" He was eyeing her closely.

Mirelle laughed softly, and drew her orange-and-black wrap closer round her.

"Send them to me, Monsieur le Comte," she said softly; "I will give them the proof they want."

Upon that she was gone, an impetuous whirlwind, her errand accomplished.

The Comte looked after her, his eyebrows delicately raised.

"She is in a fury," he murmured. "What has happened now to upset her? But she shows her hand too plainly. Does she really believe that Mr. Kettering killed his wife? She would like me to believe it. She would even like the police to believe it."

He smiled to himself. He had no intention whatsoever of going to the police. He saw various other possibilities; to judge by his smile, an agreeable vista of them.

Presently, however, his brow clouded. According to Mirelle, he was suspected by the police. That might be true or it might not. An angry woman of the type of the dancer was not likely to bother about the strict veracity of her statements. On the other hand, she might easily have obtained—inside information. In that case—his mouth set grimly—in that case he must take certain precautions.

He went into the house and questioned Hipolyte closely once more as to whether any strangers had been to the house. The valet was positive in his assurances that this was not the case. The Comte went up to his bedroom and crossed over to an old bureau that stood against the wall. He let down the lid of this, and his delicate fingers sought for a spring at the back of one of the pigeon-holes. A secret drawer flew out; in it was a small brown paper package. The Comte took this out and weighed it in his hand carefully for a minute or two. Raising his hand to his head, with a slight grimace he pulled out a single hair. This he placed on the lip of the drawer and shut it carefully. Still carrying the small parcel in his hand, he went downstairs and out of the house to the garage, where stood a scarlet two-seater car. Ten minutes later he had taken the road for Monte Carlo.

He spent a few hours at the Casino, then sauntered out into the town. Presently he re-entered the car and drove off in the direction of Mentone. Earlier in the afternoon he had noticed an inconspicuous grey car some little distance behind him. He noticed it again now. He smiled to himself. The road was climbing steadily upwards. The Comte's foot pressed hard on the accelerator. The little red car had been specially built to the Comte's design, and had a far more powerful engine than would have been suspected from its appearance. It shot ahead.

Presently he looked back and smiled; the grey car was following behind. Smothered in dust, the little red car leaped along the road. It was travelling now at a dangerous pace, but the Comte was a first-class driver. Now they were going down hill, twisting and curving unceasingly. Presently the car slackened speed, and finally came to a standstill before a Bureau de Poste. The Comte jumped out, lifted the lid of the tool chest, extracted the small brown paper parcel and hurried into the post office. Two minutes later he was driving once more in the direction of Mentone. When the grey car arrived there, the Comte was drinking English five o'clock tea on the terrace of one of the hotels.

Later, he drove back to Monte Carlo, dined there, and reached home once more at eleven o'clock. Hipolyte came out to meet him with a disturbed face.

"Ah! Monsieur le Comte has arrived. Monsieur le Comte did not telephone me, by any chance?"

The Comte shook his head.

"And yet at three o'clock I received a summons from Monsieur le Comte, to present myself to him at Nice, at the Negresco."

"Really," said the Comte; "and you went?"

"Certainly, Monsieur, but at the Negresco they knew nothing of Monsieur le Comte. He had not been there."

"Ah," said the Comte, "doubtless at that hour Marie was out doing her afternoon marketing?"

"That is so, Monsieur le Comte."

"Ah, well," said the Comte, "it is of no importance. A mistake."

He went upstairs, smiling to himself.

Once within his own room, he bolted his door and looked sharply round. Everything seemed as usual. He opened various drawers and cupboards. Then he nodded to himself. Things had been replaced almost exactly as he had left them, but not quite. It was evident that a very thorough search had been made.

He went over to the bureau and pressed the hidden spring. The drawer flew open, but the hair was no longer where he had placed it. He nodded his head several times.

"They are excellent, our French police," he murmured to himself—"excellent. Nothing escapes them."

Chapter 20

KATHERINE MAKES A FRIEND

On the following morning Katherine and Lenox were sitting on the terrace of the Villa Marguerite. Something in the nature of a friendship was springing up between them, despite the difference in age. But for Lenox, Katherine would have found life at the Villa Marguerite quite intolerable. The Kettering case was the topic of the moment. Lady Tamplin frankly exploited her guest's connection with the affair for all it was worth. The most persistent rebuffs that Katherine could administer quite failed to pierce Lady Tamplin's self-esteem. Lenox adopted a detached attitude, seemingly amused at her mother's manœuvres, and yet with a sympathetic understanding of Katherine's feelings. The situation was not helped by Chubby, whose naïve delight was unquenchable, and who introduced Katherine to all and sundry as:

"This is Miss Grey. You know that Blue Train business? She was in it up to the ears! Had a long talk with Ruth Kettering a few hours before the murder! Bit of luck for her, eh?"

A few remarks of this kind had provoked Katherine that

morning to an unusually tart rejoinder, and when they were alone together Lenox observed in her slow drawl:

"Not used to exploitation, are you? You have a lot to learn, Katherine."

"I am sorry I lost my temper. I don't, as a rule."

"It is about time you learnt to blow off steam. Chubby is only an ass; there is no harm in him. Mother, of course, is trying, but you can lose your temper with her until Kingdom come, and it won't make any impression. She will open large, sad blue eyes at you and not care a bit."

Katherine made no reply to this filial observation, and Lenox presently went on:

"I am rather like Chubby. I delight in a good murder, and besides—well, knowing Derek makes a difference."

Katherine nodded.

"So you lunched with him yesterday," pursued Lenox reflectively. "Do you like him, Katherine?"

Katherine considered for a minute or two.

"I don't know," she said very slowly.

"He is very attractive."

"Yes, he is attractive."

"What don't you like about him?"

Katherine did not reply to the question, or at any rate not directly. "He spoke of his wife's death," she said. "He said he would not pretend that it had been anything but a bit of most marvellous luck for him."

"And that shocked you, I suppose," said Lenox. She paused, and then added in rather a queer tone of voice: "He likes you, Katherine."

"He gave me a very good lunch," said Katherine, smiling.

Lenox refused to be side-tracked.

"I saw it the night he came here," she said thoughtfully. "The way he looked at you; and you are not his usual type—just the opposite. Well, I suppose it is like religion—you get it at a certain age."

"Mademoiselle is wanted at the telephone," said Marie, appearing at the window of the salon. "M. Hercule Poirot desires to speak with her."

"More blood and thunder. Go on, Katherine; go and dally with your detective."

M. Hercule Poirot's voice came neat and precise in its intonation to Katherine's ear.

"That is Mademoiselle Grey who speaks? *Bon.* Mademoiselle, I have a word for you from M. Van Aldin, the father of Madame Kettering. He wishes very much to speak with you, either at the Villa Marguerite or at his hotel, whichever you prefer."

Katherine reflected for a moment, but she decided that for Van Aldin to come to the Villa Marguerite would be both painful and unnecessary. Lady Tamplin would have hailed his advent with far too much delight. She never lost a chance to cultivate millionaires. She told Poirot that she would much rather come to Nice.

"Excellent, Mademoiselle. I will call for you myself in an auto. Shall we say in about three-quarters of an hour?"

Punctually to the moment Poirot appeared. Katherine was waiting for him, and they drove off at once.

"Well, Mademoiselle, how goes it?"

She looked at his twinkling eyes, and was confirmed in her first impression that there was something very attractive about M. Hercule Poirot.

"This is our own *roman policier*, is it not?" said Poirot. "I made you the promise that we should study it together. And me, I always keep my promises."

"You are too kind," murmured Katherine.

"Ah, you mock yourself at me; but do you want to hear the developments of the case, or do you not?"

Katherine admitted that she did, and Poirot proceeded to sketch for her a thumbnail portrait of the Comte de la Roche.

"You think he killed her," said Katherine thoughtfully.

"That is the theory," said Poirot guardedly.

"Do you yourself believe that?"

"I did not say so. And you, Mademoiselle, what do you think?"

Katherine shook her head.

"How should I know? I don't know anything about those things, but I should say that [illegible]"

"Yes," said Poirot encouragingly.

"Well—from what you say the Count does not sound the kind of man who would actually kill anybody."

"Ah! Very good," cried Poirot. "You agree with me; that is just what I have said." He looked at her sharply. "But tell me, you have met Mr. Derek Kettering?"

"I met him at Lady Tamplin's, and I lunched with him yesterday."

"A *mauvais sujet*," said Poirot, shaking his head; "but *les femmes*—they like that, eh?"

He twinkled at Katherine and she laughed.

"He is the kind of man one would notice anywhere," continued Poirot. "Doubtless you observed him on the Blue Train?"

"Yes, I noticed him."

"In the restaurant car?"

"No. I didn't notice him at meals at all. I only saw him once—going into his wife's compartment."

Poirot nodded. "A strange business," he murmured. "I believe you said you were awake, Mademoiselle, and looked out of your window at Lyons? You saw no tall dark man such as the Comte de la Roche leave the train?"

Katherine shook her head. "I don't think I saw anyone at all," she said. "There was a youngish lad in a cap and overcoat who got out, but I don't think he was leaving the train, only walking up and down the platform. There was a fat Frenchman with a beard, in pyjamas and an overcoat, who wanted a cup of coffee. Otherwise, I think there were only the train attendants."

Poirot nodded his head several times. "It is like this, you see," he confided, "the Comte de la Roche has an alibi. An alibi, it is a very pestilential thing, and always open to the gravest suspicion. But here we are!"

They went straight up to Van Aldin's suite, where they found Knighton. Poirot introduced him to Katherine. After a few commonplaces had been exchanged, Knighton said: "I will tell Mr. Van Aldin that Miss Grey is here."

He went through a second door into an adjoining room. There was a low murmur of voices, and then Van Aldin came into the room and advanced towards Katherine with outstretched hand, giving her at the same time a shrewd and penetrating glance.

"I am pleased to meet you, Miss Grey," he said simply. "I have been wanting very badly to hear what you can tell me about Ruth."

The quiet simplicity of the millionaire's manner appealed to Katherine strongly. She felt herself in the presence of a very genuine grief, the more real for its absence of outward sign.

He drew forward a chair.

"Sit here, will you, and just tell me all about it."

Poirot and Knighton retired discreetly into the other room, and Katherine and Van Aldin were left alone together. She found no difficulty in her task. Quite simply and naturally she related her conversation with Ruth Kettering, word for word as nearly as she could. He listened in silence, leaning back in his chair, with one hand shading his eyes. When she had finished he said quietly:

"Thank you, my dear."

They both sat silent for a minute or two. Katherine felt that words of sympathy would be out of place. When the millionaire spoke, it was in a different tone:

"I am very grateful to you, Miss Grey. I think you did something to ease my poor Ruth's mind in the last hours of her life. Now I want to ask you something. You know—M. Poirot will have told you—about the scoundrel that my poor girl had got herself mixed up with. He was the man of whom she spoke to you—the man she was going to meet. In your judgment, do you think she might have changed her mind after her conversation with you? Do you think she meant to go back on her word?"

"I can't honestly tell you. She had certainly come to some decision, and seemed more cheerful in consequence of it."

"She gave you no idea where she intended to meet the skunk—whether in Paris or at Hyères?"

Katherine shook her head.

"She said nothing as to that."

"Ah!" said Van Aldin thoughtfully, "and that is the important point. Well, time will show."

He got up and opened the door of the adjoining room. Poirot and Knighton came back.

Katherine declined the millionaire's invitation to lunch, and Knighton went down with her and saw her into the waiting car. He returned to find Poirot and Van Aldin deep in conversation.

"If we only knew," said the millionaire thoughtfully, "what decision Ruth came to. It might have been any of half a dozen. She might have meant to leave the train at Paris and cable to me. She may have meant to have gone on to the south of France and have an explanation with the Count there. We are in the dark—absolutely in the dark. But we have the maid's word for it that she was both startled and dismayed at the Count's appearance at the station in Paris. That was clearly not part of the preconceived plan. You agree with me, Knighton?"

The secretary started. "I beg your pardon, Mr. Van Aldin. I was not listening."

"Day-dreaming, eh?" said Van Aldin. "That's not like you. I believe that girl has bowled you over."

Knighton blushed.

"She is a remarkably nice girl," said Van Aldin thoughtfully, "very nice. Did you happen to notice her eyes?"

"Any man," said Knighton, "would be bound to notice her eyes."

Chapter 21

AT THE TENNIS

Several days had elapsed. Katherine had been for a walk by herself one morning, and came back to find Lenox grinning at her expectantly.

"Your young man has been ringing you up, Katherine!"

"Who do you call my young man?"

"A new one—Rufus Van Aldin's secretary. You seem to have made rather an impression there. You are becoming a serious breaker of hearts, Katherine. First Derek Kettering, and now this young Knighton. The funny thing is that I remember him quite well. He was in Mother's War Hospital that she ran out here. I was only a kid of about eight at the time."

"Was he badly wounded?"

"Shot in the leg, if I remember rightly—rather a nasty business. I think the doctors messed it up a bit. They said he wouldn't limp or anything, but when he left here he was still completely dot and go one."

Lady Tamplin came out and joined them.

"Have you been telling Katherine about Major Knighton?" she asked. "Such a dear fellow! Just at first I didn't remember him—one had so many—but now it all comes back."

"He was a bit too unimportant to be remembered before," said Lenox. "Now that he is a secretary to an American millionaire, it is a very different matter."

"Darling!" said Lady Tamplin in her vague reproachful voice.

"What did Major Knighton ring up about?" inquired Katherine.

"He asked if you would like to go to the tennis this afternoon. If so, he would call for you in a car. Mother and I accepted for you with *empressement*. Whilst you dally with a millionaire's secretary, you might give me a chance with the millionaire, Katherine. He is about sixty, I suppose, so that he will be looking about for a nice sweet young thing like me."

"I should like to meet Mr. Van Aldin," said Lady Tamplin earnestly; "one has heard so much of him. Those fine rugged figures of the Western world"—she broke off—"so fascinating," she murmured.

"Major Knighton was very particular to say it was Mr. Van Aldin's invitation," said Lenox. "He said it so often that I began to smell a rat. You and Knighton would make a very nice pair, Katherine. Bless you, my children."

Katherine laughed, and went upstairs to change her clothes.

Knighton arrived soon after lunch and endured manfully Lady Tamplin's transports of recognition.

When they were driving together towards Cannes he remarked to Katherine: "Lady Tamplin has changed wonderfully little."

"In manner or appearance?"

"Both. She must be, I suppose, well over forty, but she is a remarkably beautiful woman still."

"She is," agreed Katherine.

"I am very glad that you could come to-day," went on Knighton. "M. Poirot is going to be there also. What an extraordinary little man he is. Do you know him well, Miss Grey?"

Katherine shook her head. "I met him on the train on the way here. I was reading a detective novel, and I happened to say something about such things not happening in real life. Of course, I had no idea of who he was."

"He is a very remarkable person," said Knighton slowly, "and has done some very remarkable things. He has a kind of genius for going to the root of the matter, and right up to the end no one has any idea of what he is really thinking. I remember I was staying at a house in Yorkshire, and Lady Clanravon's jewels were stolen. It seemed at first to be a simple robbery, but it completely baffled the local police. I wanted them to call in Hercule Poirot, and said he was the only man who could help them, but they pinned their faith to Scotland Yard."

"And what happened?" said Katherine curiously.

"The jewels were never recovered," said Knighton drily.

"You really do believe in him?"

"I do indeed. The Comte de la Roche is a pretty wily customer. He has wriggled out of most things. But I think he has met his match in Hercule Poirot."

"The Comte de la Roche," said Katherine thoughtfully; "so you really think he did it?"

"Of course." Knighton looked at her in astonishment. "Don't you?"

"Oh yes," said Katherine hastily; "that is, I mean, if it was not just an ordinary train robbery."

"It might be, of course," agreed the other, "but it seems to me that the Comte de la Roche fits into this business particularly well."

"And yet he has an alibi."

"Oh, alibis!" Knighton laughed, his face broke into his attractive boyish smile.

"You confess that you read detective stories, Miss Grey. You must know that anyone who has a perfect alibi is always open to grave suspicion."

"Do you think that real life is like that?" asked Katherine, smiling.

"Why not? Fiction is founded on fact."

"But is rather superior to it," suggested Katherine.

"Perhaps. Anyway, if I was a criminal I should not like to have Hercule Poirot on my track."

"No more should I," said Katherine, and laughed.

They were met on arrival by Poirot. As the day was warm he was attired in a white duck suit, with a white camellia in his buttonhole.

"*Bonjour,* Mademoiselle," said Poirot. "I look very English, do I not?"

"You look wonderful," said Katherine tactfully.

"You mock yourself at me," said Poirot genially. "But no matter. Papa Poirot, he always laughs the last."

"Where is Mr. Van Aldin?" asked Knighton.

"He will meet us at our seats. To tell you the truth, my friend, he is not too well pleased with me. Oh, those Americans—the repose, the calm, they know it not! Mr. Van Aldin, he would that I fly myself in the pursuit of criminals through all the byways of Nice."

"I should have thought myself that it would not have been a bad plan," observed Knighton.

"You are wrong," said Poirot; "in these matters one needs not energy but finesse. At the tennis one meets everyone. That is so important. Ah, there is Mr. Kettering."

Derek came abruptly up to them. He looked reckless and angry, as though something had arisen to upset him. He and Knighton greeted each other with some frigidity. Poirot alone seemed unconscious of any sense of strain, and chatted pleasantly in a laudable attempt to put everyone at their ease. He paid little compliments.

"It is amazing, M. Kettering, how well you speak the French," he observed—"so well that you could be taken for a Frenchman if you chose. That is a very rare accomplishment among Englishmen."

"I wish I did," said Katherine. "I am only too well aware that my French is of a painfully British order."

They reached their seats and sat down, and almost immediately Knighton perceived his employer signalling to him from the other end of the court, and went off to speak to him.

"Me, I approve of that young man," said Poirot, sending a beaming smile after the departing secretary; "and you, Mademoiselle?"

"I like him very much."

"And you, M. Kettering?"

Some quick rejoinder was springing to Derek's lips, but he checked it as though something in the little Belgian's twinkling eyes had made him suddenly alert. He spoke carefully, choosing his words.

"Knighton is a very good fellow," he said.

Just for a moment Katherine fancied that Poirot looked disappointed.

"He is a great admirer of yours, M. Poirot," she said, and she related some of the things that Knighton had said. It amused her to see the little man plume himself like a bird, thrusting out his chest, and assuming an air of mock modesty that would have deceived no one.

"That reminds me, Mademoiselle," he said suddenly, "I have a little matter of business I have to speak to you about. When you were sitting talking to that poor lady in the train, I think you must have dropped a cigarette case."

Katherine looked rather astonished. "I don't think so," she said. Poirot drew from his pocket a cigarette case of soft blue leather, with the initial "K" on it in gold.

"No, that is not mine," Katherine said.

"Ah, a thousand apologies. It was doubtless Madame's own. 'K,' of course, stands for Kettering. We were doubtful, because she had another cigarette case in her bag, and it seemed odd that she should have two." He turned to Derek suddenly. "You do not know, I suppose, whether this was your wife's case or not?"

Derek seemed momentarily taken aback. He stammered a little in his reply: "I—I don't know. I suppose so."

"It is not yours by any chance?"

"Certainly not. If it were mine it would hardly have been in my wife's possession."

Poirot looked more ingenuous and childlike than ever.

"I thought perhaps you might have dropped it when you were in your wife's compartment," he explained guilelessly.

"I never was there. I have already told the police that a dozen times."

"A thousand pardons," said Poirot, with his most apologetic air. "It was Mademoiselle here who mentioned having seen you going in."

He stopped with an air of embarrassment.

Katherine looked at Derek. His face had gone rather white, but perhaps that was her fancy. His laugh, when it came, was natural enough.

"You made a mistake, Miss Grey," he said easily. "From what the police have told me, I gather that my own compartment was only a door or two away from that of my wife's—though I never suspected the fact at the time. You must have seen me going into my own compartment." He got up quickly as he saw Van Aldin and Knighton approaching.

"I'm going to leave you now," he announced. "I can't stand my father-in-law at any price."

Van Aldin greeted Katherine very courteously, but was clearly in a bad humour.

"You seem fond of watching tennis, M. Poirot," he growled.

"It is a pleasure to me, yes," replied Poirot placidly.

"It is as well you are in France," said Van Aldin. "We are made of sterner stuff in the States. Business comes before pleasure there."

Poirot did not take offence; indeed, he smiled gently and confidingly at the irate millionaire.

"Do not enrage yourself, I beg of you. Everyone his own methods. Me, I have always found it a delightful and pleasing idea to combine business and pleasure together."

He glanced at the other two. They were deep in conversation, absorbed in each other. Poirot nodded his head in satisfaction, and then leant towards the millionaire, lowering his voice as he did so.

"It is not only for pleasure that I am here, M. Van Aldin. Observe just opposite us that tall old man—the one with the yellow face and the venerable beard."

"Well, what of him?"

"That," Poirot said, "is M. Papopolous."

"A Greek, eh?"

"As you say—a Greek. He is a dealer in antiques of world-wide reputation. He has a small shop in Paris, and he is suspected by the police of being something more."

"What?"

"A receiver of stolen goods, especially jewels. There is nothing as to the re-cutting and re-setting of gems that he does not know. He deals with the highest in Europe and with the lowest of the riff-raff of the underworld."

Van Aldin was looking at Poirot with suddenly awakened attention.

"Well?" he demanded, a new note in his voice.

"I ask myself," said Poirot, "I, Hercule Poirot"—he thumped himself dramatically on the chest—"ask myself *why is M. Papopolous suddenly come to Nice?*"

Van Aldin was impressed. For a moment he had doubted Poirot and suspected the little man of being past his job, a *poseur* only. Now, in a moment, he switched back to his original opinion. He looked straight at the little detective.

"I must apologise to you, M. Poirot."

Poirot waved the apology aside with an extravagant gesture.

"Bah!" he cried, "all that is of no importance. Now listen, M. Van Aldin; I have news for you."

The millionaire looked sharply at him, all his interest aroused.

Poirot nodded.

"It is as I say. You will be interested. As you know, M. Van Aldin, the Comte de la Roche has been under surveillance ever since his interview with the Juge d'Instruction. The day after that, during his absence, the Villa Marina was searched by the police."

"Well," said Van Aldin, "did they find anything? I bet they didn't."

Poirot made him a little bow.

"Your acumen is not at fault, M. Van Aldin. They found nothing of an incriminating nature. It was not to be expected that they would. The Comte de la Roche, as your expressive idiom has it, was not born on the preceding day. He is an astute gentleman with great experience."

"Well, go on," growled Van Aldin.

"It may be, of course, that the Comte had nothing of a compromising nature to conceal. But we must not neglect the possibility. If, then, he has something to conceal, where is it? Not in his house—the police searched thoroughly. Not on his person, for he knows that he is liable to arrest at any minute. There remains—his car. As I say, he was under surveillance. He was followed on that day to Monte Carlo. From there he went by road to Mentone, driving himself. His car is a very powerful one, it outdistanced his pursuers, and for about a quarter of an hour they completely lost sight of him."

"And during that time you think he concealed something by the roadside?" asked Van Aldin, keenly interested.

"By the roadside, no. *Ca n'est pas pratique.* But listen now—me, I have made a little suggestion to M. Carrège. He is graciously pleased to approve of it. In each Bureau de Poste in the neighbourhood it has been seen to that there is someone who knows the Comte de la Roche by sight. Because, you see, Messieurs, the best way of hiding a thing is by sending it away by the post."

"Well?" demanded Van Aldin; his face was keenly alight with interest and expectation.

"Well—*voilà!*" With a dramatic flourish Poirot drew out from his pocket a loosely wrapped brown paper package from which the string had been removed.

"During that quarter of an hour's interval, our good gentleman mailed this."

"The address?" asked the other sharply.

Poirot nodded his head.

"Might have told us something, but unfortunately it does not. The package was addressed to one of these little newspaper shops in Paris where letters and parcels are kept until called for on payment of a small commission."

"Yes, but what is inside?" demanded Van Aldin impatiently.

Poirot unwrapped the brown paper and disclosed a square cardboard box. He looked round him.

"It is a good moment," he said quietly. "All eyes are on the tennis. Look, Monsieur!"

He lifted the lid of the box for a fraction of a second. An

exclamation of utter astonishment came from the millionaire. His face turned as white as chalk.

"My God!" he breathed, "the rubies."

He sat for a minute as though dazed. Poirot restored the box to his pocket and beamed placidly. Then suddenly the millionaire seemed to come out of his trance; he leaned across to Poirot and wrung his hand so heartily that the little man winced with pain.

"This is great," said Van Aldin. "Great! You are the goods, M. Poirot. Once and for all, you are the goods."

"It is nothing," said Poirot modestly. "Order, method, being prepared for eventualities beforehand—that is all there is to it."

"And now, I suppose, the Comte de la Roche has been arrested?" continued Van Aldin eagerly.

"No," said Poirot.

A look of utter astonishment came over Van Aldin's face.

"But why? What more do you want?"

"The Comte's alibi is still unshaken."

"But that is nonsense."

"Yes," said Poirot; "I rather think it is nonsense, but unfortunately we have to prove it so."

"In the meantime he will slip through your fingers."

Poirot shook his head very energetically.

"No," he said, "he will not do that. The one thing the Comte cannot afford to sacrifice is his social position. At all costs he must stop and brazen it out."

Van Aldin was still dissatisfied.

"But I don't see——"

Poirot raised a hand. "Grant me a little moment, Monsieur. Me, I have a little idea. Many people have mocked themselves at the little ideas of Hercule Poirot—and they have been wrong."

"Well," said Van Aldin, "go ahead. What is this little idea?"

Poirot paused for a moment and then he said:

"I will call upon you at your hotel at eleven o'clock tomorrow morning. Until then, say nothing to anyone."

Chapter 22

M. PAPOPOLOUS BREAKFASTS

M. Papopolous was at breakfast. Opposite him sat his daughter, Zia.

There was a knock at the sitting-room door, and a chasseur entered with a card which he brought to M. Papopolous. The latter scrutinised it, raised his eyebrows, and passed it over to his daughter.

"Ah!" said M. Papopolous, scratching his left ear thoughtfully, "Hercule Poirot. I wonder now."

Father and daughter looked at each other.

"I saw him yesterday at the tennis," said M. Papopolous. "Zia, I hardly like this."

"He was very useful to you once," his daughter reminded him.

"That is true," acknowledged M. Papopolous; "also he has retired from active work, so I hear."

These interchanges between father and daughter had passed in their own language. Now M. Papopolous turned to the chasseur and said in French:

"Faîtes monter ce monsieur."

A few minutes later Hercule Poirot, exquisitely attired, and swinging a cane with a jaunty air, entered the room.

"My dear M. Papopolous."

"My dear M. Poirot."

"And Mademoiselle Zia." Poirot swept her a low bow.

"You will excuse us going on with our breakfast," said M. Papopolous, pouring himself out another cup of coffee. "Your call is—ahem!—a little early."

"It is scandalous," said Poirot, "but you see, I am pressed."

"Ah!" murmured M. Papopolous, "you are on an affair then?"

"A very serious affair," said Poirot; "the death of Madame Kettering."

"Let me see," M. Papopolous looked innocently up at the

ceiling, "that was the lady who died on the Blue Train, was it not? I saw a mention of it in the papers, but there was no suggestion of foul play."

"In the interests of justice," said Poirot, "it was thought best to suppress that fact."

There was a pause.

"And in what way can I assist you, M. Poirot?" asked the dealer politely.

"*Voilà*," said Poirot, "I shall come to the point." He took from his pocket the same box that he had displayed at Cannes, and, opening it, he took out the rubies and pushed them across the table to Papopolous.

Although Poirot was watching him narrowly, not a muscle of the old man's face moved. He took up the jewels and examined them with a kind of detached interest, then he looked across at the detective inquiringly:

"Superb, are they not?" asked Poirot.

"Quite excellent," said M. Papopolous.

"How much should you say they are worth?"

The Greek's face quivered a little.

"Is it really necessary to tell you, M. Poirot?" he asked.

"You are shrewd, M. Papopolous. No, it is not. They are not, for instance, worth five hundred thousand dollars."

Papopolous laughed, and Poirot joined with him.

"As an imitation," said Papopolous, handing them back to Poirot, "they are, as I said, quite excellent. Would it be indiscreet to ask, M. Poirot, where you came across them?"

"Not at all," said Poirot; "I have no objection to telling an old friend like yourself. They were in the possession of the Comte de la Roche."

M. Papopolous' eyebrows lifted themselves eloquently.

"In-deed," he murmured.

Poirot leaned forward and assumed his most innocent and beguiling air.

"M. Papopolous," he said, "I am going to lay my cards upon the table. The original of these jewels was stolen from Madame Kettering on the Blue Train. Now I will say to you first this: *I am not concerned with the recovery of these jewels. That is the affair of the police.* I am working not for the police but for M. Van Aldin. I want to lay hands on the man who killed Madame Kettering. I am interested in the jewels only in so far as they may lead me to the man. You understand?"

The last two words were uttered with great significance. M. Papopolous, his face quite unmoved, said quietly:

"Go on."

"It seems to me probable, Monsieur, that the jewels will change hands in Nice—may already have done so."

"Ah!" said M. Papopolous.

He sipped his coffee reflectively, and looked a shade more noble and patriarchal than usual.

"I say to myself," continued Poirot, with animation, "what good fortune! My old friend, M. Papopolous, is in Nice. He will aid me."

"And how do you think I can aid you?" inquired M. Papopolous coldly.

"I said to myself, without doubt M. Papopolous is in Nice on business."

"Not at all," said M. Papopolous, "I am here for my health—by the doctor's orders."

He coughed hollowly.

"I am desolated to hear it," replied Poirot, with somewhat insincere sympathy. "But to continue. When a Russian Grand Duke, an Austrian Archduchess, or an Italian Prince wish to dispose of their family jewels—to whom do they go? To M. Papopolous, is it not? He who is famous all over the world for the discretion with which he arranges these things."

The other bowed.

"You flatter me."

"It is a great thing, discretion," mused Poirot, and was rewarded by the fleeting smile which passed across the Greek's face. "I, too, can be discreet."

The eyes of the two men met.

Then Poirot went on speaking very slowly, and obviously picking his words with care.

"I say to myself, this: if these jewels have changed hands in Nice, M. Papopolous would have heard of it. He has knowledge of all that passes in the jewel world."

"Ah!" said M. Papopolous, and helped himself to a *croissant*.

"The police, you understand," said M. Poirot, "do not enter into the matter. It is a personal affair."

"One hears rumours," admitted M. Papopolous cautiously.

"Such as?" prompted Poirot.

"Is there any reason why I should pass them on?"

"Yes," said Poirot, "I think there is. You may remember, M. Papopolous, that seventeen years ago there was a certain article in your hands, left there as security by a very—er—Prominent Person. It was in your keeping and it unaccountably disappeared. You were, if I may use the English expression, in the soup."

His eyes came gently round to the girl. She had pushed her cup and plate aside, and with both elbows on the table and her chin resting on her hands, was listening eagerly. Still keeping an eye on her he went on:

"I am in Paris at the time. You send for me. You place yourself in my hands. If I restore to you that—article, you say I shall earn your undying gratitude. *Eh bien!* I did restore it to you."

A long sigh came from M. Papopolous.

"It was the most unpleasant moment of my career," he murmured.

"Seventeen years is a long time," said Poirot thoughtfully, "but I believe that I am right in saying, Monsieur, that your race does not forget."

"A Greek?" murmured Papopolous, with an ironical smile.

"It was not as a Greek I meant," said Poirot.

There was a silence, and then the old man drew himself up proudly.

"You are right, M. Poirot," he said quietly. "I am a Jew. And, as you say, our race does not forget."

"You will aid me then?"

"As regards the jewels, Monsieur, I can do nothing."

The old man, as Poirot had done just now, picked his words carefully.

"I know nothing. I have heard nothing. But I can perhaps do you a good turn—that is, if you are interested in racing."

"Under certain circumstances I might be," said Poirot, eyeing him steadily.

"There is a horse running at Longchamps that would, I

think, repay attention. I cannot say for certain, you understand; this news passed through so many hands."

He stopped, fixing Poirot with his eye, as though to make sure that the latter was comprehending him.

"Perfectly, perfectly," said Poirot, nodding.

"The name of the horse," said M. Papopolous, leaning back and joining the tips of his fingers together, "is the Marquis. I think, but I am not sure, that it is an English horse, eh, Zia?"

"I think so too," said the girl.

Poirot got up briskly.

"I thank you, Monsieur," he said. "It is a great thing to have what the English call a tip from the stable. Au revoir, Monsieur, and many thanks."

He turned to the girl.

"Au revoir, Mademoiselle Zia. It seems to me but yesterday that I saw you in Paris. One would say that two years had passed at most."

"There is a difference between sixteen and thirty-three," said Zia ruefully.

"Not in your case," declared Poirot gallantly. "You and your father will perhaps dine with me one night."

"We shall be delighted," replied Zia.

"Then we will arrange it," declared Poirot, "and now—*je me sauve.*"

Poirot walked along the street humming a little tune to himself. He twirled his stick with a jaunty air, once or twice he smiled to himself quietly. He turned into the first Bureau de Poste he came to and sent off a telegram. He took some time in wording it, but it was in code and he had to call upon his memory. It purported to deal with a missing scarf-pin, and was addressed to Inspector Japp, Scotland Yard.

Decoded, it was short and to the point. "*Wire me everything known about man whose soubriquet is the Marquis.*"

Chapter 23

A NEW THEORY

It was exactly eleven o'clock when Poirot presented himself at Van Aldin's hotel. He found the millionaire alone.

"You are punctual, M. Poirot," he said, with a smile, as he rose to greet the detective.

"I am always punctual," said Poirot. "The exactitude—always do I observe it. Without order and method——"

He broke off. "Ah, but it is possible that I have said these things to you before. Let us come at once to the object of my visit."

"Your little idea?"

"Yes, my little idea." Poirot smiled.

"First of all, Monsieur, I should like to interview once more the maid, Ada Mason. She is here?"

"Yes, she's here."

"Ah!"

Van Aldin looked at him curiously. He rang the bell, and a messenger was despatched to find Mason.

Poirot greeted her with his usual politeness, which was never without effect on that particular class.

"Good afternoon, Mademoiselle," he said cheerfully. "Be seated, will you not, if Monsieur permits."

"Yes, yes, sit down, my girl," said Van Aldin.

"Thank you, sir," said Mason primly, and she sat down on the extreme edge of a chair. She looked bonier and more acid than ever.

"I have come to ask you yet more questions," said Poirot. "We must get to the bottom of this affair. Always I return to the question of the man in the train. You have been shown the Comte de la Roche. You say that it is possible he was the man, but you are not sure."

"As I told you, sir, I never saw the gentleman's face. That is what makes it so difficult."

Poirot beamed and nodded.

"Precisely, exactly. I comprehend well the difficulty. Now, Mademoiselle, you have been in the service of Madame Kettering two months, you say. During that time, how often did you see your master?"

Mason reflected a minute or two, and then said:

"Only twice, sir."

"And was that near to, or far away?"

"Well once, sir, he came to Curzon Street. I was upstairs, and I looked over the banisters and saw him in the hall below. I was a bit curious like, you understand, knowing the way things—er—were." Mason finished up with her discreet cough.

"And the other time?"

"I was in the Park, sir, with Annie—one of the housemaids, sir, and she pointed out the master to me walking with a foreign lady."

Again Poirot nodded.

"Now listen, Mason, this man whom you saw in the carriage talking to your mistress at the Gare de Lyon, how do you know it was not your master?"

"The master, sir? Oh, I don't think it could have been."

"But you are not sure," Poirot persisted.

"Well—I never thought of it, sir."

Mason was clearly upset at the idea.

"You have heard that your master was also on the train. What more natural than that it should be he who came along the corridor?"

"But the gentleman who was talking to the mistress must have come from outside, sir. He was dressed for the street. In an overcoat and soft hat."

"Just so, Mademoiselle, but reflect a minute. The train has just arrived at the Gare de Lyon. Many of the passengers promenade themselves upon the quay. Your mistress was about to do so, and for that purpose had doubtless put on her fur coat, eh?"

"Yes, sir," agreed Mason.

"Your master, then, does the same. The train is heated, but outside in the station it is cold. He puts on his overcoat and his hat and he walks along beside the train, and looking up at the lighted windows he suddenly sees Madame Kettering. Until then he has had no idea that she was on the train. Naturally, he mounts the carriage and goes to her compartment. She gives an exclamation of surprise at seeing him and quickly shuts the door between the two compartments since it is possible that their conversation may be of a private nature."

He leaned back in his chair and watched the suggestion slowly take effect. No one knew better than Hercule Poirot that the class to which Mason belongs cannot be hurried. He must give her time to get rid of her own preconceived ideas. At the end of three minutes she spoke:

"Well, of course, sir, it might be so. I never thought of it that way. The master is tall and dark, and just about that build. It was seeing the hat and coat that made me say it was a gentleman from outside. Yes, it might have been the master. I would not like to say either way I'm sure."

"Thank you very much, Mademoiselle. I shall not require you any further. Ah, just one thing more." He took from his pocket the cigarette case he had already shown to Katherine. "Is that your mistress's case?" he said to Mason.

"No, sir, it is not the mistress's—at least——"

She looked suddenly startled. An idea was clearly working its way to the forefront of her mind.

"Yes?" said Poirot encouragingly.

"I think, sir—I can't be sure, but I think—it is a case that the mistress bought to give to the master."

"Ah," said Poirot in a non-committal manner.

"But whether she ever did give it to him or not, I can't say, of course."

"Precisely," said Poirot, "precisely. That is all, I think, Mademoiselle. I wish you good afternoon."

Ada Mason retired discreetly, closing the door noiselessly behind her.

Poirot looked across at Van Aldin, a faint smile upon his face. The millionaire looked thunderstruck.

"You think—you think it was Derek?" he queried, "but—everything points the other way. Why, the Count has actually been caught red-handed with the jewels on him."

"No."

"But you told me——"

"What did I tell you?"

"That story about the jewels. You showed them to me."

"No."

Van Aldin stared at him.

"You mean to say you didn't show them to me?"

"No."

"Yesterday—at the tennis?"

"No."

"Are you crazy, M. Poirot, or am I?"

"Neither of us is crazy," said the detective. "You ask me a question; I answer it. You say have I not shown you the jewels yesterday? I reply—no. What I showed you, M. Van Aldin, was a first-class imitation, hardly to be distinguished except by an expert from the real ones."

Chapter 24

POIROT GIVES ADVICE

It took the millionaire some few minutes to take the thing in. He stared at Poirot as though dumbfounded. The little Belgian nodded at him gently.

"Yes," he said, "it alters the position, does it not?"

"Imitation!"

He leaned forward.

"All along, M. Poirot, you have had this idea? All along this is what you have been driving at? You never believed that the Comte de la Roche was the murderer?"

"I have had doubts," said Poirot quietly. "I said as much to you. Robbery with violence and murder"—he shook his head energetically—"no, it is difficult to picture. It does not harmonise with the personality of the Comte de la Roche."

"But you believe that he meant to steal the rubies?"

"Certainly. There is no doubt as to that. See, I will recount to you the affair as I see it. The Comte knew of the rubies and he laid his plans accordingly. He made up a romantic story of a book he was writing, so as to induce your daughter to bring them with her. He provided himself with an exact duplicate. It is clear, is it not, that substitution is what he was after. Madame, your daughter, was not an expert on jewels. It would probably be a long time before she discovered what had occurred. When she did so—well—I do not think she would prosecute the Comte. Too much would come out. He would have in his possession various letters of hers. Oh yes, a very safe scheme from the Comte's point of view—one that he has probably carried out before."

"It seems clear enough, yes," said Van Aldin musingly.

"It accords with the personality of the Comte de la Roche," said Poirot.

"Yes, but now——" Van Aldin looked searchingly at the other. "What actually happened? Tell me that, M. Poirot."

Poirot shrugged his shoulders.

"It is quite simple," he said; "someone stepped in ahead of the Comte."

There was a long pause.

Van Aldin seemed to be turning things over in his mind. When he spoke it was without beating about the bush.

"How long have you suspected my son-in-law, M. Poirot?"

"From the very first. He had the motive and the opportunity. Everyone took for granted that the man in Madame's compartment in Paris was the Comte de la Roche. I thought so, too. Then you happened to mention that you had once mistaken the Comte for your son-in-law. That told me that they were of the same height and build, and alike in colouring. It put some curious ideas in my head. The maid had only been with your daughter a short time. It was unlikely that she would know Mr. Kettering well by sight, since he had not been living in Curzon Street; also the man was careful to keep his face turned away."

"You believe he—murdered her?" said Van Aldin hoarsely.

Poirot raised a hand quickly.

"No, no, I did not say that—but it is a possibility—a very strong possibility. He was in a tight corner, a very tight corner, threatened with ruin. This was the one way out."

"But why take the jewels?"

"To make the crime appear an ordinary one committed by train robbers. Otherwise suspicion might have fallen on him straight away."

"If that is so, what has he done with the rubies?"

"That remains to be seen. There are several possibilities. There is a man in Nice who may be able to help, the man I pointed out at the tennis."

He rose to his feet and Van Aldin rose also and laid his hand on the little man's shoulder. His voice when he spoke was harsh with emotion.

"Find Ruth's murderer for me," he said, "that is all I ask."

Poirot drew himself up.

"Leave it in the hands of Hercule Poirot," he said superbly; "have no fears. I will discover the truth."

He brushed a speck of fluff from his hat, smiled reassuringly at the millionaire, and left the room. Nevertheless, as he went down the stairs some of the confidence faded from his face.

"It is all very well," he murmured to himself, "but there are difficulties. Yes, there are great difficulties." As he was passing out of the hotel he came to a sudden halt. A car had drawn up in front of the door. In it was Katherine Grey, and Derek Kettering was standing beside it talking to her earnestly. A minute or two later the car drove off and Derek remained standing on the pavement looking after it. The expression on his face was an odd one. He gave a sudden impatient gesture of the shoulders, sighed deeply, and turned to find Hercule Poirot standing at his elbow. In spite of himself he started. The two men looked at each other. Poirot steadily and unwaveringly and Derek with a kind of light-hearted defiance. There was a sneer behind the easy mockery of his tone when he spoke, raising his eyebrows slightly as he did so.

"Rather a dear, isn't she?" he asked easily.

His manner was perfectly natural.

"Yes," said Poirot thoughtfully, "that describes Mademoiselle Katherine very well. It is very English, that phrase there, and Mademoiselle Katherine, she also is very English."

Derek remained perfectly still without answering.

"And yet she is *sympathique*, is it not so?"

"Yes," said Derek; "there are not many like her."

He spoke softly, almost as though to himself. Poirot nodded significantly. Then he leant towards the other and spoke in a different tone, a quiet, grave tone that was new to Derek Kettering.

"You will pardon an old man, Monsieur, if he says to you something that you may consider impertinent. There is one of your English proverbs that I would quote to you. It says that 'it is well to be off with the old love, before being on with the new.'"

Kettering turned on him angrily.

"What the devil do you mean?"

"You enrage yourself at me," said Poirot placidly. "I expected as much. As to what I mean—I mean, Monsieur, that there is a second car with a lady in it. If you turn your head you will see her."

Derek spun round. His face darkened with anger.

"Mirelle, damn her!" he muttered. "I will soon——"

Poirot arrested the movement he was about to make.

"Is it wise what you are about to do there?" he asked warningly. His eyes shone softly with a green light in them. But Derek was past noticing the warning signs. In his anger he was completely off his guard.

"I have broken with her utterly, and she knows it," cried Derek angrily.

"You have broken with her, yes, but has *she* broken with you?"

Derek gave a sudden harsh laugh.

"She won't break with two million pounds if she can help it," he murmured brutally; "trust Mirelle for that."

Poirot raised his eyebrows.

"You have the outlook cynical," he murmured.

"Have I?" There was no mirth in his sudden wide smile. "I have lived in the world long enough, M. Poirot, to know that all women are pretty much alike." His face softened suddenly. "All save one."

He met Poirot's gaze defiantly. A look of alertness crept into his eyes, then faded again. "That one," he said, and jerked his head in the direction of Cap Martin.

"Ah!" said Poirot.

This quiescence was well calculated to provoke the impetuous temperament of the other.

"I know what you are going to say," said Derek rapidly, "the kind of life I have led, the fact that I am not worthy of her. You will say that I have no right to think even of such a thing. You will say that it is not a case of giving a dog a bad name—I know that it is not decent to be speaking like this with my wife dead only a few days, and murdered at that."

He paused for breath, and Poirot took advantage of the pause to remark in his plaintive tone:

"But, indeed, I have not said anything at all."

"But you will."

"Eh?" said Poirot.

"You will say that I have no earthly chance of marrying Katherine."

"No," said Poirot, "I would not say that. Your reputation is bad, yes, but with women—never does that deter them. If you were a man of excellent character, of strict morality who had done nothing that he should not do, and—possibly everything that he should do—*eh bien!* then I should have grave doubts of your success. Moral worth, you understand, it is not romantic. It is appreciated, however, by widows."

Derek Kettering stared at him, then he swung round on his heel and went up to the waiting car.

Poirot looked after him with some interest. He saw the lovely vision lean out of the car and speak.

Derek Kettering did not stop. He lifted his hat and passed straight on.

"*Ca y est*," said M. Hercule Poirot, "it is time, I think, that I return *chez moi*."

He found an imperturbable George pressing trousers.

"A pleasant day, Georges, somewhat fatiguing, but not without interest," he said.

George received these remarks in his usual wooden fashion.

"Indeed, sir."

"The personality of a criminal, Georges, is an interesting matter. Many murderers are men of great personal charm."

"I always heard, sir, that Dr. Crippen was a pleasant-spoken gentleman. And yet he cut up his wife like so much mince-meat."

"Your instances are always apt, Georges."

The valet did not reply, and at that moment the telephone rang. Poirot took up the receiver.

"'Allo—'allo—yes, yes, it is Hercule Poirot who speaks."

"This is Knighton. Will you hold the line a minute, M. Poirot. Mr. Van Aldin would like to speak to you."

There was a moment's pause, then the millionaire's voice came through.

"Is that you, M. Poirot? I just wanted to tell you that Mason came to me now of her own accord. She has been thinking it over, and she says that she is almost certain that the man at Paris was Derek Kettering. There was something familiar about him at the time, she says, but at the minute she could not place it. She seems pretty certain now."

"Ah," said Poirot, "thank you, M. Van Aldin. That advances us."

He replaced the receiver, and stood for a minute or two with a very curious smile on his face. George had to speak to him twice before obtaining an answer.

"Eh?" said Poirot. "What is that that you say to me?"

"Are you lunching here, sir, or are you going out?"

"Neither," said Poirot. "I shall go to bed and take a *tisane*. The expected has happened, and when the expected happens, it always causes me emotion."

Chapter 25

DEFIANCE

As Derek Kettering passed the car, Mirelle leant out.

"Dereek—I must speak to you for a moment——"

But, lifting his hat, Derek passed straight on without stopping.

When he got back to his hotel, the concierge detached himself from his wooden pen and accosted him.

"A gentleman is waiting to see you, Monsieur."

"Who is it?" asked Derek.

"He did not give his name, Monsieur, but he said his business with you was important, and that he would wait."

"Where is he?"

"In the little salon, Monsieur. He preferred it to the lounge, he said, as being more private."

Derek nodded, and turned his steps in that direction.

The small salon was empty except for the visitor, who rose and bowed with easy foreign grace as Derek entered. As it chanced, Derek had only seen the Comte de la Roche once, but found no difficulty in recognising that aristocratic nobleman, and he frowned angrily. Of all the consummate impertinence!

"The Comte de la Roche, is it not?" he said. "I am afraid you have wasted your time in coming here."

"I hope not," said the Comte agreeably. His white teeth glittered.

The Comte's charm of manner was usually wasted on his own sex. All men, without exception, disliked him heartily. Derek Kettering was already conscious of a distinct longing to kick the Count bodily out of the room. It was only the realisation that scandal would be unfortunate just at present that restrained him. He marvelled anew that Ruth could have cared, as she certainly had, for this fellow. A bounder, and worse than a bounder. He looked with distaste at the Count's exquisitely manicured hands.

"I called," said the Comte, "on a little matter of business. It would be advisable, I think, for you to listen to me."

Again Derek felt strongly tempted to kick him out, but again he refrained. The hint of a threat was not lost upon him, but he interpreted it in his own way. There were various reasons why it would be better to hear what the Comte had to say.

He sat down and drummed impatiently with his fingers on the table.

"Well," he said sharply, "what is it?"

It was not the Comte's way to come out into the open at once.

"Allow me, Monsieur, to offer you my condolences on your recent bereavement."

"If I have any impertinence from you," said Derek quietly, "you go out by that window."

He nodded his head towards the window beside the Comte, and the latter moved uneasily.

"I will send my friends to you, Monsieur, if that is what you desire," he said haughtily.

Derek laughed.

"A duel, eh? My dear Count, I don't take you seriously enough for that. But I should take a good deal of pleasure in kicking you down the Promenade des Anglais."

The Comte was not at all anxious to take offence. He merely raised his eyebrows and murmured:

"The English are barbarians."

"Well," said Derek, "what is it you have to say to me?"

"I will be frank," said the Comte, "I will come immediately to the point. That will suit us both, will it not?"

Again he smiled in his agreeable fashion.

"Go on," said Derek curtly.

The Comte looked at the ceiling, joined the tips of his fingers together, and murmured softly:

"You have come into a lot of money, Monsieur."

"What the devil has that got to do with you?"

The Comte drew himself up.

"Monsieur, my name is tarnished! I am suspected—accused—of foul crime."

"The accusation does not come from me," said Derek coldly; "as an interested party I have not expressed any opinion."

"I am innocent," said the Comte. "I swear before heaven"—he raised his hand to heaven—"that I am innocent."

"M. Carrège is, I believe, the Juge d'Instruction in charge of the case," hinted Derek politely.

The Comte took no notice.

"Not only am I unjustly suspected of a crime that I did not commit, but I am also in serious need of money."

He coughed softly and suggestively.

Derek rose to his feet.

"I was waiting for that," he said softly; "you blackmailing brute! I will not give you a penny. My wife is dead, and no scandal that you can make can touch her now. She wrote you foolish letters, I dare say. If I were to buy them from you for a round sum at this minute, I am pretty certain that you would manage to keep one or two back; and I will tell you this, M. de la Roche, blackmailing is an ugly word both in England and France. That is my answer to you. Good afternoon."

"One moment"—the Comte stretched out a hand as Derek

was turning to leave the room. "You are mistaken, Monsieur. You are completely mistaken. I am, I hope, a 'gentleman.'" Derek laughed. "Any letters that a lady might write to me I should hold sacred." He flung back his head with a beautiful air of nobility. "The proposition that I was putting before you was of quite a different nature. I am, as I said, extremely short of money, and my conscience might impel me to go to the police with certain information."

Derek came slowly back into the room.

"What do you mean?"

The Comte's agreeable smile flashed forth once more.

"Surely it is not necessary to go into details," he purred. "Seek whom the crime benefits, they say, don't they? As I said just now, you have come into a lot of money lately."

Derek laughed.

"If that is all——" he said contemptuously.

But the Comte was shaking his head.

"But it is not all, my dear sir. I should not come to you unless I had much more precise and detailed information than that. It is not agreeable, Monsieur, to be arrested and tried for murder."

Derek came close up to him. His face expressed such furious anger that involuntarily the Comte drew back a pace or two.

"Are you threatening *me*?" the young man demanded angrily.

"You shall hear nothing more of the matter," the Comte assured him.

"Of all the colossal bluffs that I have ever struck——"

The Comte raised a white hand.

"You are wrong. It is not a bluff. To convince you I will tell you this. My information was obtained from a certain lady. It is she who holds the irrefutable proof that you committed the murder."

"She? Who?"

"Mademoiselle Mirelle."

Derek drew back as though struck.

"Mirelle," he muttered.

The Comte was quick to press what he took to be his advantage.

"A bagatelle of one hundred thousand francs," he said. "I ask no more."

"Eh?" said Derek absently.

"I was saying, Monsieur, that a bagatelle of one hundred thousand francs would satisfy my—conscience."

Derek seemed to recollect himself. He looked earnestly at the Comte.

"You would like my answer now?"

"If you please, Monsieur."

"Then here it is. You can go to the devil. See?"

Leaving the Comte too astonished to speak, Derek turned on his heel and swung out of the room.

Once out of the hotel he hailed a taxi and drove to Mirelle's hotel. On inquiring, he learned that the dancer had just come in. Derek gave the concierge his card.

"Take this up to Mademoiselle and ask if she will see me."

A very brief interval elapsed, and then Derek was bidden to follow a *chasseur*.

A wave of exotic perfume assailed Derek's nostrils as he stepped over the threshold of the dancer's apartments. The room was filled with carnations, orchids, and mimosa. Mirelle was standing by the window in a *peignoir* of foamy lace.

She came towards him, her hands outstretched.

"Dereek—you have come to me. I knew you would."

He put aside the clinging arms and looked down on her sternly.

"Why did you send the Comte de la Roche to me?"

She looked at him in astonishment, which he took to be genuine.

"I? Send the Comte de la Roche to you? But for what?"

"Apparently—for blackmail," said Derek grimly.

Again she stared. Then suddenly she smiled and nodded her head.

"Of course. It was to be expected. It is what he would do, *ce type là*. I might have known it. No, indeed, Dereek, I did not send him."

He looked at her piercingly, as though seeking to read her mind.

"I will tell you," said Mirelle. "I am ashamed, but I will

tell you. The other day, you comprehend, I was mad with rage, quite mad"—she made an eloquent gesture. "My temperament, it is not a patient one. I want to be revenged on you, and so I go to the Comte de la Roche, and I tell him to go to the police and say so and so, and so and so. But have no fear, Dereek. Not completely did I lose my head; the proof rests with me alone. The police can do nothing without my word, you understand? And now—now?"

She nestled up close to him, looking at him with melting eyes.

He thrust her roughly away from him. She stood there, her breast heaving, her eyes narrowing to a cat-like slit.

"Be careful, Dereek, be very careful. You have come back to me, have you not?"

"I shall never come back to you," said Derek steadily.

"Ah!"

More than ever the dancer looked like a cat. Her eyelids flickered.

"So there is another woman? The one with whom you lunched that day. Eh! am I right?"

"I intend to ask that lady to marry me. You might as well know."

"That prim Englishwoman! Do you think that I will support that for one moment? Ah, no." Her beautiful lithe body quivered. "Listen, Dereek, do you remember that conversation we had in London? You said the only thing that could save you was the death of your wife. You regretted that she was so healthy. Then the idea of an accident came to your brain. And more than an accident."

"I suppose," said Derek contemptuously, "that it was this conversation that you repeated to the Comte de la Roche."

Mirelle laughed.

"Am I a fool? Could the police do anything with a vague story like that? See—I will give you a last chance. You shall give up this Englishwoman. You shall return to me. And then, *chéri*, never, never will I breathe——"

"Breathe what?"

She laughed softly. "You thought no one saw you——"

"What do you mean?"

"As I say, you thought no one saw you—but *I* saw you, Dereek, *mon ami; I saw you coming out of the compartment of Madame your wife just before the train got into Lyons that night.* And I know more than that. I know that when you came out of her compartment she was dead."

He stared at her. Then, like a man in a dream, he turned very slowly and went out of the room, swaying slightly as he walked.

Chapter 26

A WARNING

"And so it is," said Poirot, "that we are the good friends and have no secrets from each other."

Katherine turned her head to look at him. There was something in his voice, some undercurrent of seriousness, which she had not heard before.

They were sitting in the gardens of Monte Carlo. Katherine had come over with her friends, and they had run into Knighton and Poirot almost immediately on arrival. Lady Tamplin had seized upon Knighton and had overwhelmed him with reminiscences, most of which Katherine had a faint suspicion were invented. They had moved away together, Lady Tamplin with her hand on the young man's arm. Knighton had thrown a couple of glances back over his shoulder, and Poirot's eyes twinkled a little as he saw them.

"Of course we are friends," said Katherine.

"From the beginning we have been sympathetic to each other," mused Poirot.

"When you told me that a '*roman policier*' occurs in real life."

"And I was right, was I not?" he challenged her, with an emphatic forefinger. "Here we are, plunged in the middle of one. That is natural for me—it is my *métier*—but for you it is different. Yes," he added in a reflective tone, "for you it is different."

She looked sharply at him. It was as though he were warning her, pointing out to her some menace that she had not seen.

"Why do you say that I am in the middle of it? It is true that I had that conversation with Mrs. Kettering just before she died, but now—now all that is over. I am not connected with the case any more."

"Ah, Mademoiselle, Mademoiselle, can we ever say, 'I have finished with this or that'?"

Katherine turned defiantly round to face him.

"What is it?" she asked. "You are trying to tell me something—to convey it to me rather. But I am not clever at taking hints. I would much rather that you said anything you have to say straight out."

Poirot looked at her sadly. "*Ah, mais c'est anglais ça,*" he murmured, "everything in black and white, everything clear cut and well defined. But life, it is not like that, Mademoiselle. There are the things that are not yet, but which cast their shadow before."

He dabbed his brow with a very large silk pocket-handkerchief and murmured:

"Ah, but it is that I become poetical. Let us, as you say, speak only of facts. And, speaking of facts, tell me what you think of Major Knighton."

"I like him very much indeed," said Katherine warmly; "he is quite delightful."

Poirot sighed.

"What is the matter?" asked Katherine.

"You reply so heartily," said Poirot. "If you had said in an indifferent voice, 'Oh, quite nice,' *eh bien*, do you know I should have been better pleased."

Katherine did not answer. She felt slightly uncomfortable. Poirot went on dreamily:

"And yet, who knows? With *les femmes*, they have so many ways of concealing what they feel—and heartiness is perhaps as good a way as any other."

He sighed.

"I don't [illegible]—" began Katherine.

He interrupted her.

"You do not see why I am being so impertinent, Mademoiselle? I am an old man, and now and then—not very often—I come across someone whose welfare is dear to me. We are friends, Mademoiselle. You have said so yourself. And it is just this—I should like to see you happy."

Katherine stared very straight in front of her. She had a cretonne sunshade with her, and with its point she traced little designs in the gravel at her feet.

"I have asked you a question about Major Knighton, now I will ask you another. Do you like Mr. Derek Kettering?"

"I hardly know him," said Katherine.

"That is not an answer, that."

"I think it is."

He looked at her, struck by something in her tone. Then he nodded his head gravely and slowly.

"Perhaps you are right, Mademoiselle. See you, I who speak to you have seen much of the world, and I know that there are two things which are true. A good man may be ruined by his love for a bad woman—but the other way holds good also. A bad man may equally be ruined by his love for a good woman."

Katherine looked up sharply.

"When you say ruined——"

"I mean from his point of view. One must be whole-hearted in crime as in everything else."

"You are trying to warn me," said Katherine in a low voice. "Against whom?"

"I cannot look into your heart, Mademoiselle; I do not think you would let me if I could. I will just say this. There are men who have a strange fascination for women."

"The Comte de la Roche," said Katherine, with a smile.

"There are others—more dangerous than the Comte de la Roche. They have qualities that appeal—recklessness, daring, audacity. You are fascinated, Mademoiselle; I see that, but I think that it is no more than that. I hope so. This man of whom I speak, the emotion he feels is genuine enough, but all the same——"

"Yes?"

He got up and stood looking down at her. Then he spoke in a low, distinct voice:

"You could, perhaps, love a thief, Mademoiselle, *but not a murderer.*"

He wheeled sharply away on that and left her sitting there. He heard the little gasp she gave and paid no attention. He had said what he meant to say. He left her there to digest that last unmistakable phrase.

Derek Kettering, coming out of the Casino into the sunshine, saw her sitting alone on the bench and joined her.

"I have been gambling," he said, with a light laugh, "gambling unsuccessfully. I have lost everything—everything, that is, that I have with me."

Katherine looked at him with a troubled face. She was aware at once of something new in his manner, some hidden excitement that betrayed itself in a hundred different infinitesimal signs.

"I should think you were always a gambler. The spirit of gambling appeals to you."

"Every day and in every way a gambler? You are about right. Don't *you* find something stimulating in it? To risk all on one throw—there is nothing like it."

Calm and stolid as she believed herself to be, Katherine felt a faint answering thrill.

"I want to talk to you," went on Derek, "and who knows when I may have another opportunity? There is an idea going about that I murdered my wife—no, please don't interrupt. It is absurd, of course." He paused for a minute or two, then went on, speaking more deliberately. "In dealing with the police and Local Authorities here I have had to pretend to—well—a certain decency. I prefer not to pretend with you. I meant to marry money. I was on the look out for money when I first met Ruth Van Aldin. She had the look of a slim Madonna about her, and —I—well—I made all sorts of good resolutions—and was bitterly disillusioned. My wife was in love with another man when she married me. She never cared for me in the least. Oh, I am not complaining; the thing was a perfectly respectable bargain. She wanted Leconbury and I wanted money. The trouble arose simply through Ruth's American blood. Without caring a pin for me, she would have liked me to be continually dancing attendance. Time and again she as good as told me that she had bought me and that I belonged to her. The result was that I behaved abominably to her. My father-in-law will tell you that, and he is quite right. At the time of Ruth's death, I was faced with absolute disaster." He laughed suddenly. "One *is* faced with absolute disaster when one is up against a man like Rufus Van Aldin."

"And then?" asked Katherine in a low voice.

"And then," Derek shrugged his shoulders, "Ruth was murdered—very providentially."

He laughed, and the sound of his laugh hurt Katherine. She winced.

"Yes," said Derek, "that wasn't in very good taste. But it is quite true. Now I am going to tell you something more. From the very first moment I saw you I knew you were the only woman in the world for me. I was—afraid of you. I thought you might bring me bad luck."

"Bad luck?" said Katherine sharply.

He stared at her. "Why do you repeat it like that? What have you got in your mind?"

"I was thinking of things that people have said to me."

Derek grinned suddenly. "They will say a lot to you about me, my dear, and most of it will be true. Yes, and worse things too—things that I shall never tell you. I have been a gambler always—and I have taken some long odds. I shan't confess to you now or at any other time. The past is done with. There is one thing I do wish you to believe. I swear to you solemnly that I did not kill my wife."

He said the words earnestly enough, yet there was somehow a theatrical touch about them. He met her troubled gaze and went on:

"I know. I lied the other day. It *was* my wife's compartment I went into."

"Ah," said Katherine.

"It's difficult to explain just why I went in, but I'll try. I did it on an impulse. You see, I was more or less spying on my wife. I kept out of sight on the train. Mirelle had told me that my wife was meeting the Comte de la Roche in Paris. Well, as far as I had seen, that was not so. I felt ashamed, and I thought suddenly that it would be a good thing to have it out with her once and for all, so I pushed open the door and went in."

He paused.

"Yes," said Katherine gently.

"Ruth was lying on the bunk asleep—her face was turned away from me—I could only see the back of her head. I could have woken her up, of course. But suddenly I felt a reaction. What, after all, was there to say that we hadn't both of us said a hundred times before? She looked so peaceful lying there. I left the compartment as quietly as I could."

"Why lie about it to the police?" asked Katherine.

"Because I'm not a complete fool. I've realised from the beginning that, from the point of view of motive, I'm the ideal murderer. If I once admitted that I had been in her compartment just before she was murdered, I'd do for myself once and for all."

"I see."

Did she see? She could not have told herself. She was feeling the magnetic attraction of Derek's personality, but there was something in her that resisted, that held back . . .

"Katherine——"

"I——"

"You know that I care for you. Do—do you care for me?"

"I—I don't know."

Weakness there. Either she knew or she did not know. If —if only——

She cast a look round desperately as though seeking something that would help her. A soft colour rose in her cheeks as a tall fair man with a limp came hurrying along the path towards them—Major Knighton.

There was relief and an unexpected warmth in her voice as she greeted him.

Derek stood up, scowling, his face black as a thunder-cloud.

"Lady Tamplin having a flutter?" he said easily. "I must join her and give her the benefit of my system."

He swung round on his heel and left them together. Katherine sat down again. Her heart was beating rapidly and unevenly, but as she sat there, talking commonplaces to the quiet, rather shy man beside her, her self-command came back.

Then she realised with a shock that Knighton also was

laying bare his heart, much as Derek had done, but in a very different manner.

He was shy and stammering. The words came haltingly with no eloquence to back them.

"From the first moment I saw you—I—I ought not to have spoken so soon—but Mr. Van Aldin may leave here any day, and I might not have another chance. I know you can't care for me so soon—that is impossible. I dare say it is presumption anyway on my part. I have private means, but not very much—no, please don't answer now. I know what your answer would be. But in case I went away suddenly I just wanted you to know—that I care."

She was shaken—touched. His manner was so gentle and appealing.

"There's one thing more. I just wanted to say that if—if you are ever in trouble, anything that I can do——"

He took her hand in his, held it tightly for a minute, then dropped it and walked rapidly away towards the Casino without looking back.

Katherine sat perfectly still, looking after him. Derek Kettering—Richard Knighton—two men so different—so very different. There was something kind about Knighton, kind and trustworthy. As to Derek——

Then suddenly Katherine had a very curious sensation. She felt that she was no longer sitting alone on the seat in the Casino gardens, but that someone was standing beside her, and that that someone was the dead woman, Ruth Kettering. She had a further impression that Ruth wanted—badly—to tell her something. The impression was so curious, so vivid, that it could not be driven away. She felt absolutely certain that the spirit of Ruth Kettering was trying to convey something of vital importance to her. The impression faded. Katherine got up, trembling a little. What was it that Ruth Kettering had wanted so badly to say?

Chapter 27

INTERVIEW WITH MIRELLE

When Knighton left Katherine he went in search of Hercule Poirot, whom he found in the Rooms, jauntily placing the minimum stake on the even numbers. As Knighton joined him, the number thirty-three turned up, and Poirot's stake was swept away.

"Bad luck!" said Knighton; "are you going to stake again?"

Poirot shook his head.

"Not at present."

"Do you feel the fascination of gambling?" asked Knighton curiously.

"Not at roulette."

Knighton shot a swift glance at him. His own face became troubled. He spoke haltingly, with a touch of deference.

"I wonder, are you busy, M. Poirot? There is something I would like to ask you about."

"I am at your disposal. Shall we go outside? It is pleasant in the sunshine."

They strolled out together, and Knighton drew a deep breath.

"I love the Riviera," he said. "I came here first twelve years ago, during the War, when I was sent to Lady Tamplin's Hospital. It was like Paradise, coming from Flanders to this."

"It must have been," said Poirot.

"How long ago the War seems now!" mused Knighton.

They walked on in silence for some little way.

"You have something on your mind?" said Poirot.

Knighton looked at him in some surprise.

"You are quite right," he confessed. "I don't know how you knew it, though."

"It showed itself only too plainly," said Poirot drily.

"I did not know that I was so transparent."

"It is my business to observe the physiognomy," the little man explained, with dignity.

"I will tell you, M. Poirot. You have heard of this dancer woman—Mirelle?"

"She who is the *chère amie* of M. Derek Kettering?"

"Yes, that is the one; and, knowing this, you will understand that Mr. Van Aldin is naturally prejudiced against her. She wrote to him, asking for an interview. He told me to dictate a curt refusal, which of course I did. This morning she came to the hotel and sent up her card, saying that it was urgent and vital that she should see Mr. Van Aldin at once."

"You interest me," said Poirot.

"Mr. Van Aldin was furious. He told me what message to send down to her. I ventured to disagree with him. It seemed to me both likely and probable that this woman Mirelle might give us valuable information. We know that she was on the Blue Train, and she may have seen or heard something that it might be vital for us to know. Don't you agree with me, M. Poirot?"

"I do," said Poirot drily. "M. Van Aldin, if I may say so, behaved exceedingly foolishly."

"I am glad you take that view of the matter," said the secretary. "Now I am going to tell you something, M. Poirot. So strongly did I feel the unwisdom of Mr. Van Aldin's attitude that I went down privately and had an interview with the lady."

"*Eh bien?*"

"The difficulty was that she insisted on seeing Mr. Van Aldin himself. I softened his message as much as I possibly could. In fact—to be candid—I gave it in a very different form. I said that Mr. Van Aldin was too busy to see her at present, but that she might make any communication she wished to me. That, however, she could not bring herself to do, and she left without saying anything further. But I have a strong impression, M. Poirot, that that woman knows something."

"This is serious," said Poirot quietly. "You know where she is staying?"

"Yes." Knighton mentioned the name of the hotel.

"Good," said Poirot; "we will go there immediately."

The secretary looked doubtful.

"And Mr. Van Aldin?" he queried doubtfully.

"M. Van Aldin is an obstinate man," said Poirot drily. "I do not argue with obstinate men. I act in spite of them. We will go and see the lady immediately. I will tell her that you are empowered by M. Van Aldin to act for him, and you will guard yourself well from contradicting me."

Knighton still looked slightly doubtful, but Poirot took no notice of his hesitation.

At the hotel, they were told that Mademoiselle was in, and Poirot sent up both his and Knighton's cards, with "From Mr. Van Aldin" pencilled upon them.

Word came down that Mademoiselle Mirelle would receive them.

When they were ushered into the dancer's apartments, Poirot immediately took the lead.

"Mademoiselle," he murmured, bowing very low, "we are here on behalf of M. Van Aldin."

"Ah! And why did he not come himself?"

"He is indisposed," said Poirot mendaciously; "the Riviera throat, it has him in its grip, but me I am empowered to act for him, as is Major Knighton, his secretary. Unless, of course, Mademoiselle would prefer to wait a fortnight or so."

If there was one thing of which Poirot was tolerably certain, it was that to a temperament such as Mirelle's the mere word "wait" was anathema.

"*Eh bien*, I will speak, Messieurs," she cried. "I have been patient. I have held my hand. And for what? That I should be insulted! Yes, insulted! Ah! Does he think to treat Mirelle like that? To throw her off like an old glove. I tell you never has a man tired of me. Always it is I who tire of them."

She paced up and down the room, her slender body trembling with rage. A small table impeded her free passage, and she flung it from her into a corner, where it splintered against the wall.

"That is what I will do to him," she cried, "and that!"

Picking up a glass bowl filled with lilies she flung it into the grate, where it smashed into a hundred pieces.

Knighton was looking at her with cold British disapproval.

He felt embarrassed and ill at ease. Poirot, on the other hand, with twinkling eyes was thoroughly enjoying the scene.

"Ah, it is magnificent!" he cried. "It can be seen—Madame has a temperament."

"I am an artist," said Mirelle; "every artist has a temperament. I told Dereek to beware, and he would not listen." She whirled round on Poirot suddenly. "It is true, is it not, that he wants to marry that English miss?"

Poirot coughed.

"*On m'a dit*," he murmured, "that he adores her passionately."

Mirelle came towards them.

"He murdered his wife," she screamed. "There—now you have it! He told me beforehand that he meant to do it. He had got to an *impasse*—zut! he took the easiest way out."

"You say that M. Kettering murdered his wife."

"Yes, yes, yes. Have I not told you so?"

"The police," murmured Poirot, "will need proof of that—er—statement."

"I tell you I saw him come out of her compartment that night on the train."

"When?" asked Poirot sharply.

"Just before the train reached Lyons."

"You will swear to that, Mademoiselle?"

It was a different Poirot who spoke now, sharp and decisive.

"Yes."

There was a moment's silence. Mirelle was panting, and her eyes, half defiant, half frightened, went from the face of one man to the other.

"This is a serious matter, Mademoiselle," said the detective. "You realise how serious?"

"Certainly I do."

"That is well," said Poirot. "Then you understand, Mademoiselle, that no time must be lost. You will, perhaps, accompany us immediately to the office of the Examining Magistrate."

Mirelle was taken aback. She hesitated, but, as Poirot had foreseen, she had no loophole for escape.

"Very well," she muttered, "I will fetch a coat."

Left alone together, Poirot and Knighton exchanged glances.

"It is necessary to act while—how do you say it?—the iron is hot," murmured Poirot. "She is temperamental; in an hour's time, maybe, she will repent, and she will wish to draw back. We must prevent that at all costs."

Mirelle reappeared, wrapped in a sand-coloured velvet wrap trimmed with leopard skin. She looked not altogether unlike a leopardess, tawny and dangerous. Her eyes still flashed with anger and determination.

They found M. Caux and the Examining Magistrate together. A few brief introductory words from Poirot, and Mademoiselle Mirelle was courteously entreated to tell her tale. This she did in much the same words as she had done to Knighton and Poirot, though with far more soberness of manner.

"This is an extraordinary story, Mademoiselle," said M. Carrège slowly. He leant back in his chair, adjusted his pince-nez, and looked keenly and searchingly at the dancer through them.

"You wish us to believe M. Kettering actually boasted of the crime to you beforehand?"

"Yes, yes. She was too healthy, he said. If she were to die it must be an accident—he would arrange it all."

"You are aware, Mademoiselle," said M. Carrège sternly, "that you are making yourself out to be an accessory before the fact?"

"Me? But not the least in the world, Monsieur. Not for a moment did I take that statement seriously. Ah no indeed! I know men, Monsieur; they say many wild things. It would be an odd state of affairs if one were to take all they said *au pied de la lettre*."

The Examining Magistrate raised his eyebrows.

"We are to take it, then, that you regarded M. Kettering's threats as mere idle words? May I ask, Mademoiselle, what made you throw up your engagements in London and come out to the Riviera?"

Mirelle looked at him with melting black eyes.

"I wished to be with the man I loved," she said simply. "Was it so unnatural?"

Poirot interpolated a question gently.

"Was it, then, at M. Kettering's wish that you accompanied him to Nice?"

Mirelle seemed to find a little difficulty in answering this. She hesitated perceptibly before she spoke. When she did, it was with a haughty indifference of manner.

"In such matters I please myself, Monsieur," she said.

That the answer was not an answer at all was noted by all three men. They said nothing.

"When were you first convinced that M. Kettering had murdered his wife?"

"As I tell you, Monsieur, I saw M. Kettering come out of his wife's compartment just before the train drew in to Lyons. There was a look on his face—ah! at the moment I could not understand it—a look haunted and terrible. I shall never forget it."

Her voice rose shrilly, and she flung out her arms in an extravagant gesture.

"Quite so," said M. Carrège.

"Afterwards, when I found that Madame Kettering was dead when the train left Lyons, then—then I knew!"

"And still—you did not go to the police, Mademoiselle," said the Commissary mildly.

Mirelle glanced at him superbly; she was clearly enjoying herself in the rôle she was playing.

"Shall I betray my lover?" she asked. "Ah no; do not ask a woman to do that."

"Yet now——" hinted M. Caux.

"Now it is different. He has betrayed me! Shall I suffer that in silence? . . ."

The Examining Magistrate checked her.

"Quite so, quite so," he murmured soothingly. "And now, Mademoiselle, perhaps you will read over the statement of what you have told us, see that it is correct, and sign it."

Mirelle wasted no time on the document.

"Yes, yes," she said, "it is correct." She rose to her feet. "You require me no longer, Messieurs?"

"At present, no, Mademoiselle."

"And Dereek will be arrested?"

"At once, Mademoiselle."

Mirelle laughed cruelly and drew her fur draperies closer about her.

"He should have thought of this before he insulted me," she cried.

"There is one little matter"—Poirot coughed apologetically—"just a matter of detail."

"Yes?"

"What makes you think that Madame Kettering was dead when the train left Lyons?"

Mirelle stared.

"But she *was* dead."

"Was she?"

"Yes, of course. I——"

She came to an abrupt stop. Poirot was regarding her intently, and he saw the wary look that came into her eyes.

"I have been told so. Everybody says so."

"Oh," said Poirot, "I was not aware that the fact had been mentioned outside the Examining Magistrate's office."

Mirelle appeared somewhat discomposed.

"One hears those things," she said vaguely; "they get about. Somebody told me. I can't remember who it was."

She moved to the door. M. Caux sprang forward to open it for her, and as he did so, Poirot's voice rose gently once more.

"And the jewels? Pardon, Mademoiselle. Can you tell me anything about those?"

"The jewels? What jewels?"

"The rubies of Catherine the Great. Since you hear so much, you must have heard of them."

"I know nothing about any jewels," said Mirelle sharply.

She went out, closing the door behind her. M. Caux came back to his chair; the Examining Magistrate sighed.

"What a fury!" he said, "but *diablement chic*. I wonder if she is telling the truth? I think so."

"There is *some* truth in her story, certainly," said Poirot. "We have confirmation of it from Miss Grey. She was looking down the corridor a short time before the train reached Lyons, and she saw M. Kettering go into his wife's compartment."

"The case against him seems quite clear," said the Commissary, sighing: "it is a thousand pities," he murmured.

"How do you mean?" asked Poirot.

"It has been the ambition of my life to lay the Comte de la Roche by the heels. This time, *ma foi,* I thought we had got him. This other—it is not nearly so satisfactory."

M. Carrège rubbed his nose.

"If anything goes wrong," he observed cautiously, "it will be most awkward. M. Kettering is of the aristocracy. It will get into the newspapers. If we have made a mistake——" He shrugged his shoulders forebodingly.

"The jewels now," said the Commissary, "what do you think he has done with them?"

"He took them for a plant, of course," said M. Carrège; "they must have been a great inconvenience to him and very awkward to dispose of."

Poirot smiled.

"I have an idea of my own about the jewels. Tell me, Messieurs, what do you know of a man called the Marquis?"

The Commissary leant forward excitedly.

"The Marquis," he said, "the Marquis? Do you think he is mixed up in this affair, M. Poirot?"

"I ask you what you know of him."

The Commissary made an expressive grimace.

"Not as much as we should like to," he observed ruefully. "He works behind the scenes, you understand. He has underlings who do his dirty work for him. But he is someone high up. That we are sure of. He does not come from the criminal classes."

"A Frenchman?"

"Y—es. At least we believe so. But we are not sure. He has worked in France, in England, in America. There was a series of robberies in Switzerland last autumn which were laid at his door. By all accounts he is a *grand seigneur*, speaking French and English with equal perfection, and his origin is a mystery."

Poirot nodded and rose to take his departure.

"Can you tell us nothing more, M. Poirot?" urged the Commissary.

"At present, no," said Poirot, "but I may have news awaiting me at my hotel."

M. Carrège looked uncomfortable. "If the Marquis is concerned in this——" he began, and then stopped.

"It upsets our ideas," complained M. Caux.

"It does not upset mine," said Poirot. "On the contrary, I think it agrees with them very well. Au revoir, Messieurs; if news of any importance comes to me I will communicate it to you immediately."

He walked back to his hotel with a grave face. In his absence, a telegram had come for him. Taking a paper-cutter from his pocket, he slit it open. It was a long telegram, and he read it over twice before slowly putting it in his pocket. Upstairs, George was awaiting his master.

"I am fatigued, Georges, much fatigued. Will you order for me a small pot of chocolate?"

The chocolate was duly ordered and brought, and George set it at the little table at his master's elbow. As he was preparing to retire, Poirot spoke:

"I believe, Georges, that you have a good knowledge of the English aristocracy?" murmured Poirot.

George smiled apologetically.

"I think that I might say that I have, sir," he replied.

"I suppose that it is your opinion, Georges, that criminals are invariably drawn from the lower orders?"

"Not always, sir. There was great trouble with one of the Duke of Devize's younger sons. He left Eton under a cloud, and after that he caused great anxiety on several occasions. The police would not accept the view that it was kleptomania. A very clever young gentleman, sir, but vicious through and through, if you take my meaning. His Grace shipped him to Australia, and I hear he was convicted out there under another name. Very odd, sir, but there it is. The young gentleman, I need hardly say, was not in want financially."

Poirot nodded his head slowly.

"Love of excitement," he murmured, "and a little kink in the brain somewhere. I wonder now——"

He drew out the telegram from his pocket and read it again.

"Then there was Lady Mary Fox's daughter," continued the valet in a mood of reminiscence. "Swindled tradespeople something shocking, she did. Very worrying to the best families, if I may say so, and there are many other queer cases I could mention."

"You have a wide experience, Georges," murmured Poirot. "I often wonder having lived so exclusively with titled families that you demean yourself by coming as a valet to me. I put it down to love of excitement on your part."

"Not exactly, sir," said George. "I happened to see in *Society Snippets* that you had been received at Buckingham Palace. That was just when I was looking for a new situation. His Majesty, so it said, had been most gracious and friendly and thought very highly of your abilities."

"Ah," said Poirot, "one always likes to know the reason for things."

He remained in thought for a few moments and then said:

"You rang up Mademoiselle Papopolous?"

"Yes, sir; she and her father will be pleased to dine with you to-night."

"Ah," said Poirot thoughtfully. He drank off his chocolate, set the cup and saucer neatly in the middle of the tray, and spoke gently, more to himself than to the valet.

"The squirrel, my good Georges, collects nuts. He stores them up in the autumn so that they may be of advantage to him later. To make a success of humanity, Georges, we must profit by the lessons of those below us in the animal kingdom. I have always done so. I have been the cat, watching the mouse hole. I have been the good dog following up the scent, and not taking my nose from the trail. And also, my good Georges, I have been the squirrel. I have stored away the little fact here, the little fact there. I go now to my store and I take out one particular nut, a nut that I stored away—let me see, seventeen years ago. You follow me, Georges?"

"I should hardly have thought, sir," said George, "that nuts would have kept so long as that, though I know one can do wonders with preserving bottles."

Poirot looked at him and smiled.

Chapter 28

POIROT PLAYS THE SQUIRREL

Poirot started to keep his dinner appointment with a margin of three-quarters of an hour to spare. He had an object in this. The car took him, not straight to Monte Carlo, but to Lady Tamplin's house at Cap Martin, where he asked for Miss Grey. The ladies were dressing and Poirot was shown into a small salon to wait, and here, after a lapse of three or four minutes, Lenox Tamplin came to him.

"Katherine is not quite ready yet," she said. "Can I give her a message, or would you rather wait until she comes down?"

Poirot looked at her thoughtfully. He was a minute or two in replying, as though something of great weight hung upon his decision. Apparently the answer to such a simple question mattered.

"No," he said at last, "No, I do not think it is necessary that I should wait to see Mademoiselle Katherine. I think, perhaps, that it is better that I should not. These things are sometimes difficult."

Lenox waited politely, her eyebrows slightly raised.

"I have a piece of news," continued Poirot. "You will, perhaps, tell your friend. M. Kettering was arrested to-night for the murder of his wife."

"You want me to tell Katherine that?" asked Lenox. She breathed rather hard, as though she had been running; her face, Poirot thought, looked white and strained—rather noticeably so.

"If you please, Mademoiselle."

"Why?" said Lenox. "Do you think Katherine will be upset? Do you think she cares?"

"I don't know, Mademoiselle," said Poirot. "See, I admit it frankly. As a rule I know everything, but in this case, I—well, I do not. You, perhaps, know better than I do."

"Yes," said Lenox, "I know—but I am not going to tell you all the same."

She paused for a minute or two, her dark brows drawn together in a frown.

"You believe he did it?" she said abruptly.

Poirot shrugged his shoulders.

"The police say so."

"Ah," said Lenox, "hedging, are you? So there is something to hedge about."

Again she was silent, frowning. Poirot said gently:

"You have known Derek Kettering a long time, have you not?"

"Off and on ever since I was a kid," said Lenox gruffly. Poirot nodded his head several times without speaking.

With one of her brusque movements Lenox drew forward a chair and sat down on it, her elbows on the table and her face supported by her hands. Sitting thus, she looked directly across the table at Poirot.

"What have they got to go on?" she demanded. "Motive, I suppose. Probably came into money at her death."

"He came into two million."

"And if she had not died he would have been ruined?"

"Yes."

"But there must have been more than that," persisted Lenox. "He travelled by the same train, I know, but—that would not be enough to go on by itself."

"A cigarette case with the letter 'K' on it which did not belong to Mrs. Kettering was found in her carriage, and he was seen by two people entering and leaving the compartment just before the train got into Lyons."

"What two people?"

"Your friend Miss Grey was one of them. The other was Mademoiselle Mirelle, the dancer."

"And he, Derek, what has he got to say about it?" demanded Lenox sharply.

"He denies having entered his wife's compartment at all," said Poirot.

"Fool!" said Lenox crisply, frowning. "Just before Lyons, you say? Does nobody know when—when she died?"

"The doctors' evidence necessarily cannot be very definite," said Poirot; "they are inclined to think that death was unlikely to have occurred after leaving Lyons. And we know this much, that a few moments after leaving Lyons Mrs. Kettering was dead."

"How do you know that?"

Poirot was smiling rather oddly to himself.

"Someone else went into her compartment and found her dead."

"And they did not rouse the train?"

"No."

"Why was that?"

"Doubtless they had their reasons."

Lenox looked at him sharply.

"Do you know the reason?"

"I think so—yes."

Lenox sat still turning things over in her mind. Poirot watched her in silence. At last she looked up. A soft colour had come into her cheeks and her eyes were shining.

"You think someone on the train must have killed her, but that need not be so at all. What is to stop anyone swinging themselves on to the train when it stopped at Lyons? They could go straight to her compartment, strangle her, and take the rubies and drop off the train again without anyone being the wiser. She may have been actually killed while the train was in Lyons station. Then she would have been alive when Derek went in, and dead when the other person found her."

Poirot leant back in his chair. He drew a deep breath. He looked across at the girl and nodded his head three times, then he heaved a sigh.

"Mademoiselle," he said, "what you have said there is very just—very true. I was struggling in the darkness, and you have shown me a light. There was a point that puzzled me and you have made it plain."

He got up.

"And Derek?" said Lenox.

"Who knows?" said Poirot, with a shrug of his shoulders. "But I will tell you this, Mademoiselle. I am not satisfied; no, I, Hercule Poirot, am not yet satisfied. It may be that this very night I shall learn something more. At least, I go to try."

"You are meeting someone?"

"Yes."

"Someone who knows something?"

"Someone who might know something. In these matters one must leave no stone unturned. Au revoir, Mademoiselle."

Lenox accompanied him to the door.

"Have I—helped?" she asked.

Poirot's face softened as he looked up at her standing on the doorstep above him.

"Yes, Mademoiselle, you have helped. If things are very dark, always remember that."

When the car had driven off he relapsed into a frowning absorption, but in his eyes was that faint green light which was always the precursor of the triumph to be.

He was a few minutes late at the rendezvous, and found that M. Papopolous and his daughter had arrived before him. His apologies were abject, and he outdid himself in politeness and small attentions. The Greek was looking particularly benign and noble this evening, a sorrowful patriarch of blameless life. Zia was looking handsome and good humoured. The dinner was a pleasant one. Poirot was his best and most sparkling self. He told anecdotes, he made jokes, he paid graceful compliments to Zia Papopolous, and he told many interesting incidents of his career. The menu was a carefully selected one, and the wine was excellent.

At the close of dinner M. Papopolous inquired politely:

"And the tip I gave you? You have had your little flutter on the horse?"

"I am in communication with—er—my bookmaker," replied Poirot.

The eyes of the two men met.

"A well-known horse, eh?"

"No," said Poirot; "it is what our friends, the English, call a dark horse."

"Ah!" said M. Papopolous thoughtfully.

"Now we must step across to the Casino and have our little flutter at the roulette table," cried Poirot gaily.

At the Casino the party separated, Poirot devoting himself solely to Zia, whilst Papopolous himself drifted away.

Poirot was not fortunate, but Zia had a run of good luck, and had soon won a few thousand francs.

"It would be as well," she observed drily to Poirot, "if I stopped now."

Poirot's eyes twinkled.

"Superb!" he exclaimed. "You are the daughter of your father, Mademoiselle Zia. To know when to stop. Ah! that is the art."

He looked round the rooms.

"I cannot see your father anywhere about," he remarked carelessly. "I will fetch your cloak for you, Mademoiselle, and we will go out in the gardens."

He did not, however, go straight to the cloakroom. His sharp eyes had seen but a little while before the departure of M. Papopolous. He was anxious to know what had become of the wily Greek. He ran him to earth unexpectedly in the big entrance hall. He was standing by one of the pillars, talking to a lady who had just arrived. The lady was Mirelle.

Poirot sidled unostentatiously round the room. He arrived at the other side of the pillar, and unnoticed by the two who were talking together in an animated fashion—or rather, that is to say, the dancer was talking, Papopolous contributing an occasional monosyllable and a good many expressive gestures.

"I tell you I must have time," the dancer was saying. "If you give me time I will get the money."

"To wait"—the Greek shrugged his shoulders—"it is awkward."

"Only a very little while," pleaded the other. "Ah! but you must! A week—ten days—that is all I ask. You can be sure of your affair. The money will be forthcoming."

Papopolous shifted a little and looked round him uneasily—to find Poirot almost at his elbow with a beaming innocent face.

"*Ah! vous voilà*, M. Papopolous. I have been looking for you. It is permitted that I take Mademoiselle Zia for a little turn in the gardens? Good evening, Mademoiselle." He bowed very low to Mirelle. "A thousand pardons that I did not see you immediately."

The dancer accepted his greetings rather impatiently. She was plainly annoyed at the interruption of her *tête-à-tête*. Poirot was quick to take the hint. Papopolous had already murmured: "Certainly—but certainly," and Poirot withdrew forthwith.

He fetched Zia's cloak, and together they strolled out into the gardens.

"This is where the suicides take place," said Zia.

Poirot shrugged his shoulders. "So it is said. Men are foolish, are they not, Mademoiselle? To eat, to drink, to breathe the good air, it is a very pleasant thing, Mademoiselle. One is foolish to leave all that simply because one has no money—or because the heart aches. *L'amour*, it causes many fatalities, does it not?"

Zia laughed.

"You should not laugh at love, Mademoiselle," said Poirot, shaking an energetic forefinger at her. "You who are young and beautiful."

"Hardly that," said Zia; "you forget that I am thirty-three, M. Poirot. I am frank with you, because it is no good being otherwise. As you told my father it is exactly seventeen years since you aided us in Paris that time."

"When I look at you, it seems much less," said Poirot gallantly. "You were then very much as you are now, Mademoiselle, a little thinner, a little paler, a little more serious. Sixteen years old and fresh from your *pension*. Not quite the *petite pensionnaire*, not quite a woman. You were very delicious, very charming, Mademoiselle Zia; others thought so too, without doubt."

"At sixteen," said Zia, "one is simple and a little fool."

"That may be," said Poirot; "yes, that well may be. At sixteen one is credulous, is one not? One believes what one is told."

If he saw the quick sideways glance that the girl shot at him, he pretended not to have done so. He continued dreamily: "It was a curious affair that, altogether. Your father, Mademoiselle, has never understood the true inwardness of it."

"No?"

"When he asked me for details, for explanations, I said to him thus: 'Without scandal, I have got back for you that which was lost. You must ask no questions.' Do you know, Mademoiselle, why I said these things?"

"I have no idea," said the girl coldly.

"It was because I had a soft spot in my heart for a little *pensionnaire*, so pale, so thin, so serious."

"I don't understand what you are talking about," cried Zia angrily.

"Do you not, Mademoiselle? Have you forgotten Antonio Pirezzio?" He heard the quick intake of her breath—almost a gasp.

"He came to work as an assistant in the shop, but not thus could he have got hold of what he wanted. An assistant can lift his eyes to his master's daughter, can he not? If he is young and handsome with a glib tongue. And since they cannot make love all the time, they must occasionally talk of things that interest them both—such as that very interesting thing which was temporarily in M. Papopolous' possession. And since, as you say, Mademoiselle, the young are foolish and credulous, it was easy to believe him and to give him a sight of that particular thing, to show him where it was kept. And afterwards when it is gone—when the unbelievable catastrophe has happened. Alas! the poor little *pensionnaire*. What a terrible position she is in. She is frightened, the poor little one. To speak or not to speak? And then there comes along that excellent fellow, Hercule Poirot. Almost a miracle it must have been, the way things arranged themselves. The priceless heirlooms are restored and there are no awkward questions."

Zia turned on him fiercely.

"You have known all the time? Who told you? Was it—was it Antonio?"

Poirot shook his head.

"No one told me," he said quietly. "I guessed. It was a good guess, was it not, Mademoiselle? You see, unless you are good at guessing, it is not much use being a detective."

The girl walked along beside him for some minutes in silence. Then she said in a hard voice:

"Well, what are you going to do about it; are you going to tell my father?"

"No," said Poirot sharply. "Certainly not."

She looked at him curiously.

"You want something from me?"

"I want your help, Mademoiselle."

"What makes you think that I can help you?"

"I do not think so. I only hope so."

"And if I do not help you, then—you will tell my father?"

"But no, but no! Debarrass yourself of that idea, Mademoiselle. I am not a blackmailer. I do not hold your secret over your head and threaten you with it."

"If I refuse to help you——?" began the girl slowly.

"Then you refuse, and that is that."

"Then why——?" she stopped.

"Listen, and I will tell you why. Women, Mademoiselle, are generous. If they can render a service to one who has rendered a service to them, they will do it. I was generous once to you, Mademoiselle. When I might have spoken, I held my tongue."

There was another silence; then the girl said, "My father gave you a hint the other day."

"It was very kind of him."

"I do not think," said Zia slowly, "that there is anything that I can add to that."

If Poirot was disappointed he did not show it. Not a muscle of his face changed.

"*Eh bien!*" he said cheerfully, "then we must talk of other things."

And he proceeded to chat gaily. The girl was *distraite*, however, and her answers were mechanical and not always to the point. It was when they were approaching the Casino once more that she seemed to come to a decision.

"M. Poirot?"

"Yes, Mademoiselle?"

"I—I should like to help you if I could."

"You are very amiable, Mademoiselle—very amiable."

Again there was a pause. Poirot did not press her. He was quite content to wait and let her take her own time.

"Ah bah," said Zia, "after all, why should I not tell you? My father is cautious—always cautious in everything he says. But I know that with you it is not necessary. You have told us it is only the murderer you seek, and that you are not concerned over the jewels. I believe you. You were quite right when you guessed that we were in Nice because of the rubies. They have been handed over here according to plan. My father has them now. He gave you a hint the other day as to who our mysterious client was."

"The Marquis?" murmured Poirot softly.

"Yes, the Marquis."

"Have you ever seen the Marquis, Mademoiselle Zia?"

"Once," said the girl. "But not very well," she added. "It was through a keyhole."

"That always presents difficulties," said Poirot sympathetically, "but all the same you saw him. You would know him again?"

Zia shook her head.

"He wore a mask," she explained.

"Young or old?"

"He had white hair. It may have been a wig, it may not. It fitted very well. But I do not think he was old. His walk was young, and so was his voice."

"His voice?" said Poirot thoughtfully. "Ah, his voice! Would you know it again, Mademoiselle Zia?"

"I might," said the girl.

"You were interested in him, eh? It was that that took you to the keyhole?"

Zia nodded.

"Yes, yes. I was curious. One had heard so much—he is not the ordinary thief—he is more like a figure of history or romance."

"Yes," said Poirot thoughtfully; "yes, perhaps so."

"But it is not this that I meant to tell you," said Zia. "It was just one other little fact that I thought might be—well—useful to you."

"Yes?" said Poirot encouragingly.

"The rubies, as I say, were handed over to my father here at Nice. I did not see the person who handed them over, but——"

"Yes?"

"I know one thing. *It was a woman.*"

Chapter 29

A LETTER FROM HOME

"DEAR KATHERINE,—Living among grand friends as you are doing now, I don't suppose you will care to hear any of our news; but as I always thought you were a sensible girl, perhaps you are a trifle less swollen-headed than I suppose. Everything goes on much the same here. There was great trouble about the new curate, who is scandalously high. In my view, he is neither more nor less than a Roman. Everybody has spoken to the Vicar about it, but you know what the Vicar is—all Christian charity and no proper spirit. I have had a lot of trouble with maids lately. That girl Annie was no good—skirts up to her knees and wouldn't wear sensible woollen stockings. Not one of them can bear being spoken to. I have had a lot of pain with my rheumatism one way and another, and Dr. Harris persuaded me to go and see a London specialist—a waste of three guineas and a railway fare, as I told him; but by waiting until Wednesday I managed to get a cheap return. The London doctor pulled a long face and talked all round about and never straight out, until I said to him, 'I'm a plain woman, Doctor, and I like things to be plainly stated. Is it cancer, or is it not?' And then, of course, he had to say it was. They say a year with care, and not too much pain, though I'm sure I can bear pain as well as any other Christian woman. Life seems rather lonely at times, with most of my friends dead or gone before. I wish you were in St. Mary Mead, my dear, and that is a fact. If you hadn't come into this money and gone off into grand society, I would have offered you double the salary poor Jane gave you to come and look after me; but there—there's no good wanting what we can't get. However, if things should go ill with you—and that is always possible. I have heard no end of tales of bogus noblemen marrying girls and getting hold of their money and then leaving them at the church door. I dare say you are too sensible for anything of the kind to happen to you, but one never knows; and never having had much attention of any kind it might easily go to your head now. So just in case, my dear, remember there is always a home for you here; and though a plain-spoken woman I am a warm-hearted one too.—Your affectionate old friend,

"AMELIA VINER.

"PS.—I saw a mention of you in the paper with your cousin, Viscountess Tamplin, and I cut it out and put it with my cuttings. I prayed for you on Sunday that you might be kept from pride and vainglory."

Katherine read this characteristic epistle through twice, then she laid it down and stared out of her bedroom window across the blue waters of the Mediterranean. She felt a curious lump in her throat. A sudden wave of longing for St. Mary Mead swept over her. So full of familiar, everyday, stupid little things—and yet—home. She felt very inclined to lay her head down on her arms and indulge in a real good cry.

Lenox, coming in at the moment, saved her.

"Hello, Katherine," said Lenox. "I say—what is the matter?"

"Nothing," said Katherine, grabbing up Miss Viner's letter and thrusting it into her handbag.

"You looked rather queer," said Lenox. "I say—I hope you don't mind—I rang up your detective friend, M. Poirot, and asked him to lunch with us in Nice. I said you wanted to see him, as I thought he might not come for me."

"Did you want to see him then?" asked Katherine.

"Yes," said Lenox. "I have rather lost my heart to him. I never met a man before whose eyes were really green like a cat's."

"All right," said Katherine. She spoke listlessly. The last few days had been trying. Derek Kettering's arrest had been the topic of the hour, and the Blue Train Mystery had been thrashed out from every conceivable standpoint.

"I have ordered the car," said Lenox, "and I have told Mother some lie or other—unfortunately I can't remember exactly what; but it won't matter, as she never remembers. If she knew where we were going, she would want to come too, to pump M. Poirot."

The two girls arrived at the Negresco to find Poirot waiting.

He was full of Gallic politeness, and showered so many compliments upon the two girls that they were soon helpless with laughter; yet for all that the meal was not a gay one. Katherine was dreamy and distracted, and Lenox made bursts of conversation, interspersed by silences. As they were sitting on the terrace sipping their coffee she suddenly attacked Poirot bluntly.

"How are things going? You know what I mean?"

Poirot shrugged his shoulders. "They take their course," he said.

"And you are just letting them take their course?"

He looked at Lenox a little sadly.

"You are young, Mademoiselle, but there are three things that cannot be hurried—*le bon Dieu*, Nature, and old people."

"Nonsense!" said Lenox. "You are not old."

"Ah, it is pretty, what you say there."

"Here is Major Knighton," said Lenox.

Katherine looked round quickly and then turned back again.

"He is with Mr. Van Aldin," continued Lenox. "There is something I want to ask Major Knighton about. I won't be a minute."

Left alone together, Poirot bent forward and murmured to Katherine:

"You are *distraite*, Mademoiselle; your thoughts, they are far away, are they not?"

"Just as far as England, no farther."

Guided by a sudden impulse, she took the letter she had received that morning and handed it across to him to read.

"That is the first word that has come to me from my old life; somehow or other—it hurts."

He read it through and then handed it back to her.

"So you are going back to St. Mary Mead?" he said.

"No, I am not," said Katherine; "why should I?"

"Ah," said Poirot, "it is my mistake. You will excuse me one little minute."

He strolled across to where Lenox Tamplin was talking to Van Aldin and Knighton. The American looked old and haggard. He greeted Poirot with a curt nod but without any other sign of animation.

As he turned to reply to some observation made by Lenox, Poirot drew Knighton aside.

"M. Van Aldin looks ill," he said.

"Do you wonder?" asked Knighton. "The scandal of Derek Kettering's arrest has about put the lid on things, as far as he is concerned. He is even regretting that he asked you to find out the truth."

"He should go back to England," said Poirot.

"We are going the day after to-morrow."

"That is good news," said Poirot.

He hesitated, and looked across the terrace to where Katherine was sitting.

"I wish," he murmured, "that you could tell Miss Grey that."

"Tell her what?"

"That you—I mean that M. Van Aldin is returning to England."

Knighton looked a little puzzled, but he readily crossed the terrace and joined Katherine.

Poirot saw him go with a satisfied nod of the head, and then joined Lenox and the American. After a minute or two they joined the others. Conversation was general for a few minutes, then the millionaire and his secretary departed. Poirot also prepared to take his departure.

"A thousand thanks for your hospitality, Mesdemoiselles," he cried; "it has been a most charming luncheon. *Ma foi*, I needed it!" He swelled out his chest and thumped it. "I am now a lion—a giant. Ah, Mademoiselle Katherine, you have not seen me as I can be. You have seen the gentle, the calm Hercule Poirot; but there is another Hercule Poirot. I go now to bully, to threaten, to strike terror into the hearts of those who listen to me."

He looked at them in a self-satisfied way, and they both appeared to be duly impressed, though Lenox was biting her underlip, and the corners of Katherine's mouth had a suspicious twitch.

"And I shall do it," he said gravely. "Oh yes, I shall succeed."

He had gone but a few steps when Katherine's voice made him turn.

"M. Poirot, I—I want to tell you. I think you were quite right in what you said. I am going back to England almost immediately."

Poirot stared at her very hard, and under the directness of his scrutiny she blushed.

"I see," he said gravely.

"I don't believe you do," said Katherine.

"I know more than you think, Mademoiselle," he said quietly.

He left her, with an odd little smile upon his lips. Entering a waiting car, he drove to Antibes.

Hipolyte, the Comte de la Roche's wooden-faced man-servant, was busy at the Villa Marina polishing his master's beautiful cut table glass. The Comte de la Roche himself had gone to Monte Carlo for the day. Chancing to look out of the window, Hipolyte espied a visitor walking briskly up to the hall door, a visitor of so uncommon a type that Hipolyte, experienced as he was, had some difficulty in placing him. Calling to his wife, Marie, who was busy in the kitchen, he drew her attention to what he called *ce type là*.

"It is not the police again?" said Marie anxiously.

"Look for yourself," said Hipolyte.

Marie looked.

"Certainly not the police," she declared. "I am glad."

"They have not really worried us much," said Hipolyte. "In fact, but for Monsieur le Comte's warning, I should never have guessed that stranger at the wine-shop to be what he was."

The hall bell pealed and Hipolyte, in a grave and decorous manner, went to open the door.

"M. le Comte, I regret to say, is not at home."

The little man with the large moustaches beamed placidly.

"I know that," he replied. "You are Hipolyte Flavelle, are you not?"

"Yes, Monsieur, that is my name."

"And you have a wife, Marie Flavelle?"

"Yes, Monsieur, but——"

"I desire to see you both," said the stranger, and he stepped nimbly past Hipolyte into the hall.

"Your wife is doubtless in the kitchen," he said. "I will go there."

Before Hipolyte could recover his breath, the other had selected the right door at the back of the hall and passed along the passage and into the kitchen, where Marie paused open-mouthed to stare at him.

"*Voilà*," said the stranger, and sank into a wooden arm-chair; "I am Hercule Poirot."

"Yes, Monsieur?"

"You do not know the name?"

"I have never heard it," said Hipolyte.

"Permit me to say that you have been badly educated. It is the name of one of the great ones of this world."

He sighed and folded his hands across his chest.

Hipolyte and Marie were staring at him uneasily. They were at a loss what to make of this unexpected and extremely strange visitor. "Monsieur desires——?" murmured Hipolyte mechanically.

"I desire to know why you have lied to the police."

"Monsieur!" cried Hipolyte; "I—lied to the police? Never have I done such a thing."

M. Poirot shook his head.

"You are wrong," he said; "you have done it on several occasions. Let me see." He took a small notebook from his pocket and consulted it. "Ah, yes; on seven occasions at least. I will recite them to you."

In a gentle unemotional voice he proceeded to outline the seven occasions.

Hipolyte was taken aback.

"But it is not of these past lapses that I wish to speak," continued Poirot, "only, my dear friend, do not get into the habit of thinking yourself too clever. I come now to the particular lie in which I am concerned—your statement that the Comte de la Roche arrived at this villa on the morning of 14th January."

"But that was no lie, Monsieur; that was the truth. Monsieur le Comte arrived here on the morning of Tuesday, the 14th. That is so, Marie, is it not?"

Marie assented eagerly.

"Ah, yes, that is quite right. I remember it perfectly."

"Oh," said Poirot, "and what did you give your good master for *déjeuner* that day?"

"I——" Marie paused, trying to collect herself.

"Odd," said Poirot, "how one remembers some things—and forgets others."

He leant forward and struck the table a blow with his fist; his eyes flashed with anger.

"Yes, yes, it is as I say. You tell your lies and you think nobody knows. But there are two people who know. Yes—two people. One is *le bon Dieu*——"

He raised a hand to heaven, and then settling himself back in his chair and shutting his eyelids, he murmured comfortably:

"And the other is Hercule Poirot."

"I assure you, Monsieur, you are completely mistaken. Monsieur le Comte left Paris on Monday night——"

"True," said Poirot—"by the Rapide. I do not know where he broke his journey. Perhaps you do not know that. What I do know is that he arrived here on Wednesday morning, and not on Tuesday morning."

"Monsieur is mistaken," said Marie stolidly.

Poirot rose to his feet.

"Then the law must take its course," he murmured. "A pity."

"What do you mean, Monsieur?" asked Marie, with a shade of uneasiness.

"You will be arrested and held as accomplices concerned in the murder of Mrs. Kettering, the English lady who was killed."

"Murder!"

The man's face had gone chalk white, his knees knocked together. Marie dropped the rolling-pin and began to weep.

"But it is impossible—impossible. I thought——"

"Since you stick to your story, there is nothing to be said. I think you are both foolish."

He was turning towards the door when an agitated voice arrested him.

"Monsieur, Monsieur, just a little moment. I—I had no

idea that it was anything of this kind. I—I thought it was just a matter concerning a lady. There have been little awkwardnesses with the police over ladies before. But murder—that is very different."

"I have no patience with you," cried Poirot. He turned round on them and angrily shook his fist in Hipolyte's face. "Am I to stop here all day, arguing with a couple of imbeciles thus? It is the truth I want. If you will not give it to me, that is your lookout. *For the last time, when did Monsieur le Comte arrive at the Villa Marina—Tuesday morning or Wednesday morning?*"

"Wednesday," gasped the man, and behind him Marie nodded confirmation.

Poirot regarded them for a minute or two, then inclined his head gravely.

"You are wise, my children," he said quietly. "Very nearly you were in serious trouble."

He left the Villa Marina, smiling to himself.

"One guess confirmed," he murmured to himself. "Shall I take a chance on the other?"

It was six o'clock when the card of Monsieur Hercule Poirot was brought up to Mirelle. She stared at it for a moment or two, and then nodded. When Poirot entered, he found her walking up and down the room feverishly. She turned on him furiously.

"Well?" she cried. "Well? What is it now? Have you not tortured me enough, all of you? Have you not made me betray my poor Dereek? What more do you want?"

"Just one little question, Mademoiselle. After the train left Lyons, when you entered Mrs. Kettering's compartment——"

"What is that?"

Poirot looked at her with an air of mild reproach and began again.

"I say when you entered Mrs. Kettering's compartment ——"

"I never did."

"And found her——"

"I never did."

"*Ah, sacré!*"

He turned on her in a rage and shouted at her, so that she cowered back before him.

"Will you lie to me? I tell you I know what happened as well as though I had been there. You went into her compartment and you found her dead. I tell you I know it. To lie to me is dangerous. Be careful, Mademoiselle Mirelle."

Her eyes wavered beneath his gaze and fell.

"I—I didn't——" she began uncertainly, and stopped.

"There is only one thing about which I wonder," said Poirot—"I wonder, Mademoiselle, if you found what you were looking for or whether——"

"Whether what?"

"Or whether someone else had been before you."

"I will answer no more questions," screamed the dancer. She tore herself away from Poirot's restraining hand, and flinging herself down on the floor in a frenzy, she screamed and sobbed. A frightened maid came rushing in.

Hercule Poirot shrugged his shoulders, raised his eyebrows, and quietly left the room.

But he seemed satisfied.

Chapter 30

MISS VINER GIVES JUDGMENT

Katherine looked out of Miss Viner's bedroom window. It was raining, not violently, but with a quiet, well-bred persistence. The window looked out on a strip of front garden with a path down to the gate and neat little flower-beds on either side, where later roses and pinks and blue hyacinths would bloom.

Miss Viner was lying in a large Victorian bedstead. A tray with the remains of breakfast had been pushed to one side and she was busy opening her correspondence and making various caustic comments upon it.

Katherine had an open letter in her hand and was reading it through for the second time. It was dated from the Ritz Hotel, Paris.

"CHERE MADEMOISELLE KATHERINE" (It began)—"I trust that you are in good health and that the return to the English winter has not proved too depressing. Me, I prosecute my inquiries with the utmost diligence. Do not think that it is the holiday that I take here. Very shortly I shall be in England, and I hope then to have the pleasure of meeting you once more. It shall be so, shall it not? On arrival in London I shall write to you. You remember that we are the colleagues in this affair? But indeed I think you know that very well. Be assured, Mademoiselle, of my most respectful and devoted sentiments.

HERCULE POIROT."

Katherine frowned slightly. It was as though something in the letter puzzled and intrigued her.

"A choirboys' picnic indeed," came from Miss Viner, "Tommy Saunders and Albert Dykes ought to be left behind, and I shan't subscribe to it unless they are. What those two boys think they are doing in church on Sundays I don't know. Tommy sang, 'O God, make speed to save us,' and never opened his lips again, and if Albert Dykes wasn't sucking a mint humbug, my nose is not what it is and always has been."

"I know, they are awful," agreed Katherine.

She opened her second letter, and a sudden flush came to her cheeks. Miss Viner's voice in the room seemed to recede into the far distance.

When she came back to a sense of her surroundings Miss Viner was bringing a long speech to a triumphant termination.

"And I said to her, 'Not at all. As it happens, Miss Grey is Lady Tamplin's own cousin.' What do you think of that?"

"Were you fighting my battles for me? That was very sweet of you."

"You can put it that way if you like. There is nothing to me in a title. Vicar's wife or no vicar's wife, that woman is a cat. Hinting you had bought your way into Society."

"Perhaps she was not so very far wrong."

"And look at you," continued Miss Viner. "Have you come back a stuck-up fine lady, as well you might have done? No, there you are, as sensible as ever you were, with a pair of good Balbriggan stockings on and your sensible shoes. I spoke to Ellen about it only yesterday. 'Ellen,' I said, 'you look at Miss Grey. She has been hobnobbing with some of the greatest in the land, and does she go about as you do with skirts up to her knees and silk stockings that ladder when you look at them, and the most ridiculous shoes that ever I set eyes on?' "

Katherine smiled a little to herself, it had apparently been worth while to conform to Miss Viner's prejudices. The old lady went on with increasing gusto.

"It has been a great relief to me that you have not had your head turned. Only the other day I was looking for my cuttings. I have several about Lady Tamplin and her War Hospital and what not, but I cannot lay my hand upon them. I wish you would look, my dear; your eyesight is better than mine. They are all in a box in the bureau drawer."

Katherine glanced down at the letter in her hand and was about to speak, but checked herself, and going over to the bureau found the box of cuttings and began to look over them. Since her return to St. Mary Mead, her heart had gone out to Miss Viner in admiration of the old woman's stoicism and pluck. She felt that there was little she could do for her old friend, but she knew from experience how much those seemingly small trifles meant to old people.

"Here is one," she said presently. " 'Viscountess Tamplin, who is running her villa at Nice as an Officers' Hospital, has just been the victim of a sensational robbery, her jewels having been stolen. Amongst them were some very famous emeralds, heirlooms of the Tamplin family.' "

"Probably paste," said Miss Viner; "a lot of these Society women's jewels are."

"Here is another," said Katherine. "A picture of her. 'A charming camera study of Viscountess Tamplin with her little daughter Lenox.' "

"Let me look," said Miss Viner. "You can't see much of the child's face, can you? But I dare say that is just as well. Things go by contraries in this world and beautiful mothers have hideous children. I dare say the photographer realised that to take the back of the child's head was the best thing he could do for her."

Katherine laughed.

" 'One of the smartest hostesses on the Riviera this season

is Viscountess Tamplin, who has a villa at Cap Martin. Her cousin, Miss Grey, who recently inherited a vast fortune in a most romantic manner, is staying with her there.' "

"That is the one I wanted," said Miss Viner. "I expect there has been a picture of you in one of the papers that I have missed; you know the kind of thing. Mrs. Somebody or other Jones-Williams, at the something or other Point-to-Point, usually carrying a shooting-stick and having one foot lifted up in the air. It must be a trial to some of them to see what they look like."

Katherine did not answer. She was smoothing out the cutting with her finger, and her face had a puzzled, worried look. Then she drew the second letter out of its envelope and mastered its contents once more. She turned to her friend.

"Miss Viner? I wonder—there is a friend of mine, someone I met on the Riviera, who wants very much to come down and see me here."

"A man?" said Miss Viner.

"Yes."

"Who is he?"

"He is secretary to Mr. Van Aldin, the American millionaire."

"What is his name?"

"Knighton. Major Knighton."

"H'm—secretary to a millionaire. And wants to come down here. Now, Katherine, I am going to say something to you for your own good. You are a nice girl and a sensible girl, and though you have your head screwed on the right way about most things, every woman makes a fool of herself once in her life. Ten to one what this man is after is your money."

With a gesture she arrested Katherine's reply. "I have been waiting for something of this kind. What is a secretary to a millionaire? Nine times out of ten it is a young man who likes living soft. A young man with nice manners and a taste for luxury and no brains and no enterprise, and if there is anything that is a softer job than being secretary to a millionaire it is marrying a rich woman for her money. I am not saying that you might not be some man's fancy. But you are not young, and though you have a very good complexion you are not a beauty, and what I say to you is, don't make a fool of yourself; but if you are determined to do so, do see that your money is properly tied up on yourself. There, now I have finished. What have you got to say?"

"Nothing," said Katherine; "but would you mind if he did come down to see me?"

"I wash my hands of it," said Miss Viner. "I have done my duty, and whatever happens now is on your own head. Would you like him to lunch or to dinner? I dare say Ellen could manage dinner—that is, if she didn't lose her head."

"Lunch would be very nice," said Katherine. "It is awfully kind of you, Miss Viner. He asked me to ring him up, so I will do so and say that we shall be pleased if he will lunch with us. He will motor down from town."

"Ellen does a steak with grilled tomatoes pretty fairly," said Miss Viner. "She doesn't do it well, but she does it better than anything else. It is no good having a tart because she is heavy-handed with pastry; but her little castle puddings are not bad, and I dare say you could find a nice piece of Stilton at Abbot's. I have always heard that gentlemen like a nice piece of Stilton, and there is a good deal of Father's wine left, a bottle of sparkling Moselle, perhaps."

"Oh no, Miss Viner; that is really not necessary."

"Nonsense, my child. No gentleman is happy unless he drinks something with his meal. There is some good pre-war whisky if you think he would prefer that. Now do as I say and don't argue. The key of the wine-cellar is in the third drawer down in the dressing-table, in the second pair of stockings on the left-hand side."

Katherine went obediently to the spot indicated.

"The second pair, now mind," said Miss Viner. "The first pair has my diamond earrings and my filigree brooch in it."

"Oh," said Katherine, rather taken aback, "wouldn't you like them put in your jewel-case?"

Miss Viner gave vent to a terrific and prolonged snort.

"No, indeed! I have much too much sense for that sort of thing, thank you. Dear, dear, I well remember how my poor father had a safe built in downstairs. Pleased as Punch he was with it, and he said to my mother, 'Now, Mary, you bring me your jewels in their case every night and I will lock them away for you.' My mother was a very tactful woman, and she knew that gentlemen like having their own way, and she brought him the jewel-case locked up just as he said.

"And one night burglars broke in, and of course—naturally—the first thing they went for was the safe! It would be, with my father talking up and down the village and bragging about it until you might have thought he kept all King Solomon's diamonds there. They made a clean sweep, got the tankards, the silver cups, and the presentation gold plate that my father had had presented to him, *and* the jewel-case."

She sighed reminiscently. "My father was in a great state over my mother's jewels. There was the Venetian set and some very fine cameos, and some pale pink corals, and two diamond rings with quite large stones in them. And then, of course, she had to tell him that, being a sensible woman, she had kept her jewellery rolled up in a pair of corsets, and there it was still as safe as anything."

"And the jewel-case had been quite empty?"

"Oh no, dear," said Miss Viner, "it would have been too light a weight then. My mother was a very intelligent woman; she saw to that. She kept her buttons in the jewel-case, and a very handy place it was. Boot buttons in the top tray, trouser buttons in the second tray, and assorted buttons below. Curiously enough, my father was quite annoyed with her. He said he didn't like deceit. But I mustn't go chattering on; you want to go and ring up your friend, and mind you choose a nice piece of steak, and tell Ellen she is not to have holes in her stockings when she waits at lunch."

"Is her name Ellen or Helen, Miss Viner? I thought——"

Miss Viner closed her eyes.

"I can sound my h's, dear, as well as anyone, but Helen is *not* a suitable name for a servant. I don't know what the mothers in the lower classes are coming to nowadays."

The rain had cleared away when Knighton arrived at the cottage. The pale fitful sunshine shone down on it and burnished Katherine's head as she stood in the doorway to welcome him. He came up to her quickly, almost boyishly.

"I say, I hope you don't mind. I simply had to see you again soon. I hope the friend you are staying with does not mind."

"Come in and make friends with her," said Katherine.

"She can be most alarming, but you will soon find that she has the softest heart in the world."

Miss Viner was enthroned majestically in the drawing-room, wearing a complete set of the cameos which had been so providentially preserved in the family. She greeted Knighton with dignity and an austere politeness which would have damped many men. Knighton, however, had a charm of manner which was not easily set aside, and after about ten minutes Miss Viner thawed perceptibly. Luncheon was a merry meal, and Ellen, or Helen, in a new pair of silk stockings devoid of ladders, performed prodigies of waiting. Afterwards, Katherine and Knighton went for a walk, and they came back to have tea *tête-à-tête*, since Miss Viner had gone to lie down.

When the car had finally driven off Katherine went slowly upstairs. A voice called her and she went in to Miss Viner's bedroom.

"Friend gone?"

"Yes. Thank you so much for letting me ask him down."

"No need to thank me. Do you think I am the sort of old curmudgeon who never will do anything for anybody?"

"I think you are a dear," said Katherine affectionately.

"Humph," said Miss Viner, mollified.

As Katherine was leaving the room she called her back.

"Katherine?"

"Yes."

"I was wrong about that young man of yours. A man when he is making up to anybody can be cordial and gallant and full of little attentions and altogether charming. But when a man is really in love he can't help looking like a sheep. Now, whenever that young man looked at you he looked like a sheep. I take back all I said this morning. It is genuine."

Chapter 31

MR. AARONS LUNCHES

"Ah!" said Mr. Joseph Aarons appreciatively.

He took a long draught from his tankard, set it down with a sigh, wiped the froth from his lips, and beamed across the table at his host, Monsieur Hercule Poirot.

"Give me," said Mr. Aarons, "a good Porterhouse steak and a tankard of something worth drinking, and anyone can have your French fallals and whatnots, your ordoovres and your omelettes and your little bits of quail. Give me," he reiterated, "a Porterhouse steak."

Poirot, who had just complied with this request, smiled sympathetically.

"Not that there is much wrong with a steak and kidney pudding," continued Mr. Aarons. "Apple tart? Yes, I will take apple tart, thank you, Miss, and a jug of cream."

The meal proceeded. Finally, with a long sigh, Mr. Aarons laid down his spoon and fork preparatory to toying with some cheese before turning his mind to other matters.

"There was a little matter of business I think you said, Monsieur Poirot," he remarked. "Anything I can do to help you I am sure I shall be most happy."

"That is very kind of you," said Poirot. "I said to myself, 'If you want to know anything about the dramatic profession there is one person who knows all that is to be known and that is my old friend, Mr. Joseph Aarons.'"

"And you don't say far wrong," said Mr. Aarons complacently; "whether it is past, present, or future, Joe Aarons is the man to come to."

"*Précisément.* Now I want to ask you, Monsieur Aarons, what you know about a young woman called Kidd."

"Kidd? Kitty Kidd?"

"Kitty Kidd."

"Pretty smart, she was. Male impersonator, song and a dance—— That one?"

"That is the one."

"*Very* smart, she was. Made a good income. Never out of an engagement. Male impersonation mostly, but, as a matter of fact, you could not touch her as a character actress."

"So I have heard," said Poirot; "but she has not been appearing lately, has she?"

"No. Dropped right out of things. Went over to France and took up with some swell nobleman there. She quitted the stage then for good and all, I guess."

"How long ago was that?"

"Let me see. Three years ago. And she has been a loss—let me tell you that."

"She was clever?"

"Clever as a cartload of monkeys."

"You don't know the name of the man she became friends with in Paris?"

"He was a swell, I know that. A Count—or was it a Marquis? Now I come to think of it, I believe it was a Marquis."

"And you know nothing about her since?"

"Nothing. Never even run across her accidentally like. I bet she is tooling it round some of these foreign restorts. Being a Marquise to the life. You couldn't put one over on Kitty. She would give as good as she got any day."

"I see," said Poirot thoughtfully.

"I am sorry I can't tell you more, Monsieur Poirot," said the other. "I would like to be of use to you if I could. You did me a good turn once."

"Ah, but we are quits on that; you, too, did me a good turn."

"One good turn deserves another. Ha, ha!" said Mr. Aarons.

"Your profession must be a very interesting one," said Poirot.

"So-so," said Mr. Aarons non-committally. "Taking the rough with the smooth, it is all right. I don't do so badly at it, all things considered, but you have to keep your eyes skinned. Never know what the public will jump for next."

"Dancing has come very much to the fore in the last few years," murmured Poirot reflectively.

"*I* never saw anything in this Russian ballet, but people like it. Too highbrow for me."

"I met one dancer out on the Riviera—Mademoiselle Mirelle."

"Mirelle? She is hot stuff, by all accounts. There is always money going to back her—though, so far as that goes, the girl can dance; I have seen her, and I know what I am talking about. I never had much to do with her myself, but I hear she is a terror to deal with. Tempers and tantrums all the time."

"Yes," said Poirot thoughtfully; "yes, so I should imagine."

"Temperament!" said Mr. Aarons, "temperament! That is what they call it themselves. My missus was a dancer before she married me, but I am thankful to say she never had any temperament. You don't want temperament in the home, Monsieur Poirot."

"I agree with you, my friend; it is out of place there."

"A woman should be calm and sympathetic, and a good cook," said Mr. Aarons.

"Mirelle has not been long before the public, has she?" asked Poirot.

"About two and a half years, that is all," said Mr. Aarons. "Some French duke started her. I hear now that she has taken up with the ex-Prime Minister of Greece. These are the chaps who manage to put money away quietly."

"That is news to me," said Poirot.

"Oh, she's not one to let the grass grow under her feet. They say that young Kettering murdered his wife on her account. I don't know, I am sure. Anyway, he is in prison, and she had to look round for herself, and pretty smart she has been about it. They say she is wearing a ruby the size of a pigeon's egg—not that I have ever seen a pigeon's egg myself, but that is what they always call it in works of fiction."

"A ruby the size of a pigeon's egg!" said Poirot. His eyes were green and catlike. "How interesting!"

"I had it from a friend of mine," said Mr. Aarons. "But for all I know, it may be coloured glass. They are all the same, these women—they never stop telling tall stories about their jewels. Mirelle goes about bragging that it has got a curse on it. 'Heart of Fire,' I think she calls it."

"But if I remember rightly," said Poirot, "the ruby that is named 'Heart of Fire' is the centre stone in a necklace."

"There you are! Didn't I tell you there is no end to the lies women will tell about their jewellery? This is a single stone, hung on a platinum chain round her neck; but, as I said before, ten to one it is a bit of coloured glass."

"No," said Poirot gently; "no—somehow I do not think it is coloured glass."

Chapter 32

KATHERINE AND POIROT COMPARE NOTES

"You have changed, Mademoiselle," said Poirot suddenly. He and Katherine were seated opposite each other at a small table at the Savoy.

"Yes, you have changed," he continued.

"In what way?"

"Mademoiselle, these *nuances* are difficult to express."

"I am older."

"Yes, you are older. And by that I do not mean that the wrinkles and the crows' feet are coming. When I first saw you, Mademoiselle, you were a looker-on at life. You had the quiet, amused look of one who sits back in the stalls and watches the play."

"And now?"

"Now you no longer watch. It is an absurd thing, perhaps, that I say here, but you have the wary look of a fighter who is playing a difficult game."

"My old lady is difficult sometimes," said Katherine, with a smile; "but I can assure you that I don't engage in deadly contests with her. You must go down and see her some day, Monsieur Poirot. I think you are one of the people who would appreciate her pluck and her spirit."

There was a silence while the waiter deftly served them with chicken *en casserole*. When he had departed, Poirot said: "You have heard me speak of my friend Hastings?—he who said that I was a human oyster. *Eh bien*, Mademoiselle, I have met my match in you. You, far more than I, play a lone hand."

"Nonsense," said Katherine lightly.

"Never does Hercule Poirot talk nonsense. It is as I say."

Again there was a silence. Poirot broke it by inquiring:

"Have you seen any of our Riviera friends since you have been back, Mademoiselle?"

"I have seen something of Major Knighton."

"A-ha. Is that so?"

Something in Poirot's twinkling eyes made Katherine lower hers.

"So Mr. Van Aldin remains in London?"

"Yes."

"I must try to see him to-morrow or the next day."

"You have news for him?"

"What makes you think that?"

"I—wondered, that is all."

Poirot looked across at her with twinkling eyes.

"And now, Mademoiselle, there is much that you wish to ask me, I can see that. And why not? Is not the affair of the Blue Train our own '*roman policier*'?"

"Yes, there are things I should like to ask you."

"*Eh bien?*"

Katherine looked up with a sudden air of resolution.

"What were you doing in Paris, Monsieur Poirot?"

Poirot smiled slightly.

"I made a call at the Russian Embassy."

"Oh."

"I see that that tells you nothing. But I will not be a human oyster. No, I will lay my cards on the table, which is assuredly a thing that oysters never do. You suspect, do you not, that I am not satisfied with the case against Derek Kettering?"

"That is what I have been wondering. I thought, in Nice, that you had finished with the case."

"You do not say all that you mean, Mademoiselle. But I admit everything. It was I—my researches—which placed Derek Kettering where he now is. But for me the Examining

Magistrate would still be vainly trying to fasten the crime on the Comte de la Roche. *Eh bien*, Mademoiselle, what I have done I do not regret. I have only one duty—to discover the truth, and that way led straight to Mr. Kettering. But did it end there? The police say yes, but I, Hercule Poirot, am not satisfied."

He broke off suddenly. "Tell me, Mademoiselle, have you heard from Mademoiselle Lenox lately?"

"One very short, scrappy letter. She is, I think, annoyed with me for coming back to England."

Poirot nodded.

"I had an interview with her the night that Monsieur Kettering was arrested. It was an interesting interview in more ways than one."

Again he fell silent, and Katherine did not interrupt his train of thought. "Mademoiselle," he said at last, "I am now on delicate ground, yet I will say this to you. There is, I think, someone who loves Monsieur Kettering—correct me if I am wrong—and for her sake—well—for her sake I hope that I am right and the police are wrong. You know who that someone is?"

There was a pause, then Katherine said:

"Yes—I think I know."

Poirot leant across the table towards her.

"I am not satisfied, Mademoiselle; no, I am not satisfied. The facts, the main facts, led straight to Monsieur Kettering. But there is one thing that has been left out of account."

"And what is that?"

"The disfigured face of the victim. I have asked myself, Mademoiselle, a hundred times, 'Was Derek Kettering the kind of man who would deal that smashing blow after having committed the murder?' What end would it serve? What purpose would it accomplish? Was it a likely action for one of Monsieur Kettering's temperament? And, Mademoiselle, the answer to these questions is profoundly unsatisfactory. Again and again I go back to that one point—'why?' And the only things I have to help me to a solution of the problem are these."

He whipped out his pocket-book and extracted something from it which he held between his finger and thumb.

"Do you remember, Mademoiselle? You saw me take these hairs from the rug in the railway carriage."

Katherine leant forward, scrutinising the hairs keenly.

Poirot nodded his head slowly several times.

"They suggest nothing to you, I see that, Mademoiselle. And yet—I think somehow that you see a good deal."

"I have had ideas," said Katherine slowly, "curious ideas. That is why I ask you what you were doing in Paris, Monsieur Poirot."

"When I wrote to you——"

"From the Ritz?"

A curious smile came over Poirot's face.

"Yes, as you say, from the Ritz. I am a luxurious person sometimes—when a millionaire pays."

"The Russian Embassy," said Katherine, frowning. "No, I don't see where that comes in."

"It does not come in directly, Mademoiselle. I went there to get certain information. I saw a particular personage and I threatened him—yes, Mademoiselle, I, Hercule Poirot, threatened him."

"With the police?"

"No," said Poirot drily, "with the Press—a much more deadly weapon."

He looked at Katherine and she smiled at him, just shaking her head.

"Are you not just turning back into an oyster again, Monsieur Poirot?"

"No, no; I do not wish to make mysteries. See, I will tell you everything. I suspect this man of being the active party in the sale of the jewels of Monsieur Van Aldin. I tax him with it, and in the end I get the whole story out of him. I learn where the jewels were handed over, and I learn, too, of the man who paced up and down outside in the street—a man with a venerable head of white hair, but who walked with the light, springy step of a young man—and I give that man a name in my own mind—the name of 'Monsieur le Marquis.'"

"And now you have come to London to see Mr. Van Aldin?"

"Not entirely for that reason. I had other work to do.

Since I have been in London I have seen two more people—a theatrical agent and a Harley Street doctor. From each of them I have got certain information. Put these things together, Mademoiselle, and see if you can make of them the same as I do."

"I?"

"Yes, you. I will tell you one thing, Mademoiselle. There has been a doubt all along in my mind as to whether the robbery and the murder were done by the same person. For a long time I was not sure——"

"And now?"

"And now I *know*."

There was a silence. Then Katherine lifted her head. Her eyes were shining.

"I am not clever like you, Monsieur Poirot. Half the things that you have been telling me don't seem to me to point anywhere at all. The ideas that came to me came from such an entirely different angle——"

"Ah, but that is always so," said Poirot quietly. "A mirror shows the truth, but everyone stands in a different place for looking into the mirror."

"My ideas may be absurd—they may be entirely different from yours, but——"

"Yes?"

"Tell me, does this help you at all?"

He took a newspaper cutting from her outstretched hand. He read it and, looking up, he nodded gravely.

"As I told you, Mademoiselle, one stands at a different angle for looking into the mirror, but it is the same mirror and the same things are reflected there."

Katherine got up. "I must rush," she said. "I have only just time to catch my train. Monsieur Poirot——"

"Yes, Mademoiselle."

"It—it mustn't be much longer, you understand. I—I can't go on much longer."

There was a break in her voice.

He patted her hand reassuringly.

"Courage, Mademoiselle, you must not fail now; the end is very near."

Chapter 33

A NEW THEORY

"Monsieur Poirot wants to see you, sir."

"Damn the fellow!" said Van Aldin.

Knighton remained sympathetically silent.

Van Aldin got up from his chair and paced up and down.

"I suppose you have seen the cursed newspapers this morning?"

"I have glanced at them, sir."

"Still at it hammer and tongs?"

"I am afraid so, sir."

The millionaire sat down again and pressed his hand to his forehead.

"If I had had an idea of this," he groaned. "I wish to God I had never got that little Belgian to ferret out the truth. Find Ruth's murderer—that was all I thought about."

"You wouldn't have liked your son-in-law to go scot free?"

Van Aldin sighed.

"I would have preferred to take the law into my own hands."

"I don't think that would have been a very wise proceeding, sir."

"All the same—are you sure the fellow wants to see me?"

"Yes, Mr. Van Aldin. He is very urgent about it."

"Then I suppose he will have to. He can come along this morning if he likes."

It was a very fresh and debonair Poirot who was ushered in. He did not seem to see any lack of cordiality in the millionaire's manner, and chatted pleasantly about various trifles. He was in London, he explained, to see his doctor. He mentioned the name of an eminent surgeon [illegible]

"No, no, *pas la guerre*—a memory of my days in the police force, a bullet of a rascally apache."

He touched his left shoulder and winced realistically.

"I always consider you a lucky man, Monsieur Van Aldin;

you are not like our popular idea of American millionaires, martyrs to dyspepsia."

"I am pretty tough," said Van Aldin. "I lead a very simple life, you know; plain fare and not too much of it."

"You have seen something of Miss Grey, have you not?" inquired Poirot, innocently turning to the secretary.

"I—yes; once or twice," said Knighton.

He blushed slightly and Van Aldin exclaimed in surprise:

"Funny you never mentioned to me that you had seen her, Knighton."

"I didn't think you would be interested, sir."

"I like that girl very much," said Van Aldin.

"It is a thousand pities that she should have buried herself once more in St. Mary Mead," said Poirot.

"It is very fine of her," said Knighton hotly. "There are very few people who would bury themselves down there to look after a cantankerous old woman who has no earthly claim on her."

"I am silent," said Poirot, his eyes twinkling a little; "but all the same I say it is a pity. And now, Messieurs, let us come to business."

Both the other men looked at him in some surprise.

"You must not be shocked or alarmed at what I am about to say. Supposing, Monsieur Van Aldin, that, after all, Monsieur Derek Kettering did not murder his wife?"

"What?"

Both men stared at him in blank surprise.

"Supposing, I say, that Monsieur Kettering did not murder his wife?"

"Are you mad, Monsieur Poirot?"

It was Van Aldin who spoke.

"No," said Poirot, "I am not mad. I am eccentric, perhaps—at least certain people say so; but as regards my profession, I am very much, as one says, 'all there.' I ask you, Monsieur Van Aldin, whether you would be glad or sorry if what I tell you should be the case?"

Van Aldin stared at him.

"Naturally I should be glad," he said at last. "Is this an exercise in suppositions, Monsieur Poirot, or are there any facts behind it?"

Poirot looked at the ceiling.

"There is an off-chance," he said quietly, "that it might be the Comte de la Roche after all. At least I have succeeded in upsetting his alibi."

"How did you manage that?"

Poirot shrugged his shoulders modestly.

"I have my own methods. The exercise of a little tact, a little cleverness—and the thing is done."

"But the rubies," said Van Aldin, "these rubies that the Count had in his possession were false."

"And clearly he would not have committed the crime except for the rubies. But you are overlooking one point, Monsieur Van Aldin. Where the rubies were concerned, someone might have been before him."

"But this is an entirely new theory," cried Knighton.

"Do you really believe all this rigmarole, Monsieur Poirot?" demanded the millionaire.

"The thing is not proved," said Poirot quietly. "It is as yet only a theory, but I tell you this, Monsieur Van Aldin, the facts are worth investigating. You must come out with me to the south of France and go into the case on the spot."

"You really think this is necessary—that I should go, I mean?"

"I thought it would be what you yourself would wish," said Poirot.

There was a hint of reproach in his tone which was not lost upon the other.

"Yes, yes, of course," he said. "When do you wish to start, Monsieur Poirot?"

"You are very busy at present, sir," murmured Knighton.

But the millionaire had now made up his mind, and he waved the other's objections aside.

"I guess this business comes first," he said. "All right, Monsieur Poirot, to-morrow. What train?"

"We will go, I think, by the Blue Train," said Poirot, and he smiled.

Chapter 34

THE BLUE TRAIN AGAIN

"The Millionaires' Train," as it is sometimes called, swung round a curve of line at what seemed a dangerous speed. Van Aldin, Knighton, and Poirot sat together in silence. Knighton and Van Aldin had two compartments connecting with each other, as Ruth Kettering and her maid had had on the fateful journey. Poirot's own compartment was farther along the coach.

The journey was a painful one for Van Aldin, recalling as it did the most agonising memories. Poirot and Knighton conversed occasionally in low tones without disturbing him.

When, however, the train had completed its slow journey round the *ceinture* and reached the Gare de Lyon, Poirot became suddenly galvanised into activity. Van Aldin realised that part of his object in travelling by the train had been to attempt to reconstruct the crime. Poirot himself acted every part. He was in turn the maid, hurriedly shut into her own compartment, Mrs. Kettering, recognising her husband with surprise and a trace of anxiety, and Derek Kettering discovering that his wife was travelling on the train. He tested various possibilities, such as the best way for a person to conceal himself in the second compartment.

Then suddenly an idea seemed to strike him. He clutched at Van Aldin's arm.

"*Mon Dieu*, but that is something I have not thought of! We must break our journey in Paris. Quick, quick, let us alight at once."

Seizing suit-cases he hurried from the train. Van Aldin and Knighton, bewildered but obedient, followed him. Van Aldin having once more formed his opinion of Poirot's ability was slow to depart from it. At the barrier they were held up. Their tickets were in charge of the conductor of the train, a fact which all three of them had forgotten.

Poirot's explanations were rapid, fluent, and impassioned, but they produced no effect upon the stolid-faced official.

"Let us get quit of this," said Van Aldin abruptly. "I gather you are in a hurry, Monsieur Poirot. For God's sake pay the fares from Calais and let us get right on with whatever you have got on your mind."

But Poirot's flood of language had suddenly stopped dead, and he had the appearance of a man turned to stone. His arm still outflung in an impassioned gesture, remained there as though stricken with paralysis.

"I have been an imbecile," he said simply. "*Ma foi*, I lose my head nowadays. Let us return and continue our journey quietly. With reasonable luck the train will not have gone."

They were only just in time, the train moving off as Knighton, the last of the three, swung himself and his suit-case on board.

The conductor remonstrated with them feelingly, and assisted them to carry their luggage back to their compartments. Van Aldin said nothing, but he was clearly disgusted at Poirot's extraordinary conduct. Alone with Knighton for a moment or two, he remarked:

"This is a wildgoose chase. The man has lost his grip on things. He has got brains up to a point, but any man who loses his head and scuttles round like a frightened rabbit is no earthly darned good."

Poirot came to them in a moment or two, full of abject apologies and clearly so crestfallen that harsh words would have been superfluous. Van Aldin received his apologies gravely, but managed to restrain himself from making acid comments.

They had dinner on the train, and afterwards, somewhat to the surprise of the other two, Poirot suggested that they should all three sit up in Van Aldin's compartment.

The millionaire looked at him curiously.

"Is there anything that you are keeping back from us, Monsieur Poirot?"

"I?" Poirot opened his eyes in innocent surprise. "But what an idea."

Van Aldin did not answer, but he was not satisfied. The

conductor was told that he need not make up the beds. Any surprise he might have felt was obliterated by the largeness of the tip which Van Aldin handed to him. The three men sat in silence. Poirot fidgeted and seemed restless. Presently he turned to the secretary.

"Major Knighton, is the door of your compartment bolted? The door into the corridor, I mean."

"Yes; I bolted it myself just now."

"Are you sure?" said Poirot.

"I will go and make sure, if you like," said Knighton, smiling.

"No, no, do not derange yourself. I will see for myself."

He passed through the connecting door and returned in a second or two, nodding his head.

"Yes, yes, it is as you said. You must pardon an old man's fussy ways." He closed the connecting door and resumed his place in the right-hand corner.

The hours passed. The three men dosed fitfully, waking with uncomfortable starts. Probably never before had three people booked berths on the most luxurious train available, then declined to avail themselves of the accommodation they had paid for. Every now and then Poirot glanced at his watch, and then nodded his head and composed himself to slumber once more. On one occasion he rose from his seat and opened the connecting door, peered sharply into the adjoining compartment, and then returned to his seat, shaking his head.

"What is the matter?" whispered Knighton. "You are expecting something to happen, aren't you?"

"I have the nerves," confessed Poirot. "I am like the cat upon the hot tiles. Every little noise it makes me jump."

Knighton yawned.

"Of all the darned uncomfortable journeys," he murmured. "I suppose you know what you are playing at, Monsieur Poirot."

He composed himself to sleep as best he could. Both he and Van Aldin had succumbed to slumber, when Poirot, glancing for the fourteenth time at his watch, leant across and tapped the millionaire on the shoulder.

"Eh? What is it?"

"In five or ten minutes, Monsieur, we shall arrive at Lyons."

"My God!" Van Aldin's face looked white and haggard in the dim light. "Then it must have been about this time that poor Ruth was killed."

He sat staring straight in front of him. His lips twitched a little, his mind reverting back to the terrible tragedy that had saddened his life.

There was the usual long screaming sigh of the brake, and the train slackened speed and drew into Lyons. Van Aldin let down the window and leant out.

"If it wasn't Derek—if your new theory is correct, it is here that the man left the train?" he asked over his shoulder.

Rather to his surprise Poirot shook his head.

"No," he said thoughtfully, "no *man* left the train, but I think—yes, I think, a *woman* may have done so."

Knighton gave a gasp.

"A woman?" demanded Van Aldin sharply.

"Yes, a woman," said Poirot, nodding his head. "You may not remember, Monsieur Van Aldin, but Miss Grey in her evidence mentioned that a youth in a cap and overcoat descended on to the platform ostensibly to stretch his legs. Me, I think that that youth was most probably a woman."

"But who was she?"

Van Aldin's face expressed incredulity, but Poirot replied seriously and categorically:

"Her name—or the name under which she was known, for many years—is Kitty Kidd, but you, Monsieur Van Aldin, knew her by another name—*that of Ada Mason*."

Knighton sprang to his feet.

"What?" he cried.

Poirot swung round to him.

"Ah!—before I forget it." He whipped something from a pocket and held it out.

"Permit me to offer you a cigarette—out of your own cigarette-case. It was careless of you to drop it when you boarded the train on the *ceinture* at Paris."

Knighton stood staring at him as though stupefied. Then he made a movement, but Poirot flung up his hand in a warning gesture.

"No, don't move," he said in a silky voice; "the door into the next compartment is open, and you are being covered from there this minute. I unbolted the door into the corridor when we left Paris, and our friends the police were told to take their places there. As I expect you know, the French police want you rather urgently, Major Knighton—or shall we say—Monsieur le Marquis?"

Chapter 35

EXPLANATIONS

"Explanations?"

Poirot smiled. He was sitting opposite the millionaire at a luncheon table in the latter's private suite at the Negresco. Facing him was a relieved but very puzzled man. Poirot leant back in his chair, lit one of his tiny cigarettes, and stared reflectively at the ceiling.

"Yes, I will give you explanations. It began with the one point that puzzled me. You know what that point was? *The disfigured face.* It is not an uncommon thing to find when investigating a crime and it rouses an immediate question, the question of identity. That naturally was the first thing that occurred to me. Was the dead woman really Mrs. Kettering? But that line led me nowhere, for Miss Grey's evidence was positive and very reliable, so I put that idea aside. The dead woman *was* Ruth Kettering."

"When did you first begin to suspect the maid?"

"Not for some time, but one peculiar little point drew my attention to her. The cigarette-case found in the railway carriage and which she told us was one which Mrs. Kettering had given to her husband. Now that was, on the face of it, most improbable, seeing the terms they were on. It awakened a doubt in my mind as to the general veracity of Ada Mason's statements. There was the rather suspicious fact to be taken into consideration, that she had only been with her mistress for two months. Certainly it did not seem as if she could have had anything to do with the crime since she had been left behind in Paris and Mrs. Kettering had been seen alive by several people afterwards, but——"

Poirot leant forward. He raised an emphatic forefinger and wagged it with intense emphasis at Van Aldin.

"But I am a good detective. I suspect. There is nobody and nothing that I do not suspect. I believe nothing that I am told. I say to myself: how do we know that Ada Mason was left behind in Paris? And at first the answer to that question seemed completely satisfactory. There was the evidence of your secretary, Major Knighton, a complete outsider, whose testimony might be supposed to be entirely impartial, and there were the dead woman's own words to the conductor of the train. But I put the latter point aside for the moment, because a very curious idea—an idea perhaps fantastic and impossible—was growing up in my mind. If by any outside chance it happened to be true, that particular piece of testimony was worthless.

"I concentrated on the chief stumbling-block to my theory, Major Knighton's statement that he saw Ada Mason at the Ritz after the Blue Train had left Paris. That seemed conclusive enough, but yet, on examining the facts carefully, I noted two things. First, that by a curious coincidence he, too, had been exactly two months in your service. Secondly, his initial letter was the same—K.' Supposing—just supposing—that it was *his* cigarette-case which had been found in the carriage. Then, if Ada Mason and he were working together, and she recognised it when we showed it to her, would she not act precisely as she had done? At first, taken aback, she quickly evolved a plausible theory that would agree with Mr. Kettering's guilt. *Bien entendu*, that was not the original idea. The Comte de la Roche was to be the scapegoat, though Ada Mason would not make her recognition of him too certain, in case he should be able to prove an alibi. Now, if you will cast your mind back to that time, you will remember a significant thing that happened. I suggested to Ada Mason that the man she had seen was not the Comte de la Roche, but Derek Kettering. She seemed uncertain at the time, but after I had got back to my hotel you rang me up and told me that she had come to you and said that, on thinking it over, she was now quite convinced that the man in question *was* Mr. Kettering.

I had been expecting something of the kind. There could be but one explanation of this sudden certainty on her part. After leaving your hotel, she had had time to consult with somebody, and had received instructions which she acted upon. Who had given her these instructions? Major Knighton. And there was another very small point, which might mean nothing or might mean a great deal. In casual conversation Knighton had talked of a jewel robbery in Yorkshire in a house where he was staying. Perhaps a mere coincidence—perhaps another small link in the chain."

"But there is one thing I do not understand, Monsieur Poirot. I guess I must be dense or I would have seen it before now. Who was the man in the train at Paris? Derek Kettering or the Comte de la Roche?"

"That is the simplicity of the whole thing. *There was no man*. Ah—*mille tonnerres!*—do you not see the cleverness of it all? Whose word have we for it that there ever was a man there? Only Ada Mason's. And we believe in Ada Mason because of Knighton's evidence that she was left behind in Paris."

"But Ruth herself told the conductor that she had left her maid behind there," demurred Van Aldin.

"Ah! I am coming to that. We have Mrs. Kettering's own evidence there, but, on the other hand, we have not really got her evidence, because, Monsieur Van Aldin, a dead woman cannot give evidence. It is not *her* evidence, but the evidence of the conductor of the train—a very different affair altogether."

"So you think the man was lying?"

"No, no, not at all. He spoke what he thought to be the truth. But the woman who told him that she had left her maid in Paris was not Mrs. Kettering."

Van Aldin stared at him.

"Monsieur Van Aldin, Ruth Kettering was dead before the train arrived at the Gare de Lyon. It was Ada Mason, dressed in her mistress's very distinctive clothing, who purchased a dinner basket and who made that very necessary statement to the conductor."

"Impossible!"

"No, no, Monsieur Van Aldin; not impossible. *Les*

femmes, they look so much alike nowadays that one identifies them more by their clothing than by their faces. Ada Mason was the same height as your daughter. Dressed in that very sumptuous fur coat and the little red lacquer hat jammed down over her eyes, with just a bunch of auburn curls showing over each ear, it was no wonder that the conductor was deceived. He had not previously spoken to Mrs. Kettering, you remember. True, he had seen the maid just for a moment when she handed him the tickets, but his impression had been merely that of a gaunt, black-clad female. If he had been an unusually intelligent man, he might have gone so far as to say that mistress and maid were not unlike, but it is extremely unlikely that he would even think that. And remember, Ada Mason, or Kitty Kidd, was an actress, able to change her appearance and tone of voice at a moment's notice. No, no; there was no danger of his recognising the maid in the mistress's clothing, but there *was* the danger that when he came to discover the body he might realise it was not the woman he had talked to the night before. And now we see the reason for the disfigured face. The chief danger that Ada Mason ran was that Katherine Grey might visit her compartment after the train left Paris, and she provided against that difficulty by ordering a dinner basket and by locking herself in her compartment."

"But who killed Ruth—and when?"

"First, bear it in mind that the crime was planned and undertaken by the two of them—Knighton and Ada Mason, working together. Knighton was in Paris that day on your business. He boarded the train somewhere on its way round the *ceinture*. Mrs. Kettering would be surprised, but she would be quite unsuspicious. Perhaps he draws her attention to something out of the window, and as she turns to look he slips the cord round her neck—and the whole thing is over in a second or two. The door of the compartment is locked, and he and Ada Mason set to work. They strip off the dead woman's outer clothes. Mason and Knighton roll the body up in a rug and put it on the seat in the adjoining compartment amongst the bags and suit-cases. Knighton drops off the train, taking the jewel case containing the rubies with him. Since the crime is not supposed to have been committed until nearly twelve hours later he is perfectly safe, and his evidence and the supposed Mrs. Kettering's words to the conductor will provide a perfect alibi for his accomplice.

"At the Gare de Lyon Ada Mason gets a dinner basket and, shutting herself into the toilet compartment she quickly changes into her mistress's clothes, adjusts two false bunches of auburn curls, and generally makes up to resemble her as closely as possible. When the conductor comes to make up the bed, she tells him the prepared story about having left her maid behind in Paris; and whilst he is making up the berth, she stands looking out of the window, so that her back is towards the corridor and people passing along there. That was a wise precaution, because, as we know, Miss Grey was one of those passing, and she, among others, was willing to swear that Mrs. Kettering was still alive at that hour."

"Go on," said Van Aldin.

"Before getting to Lyons, Ada Mason arranged her mistress's body in the bunk, folded up the dead woman's clothes neatly on the end of it, and herself changed into a man's clothes and prepared to leave the train. When Derek Kettering entered his wife's compartment, and, as he thought, saw her asleep in her berth, the scene had been set, and Ada Mason was hidden in the next compartment waiting for the moment to leave the train unobserved. As soon as the conductor had swung himself down on to the platform at Lyons, she follows, slouching along as though just taking a breath of air. At a moment when she is unobserved, she hurriedly crosses to the other platform, and takes the first train back to Paris and the Ritz Hotel. Her name has been registered there as taking a room the night before by one of Knighton's female accomplices. She has nothing to do but wait there placidly for your arrival. The jewels are not, and never have been, in her possession. No suspicion attaches to him, and, as your secretary, he brings them to Nice without the least fear of discovery. Their delivery there to Monsieur Papopolous is already arranged for, and they are entrusted to Mason at the last moment to hand over to the Greek. Altogether a very neatly planned coup, as one would expect from a master of the game such as the Marquis."

"And you honestly mean that Richard Knighton is a well-known criminal, who has been at this business for years?"

Poirot nodded.

"One of the chief assets of the gentleman called the Marquis was his plausible, ingratiating manner. You fell a victim to his charm, Monsieur Van Aldin, when you engaged him as a secretary on such a slight acquaintanceship."

"I could have sworn that he never angled for the post," cried the millionaire.

"It was very astutely done—so astutely done that it deceived a man whose knowledge of other men is as great as yours is."

"I looked up his antecedents too. The fellow's record was excellent."

"Yes, yes; that was part of the game. As Richard Knighton his life was quite free from reproach. He was well born, well connected, did honourable service in the War, and seemed altogether above suspicion; but when I came to glean information about the mysterious Marquis, I found many points of similarity. Knighton spoke French like a Frenchman, he had been in America, France, and England at much the same time as the Marquis was operating. The Marquis was last heard of as engineering various jewel robberies in Switzerland, and it was in Switzerland that you had come across Major Knighton; and it was at precisely that time that the first rumours were going round of your being in treaty for the famous rubies."

"But why murder?" murmured Van Aldin brokenly. "Surely a clever thief could have stolen the jewels without running his head into a noose."

Poirot shook his head. "This is not the first murder that lies to the Marquis's charge. He is a killer by instinct; he believes, too, in leaving no evidence behind him. Dead men and women tell no tales.

"The Marquis had an intense passion for famous and historical jewels. He laid his plans far beforehand by installing himself as your secretary and getting his accomplice to obtain the situation of maid with your daughter, for whom he guessed the jewels were destined. And, though this was his matured and carefully thought-out plan, he did not scruple to attempt a short-cut by hiring a couple of apaches to waylay you in Paris on the night you bought the jewels. The plan failed, which hardly surprised him, I think. This plan was, so he thought, completely safe. No possible suspicion could attach to Richard Knighton. But like all great men—and the Marquis was a great man—he had his weaknesses. He fell genuinely in love with Miss Grey, and suspecting her liking for Derek Kettering, he could not resist the temptation to saddle him with the crime when the opportunity presented itself. And now, Monsieur Van Aldin, I am going to tell you something very curious. Miss Grey is not a fanciful woman by any means, yet she firmly believes that she felt your daughter's presence beside her one day in the Casino Gardens at Monte Carlo, just after she had been having a long talk with Knighton. She was convinced, she says, that the dead woman was urgently trying to tell her something, and it suddenly came to her that what the dead woman was trying to say was that Knighton was her murderer! The idea seemed so fantastic at the time that Miss Grey spoke of it to no one. But she was so convinced of its truth that she acted on it—wild as it seemed. She did not discourage Knighton's advances, and she pretended to him that she was convinced of Derek Kettering's guilt."

"Extraordinary," said Van Aldin.

"Yes, it is very strange. One cannot explain these things. Oh, by the way, there is one little point that baffled me considerably. Your secretary has a decided limp—the result of a wound that he received in the War. Now the Marquis most decidedly did not limp. That was a stumbling block. But Miss Lenox Tamplin happened to mention one day that Knighton's limp had been a surprise to the surgeon who had been in charge of the case in her mother's hospital. That suggested camouflage. When I was in London I went to the surgeon in question, and I got several technical details from him which confirmed me in that belief. I mentioned the name of that surgeon in Knighton's hearing the day before yesterday. The natural thing would have been for Knighton to mention that he had been attended by him during the War, but he said nothing—and that little point, if nothing else, gave me the last final assurance that my theory of the crime was correct. Miss Grey, too, provided me with a cutting, showing that there had been a robbery at Lady Tamplin's hospital during the time that Knighton had been there. She realised that I was on the same track as herself when I wrote to her from the Ritz in Paris.

"I had some trouble in my inquiries there, but I got what I wanted—evidence that Ada Mason arrived on the morning after the crime and not on the evening of the day before."

There was a long silence, then the millionaire stretched out a hand to Poirot across the table.

"I guess you know what this means to me, Monsieur Poirot," he said huskily. "I am sending you round a cheque in the morning, but no cheque in the world will express what I feel about what you have done for me. You are the goods, Monsieur Poirot. Every time, you are the goods."

Poirot rose to his feet; his chest swelled.

"I am only Hercule Poirot," he said modestly, "yet, as you say, in my own way I am a big man, even as you also are a big man. I am glad and happy to have been of service to you. Now I go to repair the damages caused by travel. Alas! My excellent Georges is not with me."

In the lounge of the hotel he encountered a friend—the venerable Monsieur Papopolous, his daughter Zia beside him.

"I thought you had left Nice, Monsieur Poirot," murmured the Greek as he took the detective's affectionately proffered hand.

"Business compelled me to return, my dear Monsieur Papopolous."

"Business?"

"Yes, business. And talking of business, I hope your health is better, my dear friend?"

"Much better. In fact, we are returning to Paris to-morrow."

"I am enchanted to hear such good news. You have not completely ruined the Greek ex-Minister, I hope."

"I?"

"I understand you sold him a very wonderful ruby which—strictly *entre nous*—is being worn by Mademoiselle Mirelle, the dancer?"

"Yes," murmured Monsieur Papopolous; "yes, that is so."

"A ruby not unlike the famous 'Heart of Fire.'"

"It has points of resemblance, certainly," said the Greek casually.

"You have a wonderful hand with jewels, Monsieur Papopolous. I congratulate you. Mademoiselle Zia, I am desolate that you are returning to Paris so speedily. I had hoped to see some more of you now that my business is accomplished."

"Would one be indiscreet if one asked what that business was?" asked Monsieur Papopolous.

"Not at all, not at all. I have just succeeded in laying the Marquis by the heels."

A far-away look came over Monsieur Papopolous' noble countenance.

"The Marquis?" he murmured; "now why does that seem familiar to me? No—I cannot recall it."

"You would not, I am sure," said Poirot. "I refer to a very notable criminal and jewel robber. He has just been arrested for the murder of the English lady, Madame Kettering."

"Indeed? How interesting these things are!"

A polite exchange of farewells followed, and when Poirot was out of earshot, Monsieur Papopolous turned to his daughter.

"Zia," he said, with feeling, "that man is the devil!"

"I like him."

"I like him myself," admitted Monsieur Papopolous. "But he is the devil, all the same."

Chapter 36

BY THE SEA

The mimosa was nearly over. The scent of it in the air was faintly unpleasant. There were pink geraniums twining along the balustrade of Lady Tamplin's villa, and masses of carnations below sent up a sweet, heavy perfume. The Mediterranean was at its bluest. Poirot sat on the terrace with Lenox Tamplin. He had just finished telling her the same story that he had told to Van Aldin two days before. Lenox had listened to him with absorbed attention, her brows knitted and her eyes sombre.

When he had finished she said simply:

"And Derek?"

"He was released yesterday."

"And he has gone—where?"

"He left Nice last night."

"For St. Mary Mead?"

"Yes, for St. Mary Mead."

There was a pause.

"I was wrong about Katherine," said Lenox. "I thought she did not care."

"She is very reserved. She trusts no one."

"She might have trusted me," said Lenox, with a shade of bitterness.

"Yes," said Poirot gravely, "she might have trusted you. But Mademoiselle Katherine has spent a great deal of her life listening, and those who have listened do not find it easy to talk; they keep their sorrows and joys to themselves and tell no one."

"I was a fool," said Lenox; "I thought she really cared for Knighton. I ought to have known better. I suppose I thought so because—well, I hoped so."

Poirot took her hand and gave it a little friendly squeeze. "Courage, Mademoiselle," he said gently.

Lenox looked very straight out across the sea, and her face, in its ugly rigidity, had for the moment a tragic beauty.

"Oh, well," she said at last, "it would not have done. I am too young for Derek; he is like a kid that has never grown up. He wants the Madonna touch."

There was a long silence, then Lenox turned to him quickly and impulsively. "But I *did* help, Monsieur Poirot—at any rate I did help."

"Yes, Mademoiselle. It was you who gave me the first inkling of the truth when you said that the person who committed the crime need not have been on the train at all. Before that, I could not see how the thing had been done."

Lenox drew a deep breath.

"I am glad," she said; "at any rate—that is something."

From far behind them there came a long-drawn-out scream of an engine's whistle.

"That is that damned Blue Train," said Lenox. "Trains

are relentless things, aren't they, Monsieur Poirot? People are murdered and die, but they go on just the same. I am talking nonsense, but you know what I mean."

"Yes, yes, I know. Life is like a train, Mademoiselle. It goes on. And it is a good thing that that is so."

"Why?"

"Because the train gets to its journey's end at last, and there is a proverb about that in your language, Mademoiselle."

"'Journeys end in lovers meeting.'" Lenox laughed. "That is not going to be true for me."

"Yes—yes, it is true. You are young, younger than you yourself know. Trust the train, Mademoiselle, for it is *le bon Dieu* who drives it."

The whistle of the engine came again.

"Trust the train, Mademoiselle," murmured Poirot again. "And trust Hercule Poirot—*He knows*."

THE END

Fiction

	Title	Author	Price
☐	**Options**	Freda Bright	£1.50p
☐	**The Thirty-nine Steps**	John Buchan	£1.25p
☐	**Secret of Blackoaks**	Ashley Carter	£1.50p
☐	**A Night of Gaiety**	Barbara Cartland	90p
☐	**The Sittaford Mystery**	Agatha Christie	£1.00p
☐	**Dupe**	Liza Cody	£1.25p
☐	**Lovers and Gamblers**	Jackie Collins	£2.25p
☐	**Sphinx**	Robin Cook	£1.25p
☐	**Ragtime**	E. L. Doctorow	£1.50p
☐	**Rebecca**	Daphne du Maurier	£1.75p
☐	**Flashman**	George Macdonald Fraser	£1.50p
☐	**The Moneychangers**	Arthur Hailey	£1.95p
☐	**Secrets**	Unity Hall	£1.50p
☐	**The Maltese Falcon**	Dashiell Hammett	95p
☐	**Simon the Coldheart**	Georgette Heyer	95p
☐	**The Eagle Has Landed**	Jack Higgins	£1.75p
☐	**The Master Sniper**	Stephen Hunter	£1.50p
☐	**Smiley's People**	John le Carré	£1.75p
☐	**To Kill a Mockingbird**	Harper Lee	£1.50p
☐	**The Empty Hours**	Ed McBain	£1.25p
☐	**Gone with the Wind**	Margaret Mitchell	£2.95p
☐	**The Totem**	Tony Morrell	£1.25p
☐	**Platinum Logic**	Tony Parsons	£1.75p
☐	**Rage of Angels**	Sidney Sheldon	£1.75p
☐	**The Unborn**	David Shobin	£1.50p
☐	**A Town Like Alice**	Nevile Shute	£1.50p
☐	**A Falcon Flies**	Wilbur Smith	£1.95p
☐	**The Deep Well at Noon**	Jessica Stirling	£1.75p
☐	**The Ironmaster**	Jean Stubbs	£1.75p
☐	**The Music Makers**	E. V. Thompson	£1.50p

Non-fiction

	Title	Author	Price
☐	**Extraterrestrial Civilizations**	Isaac Asimov	£1.50p
☐	**Pregnancy**	Gordon Bourne	£2.95p
☐	**Out of Practice**	Rob Buckman	95p
☐	**The 35mm Photographer's Handbook**	Julian Calder and John Garrett	£5.95p
☐	**Travellers' Britain**	Arthur Eperon	£2.95p
☐	**Travellers' Italy**	Arthur Eperon	£2.95p
☐	**The Complete Calorie Counter**	Eileen Fowler	70p